To N
with w[...]
Jim

Waverly's
Universe

Jim Trainor

Also by Jim Trainor

Grasp: Making Sense of Science and Spirituality

Waverly's Universe

A Novel

Jim Trainor

UpNorth
Press

Waverly's Universe is a work of fiction.
Characters, places and incidents are the products of the
author's imagination, and any real names or locales used in
the book are used fictitiously.

ISBN: 978-0615709215

To Mary and my three kids

Prologue

January 1990
Late night near Albuquerque, New Mexico

    She sits shoulder to shoulder with the others on the hard metal floor of the van, between her husband and child. She's uncertain how many are in here with them, a dozen, maybe more, who can tell in the darkness? They crawled into the van just after nightfall, at the end of a dirt road in the desert, and they've been on the move for many hours, stopping once, but they were not allowed to get out. Two plastic jugs of water are all they have for the long trip. The hard-eyed Mexican driver keeps his eyes on the road, never looks back at them.

    She does not know when they'll arrive, or even what their destination is.

    There are no windows behind the driver's and front passenger windows, but now, after hours of darkness, splashes of light reflect back from the windshield, briefly illuminating the sleeping passengers. Are they passing through a city? Her husband's head rests on her shoulder and she wonders if he is snoring. She longs for that familiar roar next to her, but the road noise and vibration beneath them keep her from knowing. Her sleeping child rests against her on the other side. Such a lovely child, who has not complained once during this long ordeal.

Are the others asleep? Is she the only one awake at this hour? Is she the only one so charged with anticipation and fear that she cannot sleep?

Now the van's engine is working harder and they are gently pressed toward the back doors. They must be ascending a grade. It's grown cold and she wonders what it looks like outside. Is there snow? She has never seen snow.

Images flash through her mind of the small village they left just days ago, bringing no possessions, just each other. Her husband, her child. This is everything she has in this world. Everything she needs.

She feels the rear wheels slip, then the driver regains control. Suddenly the van is turned and seems to be moving sideways. Panic surges through her. The others remain asleep. Then it spins and rolls. Everyone is now awake. There are screams. She tries to move, tries to pull her child closer, but she is pinned by bodies piling against her, arms and legs flailing. She cannot find her husband, cannot find her child.

"Dios mio, Dios mio," she cries but cannot hear her own voice. The rear doors pop open and bodies are flying, flung from the van like seeds cast into a field. She gropes toward the opening, but she is upside down, and now the roof is crushing in upon her.

The *Albuquerque Journal* reported it this way:

> January 11, 1990 — In the predawn hours on Monday, a van
> carrying seventeen illegal immigrants spun out of control on
> the icy stretches of eastbound I-40, ten miles east of the city
> near the Cedar Crest exit. It apparently rolled several times
> before landing on its roof in the westbound lane. The driver
> and all passengers were killed. Their identities and country
> of origin are unknown at this time. Traffic in both directions
> was blocked for several hours. Officials from Immigration
> and Naturalization Services are investigating the accident.

They all died.
All except one.

Chapter 1

Thursday, October 13, 2011
Los Alamos, New Mexico

He could run away right now. Get back in his car, head north and be in Canada by tomorrow. He could start a new life there. There are good reasons to go. Josh Waverly's body straightens and his pulse quickens, as the familiar fantasy unfolds. But then he turns his eyes back toward the nearby sprawl of the national laboratory, and his shoulders droop back into their normal slouch. He sighs. He will not leave.

Josh stands in the parking lot of City Auto Parts, in the heart of the small business district. He sees no clouds over the Jemez Mountains, just beyond the Lab buildings, but he knows it's going to rain soon. These dull aches in his bum leg always let him know. He pushes his way through the glass doors of the store, careful to touch only the edge of the handle that's not streaked with black grease. The place is nearly empty. The girl behind the register is busy texting on her phone and doesn't look up as Josh makes his way toward the parts counter in the rear.

Josh hates these places, but he needs new wiper blades. Sure, he could let the blades go for now, but it's not like Josh to let things slip. With the rain coming, he needs to be ready, even though this is taking him away from his preparation for the afternoon ordeal that awaits, almost suffocating him if he allows his mind to dwell on it.

He takes one of the tall metal stools along the counter and leans forward on the unpainted-Masonite counter top like a car repair pro who knows what he's doing. In truth Josh knows nothing about car maintenance, unless you count his occasionally tuning into *Car Talk* on NPR or knowing the location of the nearest Jiffy Lube.

Another guy, who obviously does know something about auto repair, also sits at the counter, two stools down. He's hollering to the clerk, who's poking around out of sight among the rows of shelves in the back, saying something like, "If you ain't got the 325, I can probably make do with a 315. Either way, it's gotta take a 22 inch torque." The man's huge biceps bulge from his black muscle shirt. A large tattoo proclaims, "Don't Mess with Texas."

Josh can't help but compare his arms to the guy getting the 325, whatever a 325 is. Josh's arms, slender and almost hairless, must make it apparent that he's never been in the Marines, or kicked some butt in a bar-room brawl, or torn down a '57 Ford V8.

The man with the tattoo swivels his stool toward Josh, but Josh keeps his eyes cast downward. He has no intention of messing with Texas.

"How's it hangin', dude?"

"Uh, fine thanks." Josh doesn't look up, doesn't want to risk that his look might be taken the wrong way.

"What you gettin'?"

"Just wiper blades."

"Why you sittin' here? The blades are on that rack behind you. Walked right past 'em."

"Oh, I must have missed them, thanks." Josh gets up from the stool.

"What kinda wheels you got?"

"A Prius." He knows this isn't the best answer.

But Tex just grunts and returns his attention to the clerk in back.

Josh finds his wiper blades and heads for the cashier. The girl is still texting and at first doesn't see him approach. She wears a blue smock with a City Auto Parts logo and a plastic name tag that says, 'Hi, I'm Mandy.' When she finally notices Josh, Mandy quickly ditches her phone, flashes him a bright smile, and runs the wipers over a scanner. "I noticed you were talking to Bucky," she says.

"Who?" Josh is anxious to get back to the familiar sanctuary of his office at the Lab.

"The guy in the muscle shirt." She casts a longing glance towards the parts counter.

"Oh yeah, him. He's getting a 325."

Without taking her eyes off Bucky, her voice turns wistful, "I wish he'd talk to me."

For an instant the catchlight in Mandy's eyes reminds Josh of the girl in Building 28, but he quickly banishes the thought. He cannot afford this distraction today. He says to Mandy, "I'm sure he'd like to talk with you," trying to offer her a little hope, but of course he knows nothing about either of them. Yet, Josh is certain that somehow Mandy and Bucky will do okay. Unlike himself, who faces annihilation this afternoon.

&ze&

Stilwell Ferguson eyes himself in the rearview mirror and considers how he's been short changed by life. With a name like his, shouldn't it be Senator Stilwell Ferguson? And his looks match his name. A wide chiseled face that looks like presidential material. But life has not treated him fairly, and here he sits at a drive-in slot at the Sonic on the main drag in Los Alamos, watching the lunch-hour rush into town from the Lab. Next to Ferguson in the front seat of the gray Nissan is Jesse Smith, sucking loudly on his giant cherry limeade. His pale face is deeply pitted from some childhood acne attack and his stringy blond hair looks filthy. His forehead slopes at an angle that reminds Stilwell of some prehistoric man he'd seen in one of his high school text books. Stilwell bristles that he has to work with a knuckle dragger like Smith. But he has to admit that Smith is good at what he does.

Smith finishes off the limeade and tosses the plastic cup into the back seat. "Hey," protests Ferguson, "Let's keep the car a little nice, okay? Throw your garbage in the trash can, you dumb slob."

"What difference does it make?" grunts Smith, "This car sucks. Why can't we get one of those black SUVs with dark windows all around? Maybe a TV inside."

Smith is an idiot, but this is not news to Stilwell. "You've seen too many hit-man movies. This car's perfect for us." He waves his hand in a panoramic arc around the interior of the '93 Maxima, which he keeps spotlessly clean despite the car's nondescript exterior. "Your stealth Hummer would stick out like a sore thumb." But Smith just grunts again and makes no move to retrieve the empty cup from the back seat. *Was it Cro-Magnon man?*

Ferguson finishes the last of his burger, washes it down with a swig of Diet Coke, then places the cup in the middle cup holder for later. "Better hit it. He'll be there in an hour."

Smith grunts again as Ferguson backs out and drives off toward the mountains. Twelve miles west of the Lab, along a dirt road leading to a wilderness campground, Stilwell pulls into the designated place. "You got the money in back?" asks the clueless Smith.

"There'll be no money this time," and even the slow-witted Smith understands and grins.

Fifteen minutes later, a dust plume from down the road announces the arrival of a car. It pulls in with a screech of tires, as the driver, going too fast, has almost missed the turnout. A man jumps out, runs his hand through his hair, and does a quick three-sixty as if checking out the place.

Quickly he approaches Ferguson and Smith, standing beside the old Nissan.

"So Louie," Stilwell says, "looks like you got new wheels."

"Yeah," says Louie Wessel, glancing over his shoulder at the new Vette. He sounds out of breath. His face is clammy with sweat. Even on this warm day, Louie wears a slim leather jacket, which looks expensive, with sleeves pushed half-way up to the elbows.

"So, tell me Louie," Stilwell asks in his comforting monotone, his fireside-chat tone, "You getting the stuff out okay?"

Louie breathes out a nervous sigh. "So, there's been a little delay. The Lab's just started a new audit, and I heard they may be looking into some inconsistencies in my department." Louie talks fast. "So I gotta lay low for awhile. Hope you guys don't mind." His dark Oakleys hide eyes that are no doubt darting between Stilwell and Smith.

"What kind of inconsistencies, Louie?" Stilwell's voice remains steady and deep.

"Look, I don't know, okay? They're a bunch of bureaucrat bean counters, I'm not too worried. The Lab's a big place."

"Maybe you should be worried, Louie."

"Nah, I got myself covered. I planted a little what-you-might-call incriminating evidence on this girl in my department. If the heat comes down, it'll go directly to her." Louie lets out a laugh, like he's pulled off a brilliant move.

"You telling me you involved someone else in this?"

"She's not involved, not unless the Feds come in on this. And then I got us covered."

"You shouldn't have done that, Louie, not without consulting me."

"What? I was sure you'd approve." There's a trace of panic in Louie's voice now. "Look, I was only trying to do the right thing here, protect the operation. FYI, I'm the guy taking all the risks here. You guys need to cut me a little slack."

"And who is this girl you involved, Louie?"

"Just some dumb broad in my department. You don't need to worry about it." Louie is trying to project confidence, but his voice is now louder and shaky.

"Who is she, Louie?" Stilwell's words are slow and firm.

Louie mumbles a name, looking down.

Stilwell takes note of the name, then smiles at Wessel. "Louie, let's not get all worked up about this. So you made a little mistake. Not a big deal. We're all professionals here. Stuff happens, right?" It's Stilwell's most soothing voice, the reassuring voice of a trusted colleague.

Stilwell steps toward Louie and places a collegial hand on his shoulder, as he gives Jesse a subtle nod. Wessel seems to relax. "Hey, I knew you guys would understand." Jesse has now slipped behind Wessel, carrying the heavy shovel he's removed from the Nissan. Louie lets out a cocky little laugh. "After all, I'm a key player in all this, no Louie Wessel, no stuff." Smith brings the spade of the shovel down hard on Louie Wessel's head. He grunts as he falls forward, spread eagled in front of his new Corvette.

At the moment of impact, Stilwell Ferguson doesn't even blink, the smile never leaving his face. The woman. More work to take care of. There can be no loose ends. But that doesn't keep him from savoring the scene before him. Maybe he hadn't become a senator, but his job sure does have some moments of pure satisfaction.

❧❧

Blood fills her windshield. When the Spanish conquistadors first saw the high peaks in the east, turned crimson by the late afternoon sun, they named them Sangre de Cristo, the Blood of Christ. This same panorama warms Evangelina Gomez on her long daily drive home from the Lab, down the winding road from Los Alamos, across the valley of the Rio Grande, then up into the rolling foothills on the eastern side, to her village of Rinconada.

Her body sags when she finally pulls in beneath the canopy of cottonwoods that shade the small low-slung adobe house her father calls his hacienda. She remains in the car for several moments, allowing the tension of the day to ooze away, before going in to greet the joy of her life.

"Hi Papa. How's my little angel today?" she bubbles, as she enters the living room. Esteban Gomez sits with his feet up on the narrow banco in front of the kiva fireplace, even though it's not lit on this balmy afternoon.

"Hey, Vangie, your mama's got a great supper almost ready. And your little angel, she's in the kitchen with Mama."

Evangelina goes right on into the kitchen and scoops up her daughter. "Hey you, little angel cakes! You look so beautiful today!"

Serena squeals, "Mommy's home!"

Grace Gomez turns her small round shoulders away from the large gas stove. "Honey, how was your day?"

"Okay, I guess. Work is work."

"Did you talk to that boss about a promotion?"

Evangelina rolls her eyes. "Mama, I just barely got in the door. But no, I didn't, but —"

"All I'm saying is that you're the best they've got, and maybe they're just waiting for you to say you'd like something more. That's all I'm saying."

Evangelina sighs, "And my mother is the one who knows who their best employee is."

"Well, I do know how smart you are. Bet they don't have any other valedictorians working there."

But Evangelina has turned her attention to Serena. "And what's my little girl been up to today?"

"I've been helping Nana, right Nana?"

"She has!" says Grace, switching to her cheery *abuela* voice. "Now that you're four, I expect you'll be cooking us supper some night pretty soon."

"Oh, can I?" She's now squirming in Evangelina's arms and feeling heavy. Evangelina sighs through her smile. The days of carrying her daughter around in her arms are nearly gone.

"Well it won't be long, young lady," laughs Grace.

The aroma of grilled poblano peppers is now attacking Evangelina's senses with their warm pungency, so good her knees almost buckle. It will be chile rellenos tonight, her favorite. Because Evangelina knows how your world can be shattered in an instant, she is grateful for the things that never change. She wonders how she got to be so blessed.

అుప

Josh stands braced and barely breathing, like an infantryman preparing to charge from his trench into gunfire, at the rear of the Space Physics auditorium. It's only about a third full for the Thursday afternoon department seminar, and his presentation begins in five minutes. He checks his shirt to see if the building perspiration shows. If it were up to Josh, he'd never have to talk in front of an audience. He doesn't consider himself a gifted speaker, certainly not like his father was. He's not good at thinking on his feet and questions easily get him tied up in knots.

Josh worked a good part of the week getting his talk ready and went at it without a break today, other than his foray out for the wiper blades, because some of the staff love nothing better than tearing apart every little detail, even the work of a colleague. He looks down at his notes. The title of his seminar, Systematics of Germanium Gamma Ray Detector Calibrations in the 1 GeV to 1 TeV Energy Range, doesn't sound so catchy now. In fact, some people might say this work is repetitious and boring. He remembers one colleague saying you needed the personality of an old maid to do such work, and he bristles that somebody might consider him an old maid.

He tries to think of something to get himself pumped up, but all that comes to mind is the unpleasant conversation he had with the department secretary this morning, as she was helping him get his PowerPoint slides together. Paging through the talk, she said, "This looks like gobbledy-gook to me. Can you explain it to me in terms a mere mortal might understand?"

Josh had launched into a description of his work, how he measures the minute electrical signals produced when a high-energy electromagnetic wave like an x-ray or gamma ray impinges on a sensitive crystal like germanium. He hadn't gotten very far before he saw the secretary's eyes glaze over, as she began to fiddle with other things on her desk.

Interrupting him, she said, "So, you're saying your work is like holding a meat thermometer under hot water to see how far the needle moves, but never actually using it to cook anything." Geez, he didn't need to think about that right now.

Hal Gullickson, who'll introduce Josh, approaches with a sense of urgency. As annoying as Hal can be, he's the closest thing to a friend Josh has at the Lab, maybe because he's the only other single man in the group. "All set, Josh?" he asks, rubbing his hands together with mock anticipation.

"As all set as I'm going to get," Josh laughs, as a surge of acid churns in his stomach.

"Hey, don't forget we're going out tonight. I've some new moves I wanna show you."

Josh cringes. He's not sure why he lets Hal drag him along on these bar-hopping sorties, but he'll worry about that later.

Hal steps before the crowd, clicks on the mike and says, "Good afternoon everybody. It's a pleasure to introduce our own Josh Waverly, who's going to talk to us about parallel universes." He pauses, waiting for laughs, but there are only a few chuckles in the audience.

Josh winces at this too familiar joke.

"Oops," Hal continues, "Wrong Waverly. Today we get the younger Waverly, but great nonetheless. And he'll be presenting his work on gamma ray detector calibrations. Now, some might say this research isn't as sexy as parallel universes, but in fact a whole branch of astrophysics depends upon the work Josh does, the cosmologists who study the origin of cosmic rays, the space scientists who design satellite experiments, using his detectors to measure emissions from black holes. Those guys have the glamour, sure, but where would they be without the detectors that Josh provides them? Let's welcome Josh."

Josh limps slowly toward the microphone, while Hal tries for more humor, "It may take a few minutes, folks. Josh's old football injury seems to be acting up today." More laughter.

The lights dim as Josh flicks on the projector and begins. He doesn't leave out any of the details, and by the time he wraps up an hour later, a third of the audience has slipped out and probably half of those remaining are asleep. There is meager applause. Josh handles a few perfunctory questions, then that's it. No merciless attacks, in fact not much of a response at all.

"Let's thank our speaker again, everybody!" Hal says with such gusto that the last of the nappers are now awake.

More meager applause. Then turning to Josh he says, "Nice job, Bro!"

"Thanks, and in the future let's dispense with the parallel universe jokes, okay? It gets old being compared to my father all the time."

"Q. E. D., Bro." An annoying habit of Hal's is this Q. E. D. business. It's an abbreviation for a Latin phrase, meaning *it has been demonstrated,* used at the conclusion of a mathematical proof, but the problem is that no one who's not a mathematician or physicist will have a clue what Hal's talking about. And what's with the "Bro"? Hal, with an overly-large shiny red forehead taking up most of the acreage of his face between his coke-bottle horn-rims and his receding hairline, looks like the last guy who should be calling anybody Bro.

Unfazed, Hal continues. "So, I'll pick you up around seven, okay? Head into Santa Fe. There's a bar at Casa Bonita. Thought we'd grab a snack, then we'll just see where opportunity takes us after that. And tonight we're going to have fun. Got it? F. U. N."

"Casa Bonita? That's expensive, isn't it?" Josh often drives through Santa Fe on his way to the airport in Albuquerque to catch a flight to some lab, where he'll pull all-nighters calibrating detectors. He sometimes hits McDonald's to grab some fast food at the drive-through window or Wal-Mart to pick up essentials he can't get in Los Alamos. But he skips the famous historical district, the trendy galleries, the upscale shops and the gourmet restaurants like Casa Bonita.

"Sure, Bro," Hal beams, "the restaurant can set you back a wad, but we're heading for the bar just across the alley. Plate of nachos, eight bucks. You can handle that, or is that beyond the allowance your mommy gave you?"

Josh nods, backing away, anxious to be alone to recover from the seminar ordeal.

❧❦

Though her head barely clears the table top, Serena places the flatware just right, proud of her skills and saying each step out loud. "Fork on the left, spoon and knife on the right." Evangelina studies her beautiful daughter, her coal black hair, smooth light brown skin and large brown eyes that radiate warmth. She wonders if this is how she looked at Serena's age, but there are no pictures of her earliest years.

Evangelina runs her fingers over the smooth worn surface of the pine supper table her father made long ago, its familiar texture an icon for this comfortable family she loves. These evenings at home are a healing tonic for a job that is exhausting and boring, but she is grateful for her job, mindful that a year ago she was cleaning other people's houses.

Grace's chile rellenos are as great as ever, and her sopapillas, drenched in honey, bring oohs and ahs. "Mama, I've said it a million times. You need to start your own restaurant."

"Vangie, they've already got too many restaurants. And there's a lot of mamacitas out there who can cook circles around me."

"Nobody can make rellenos like yours, Mama," Esteban chimes in.

Grace glows. "Well, I've got my hands full just keeping the three of you fed!"

Esteban, finishing off another sopapilla, says, "So, Vangie, you should have seen that daughter of yours this afternoon. We were out in the back, I was working on the garden, when Serena pipes up, 'Grampa, want to see me run?' Sure, I say. So she takes off, runs all the way to the acequia. How far you think that is, Grace? Two hundred feet? Anyway, I couldn't believe how fast she is. Takes after her mother, I'd say. Looks like another track star in the family."

"And Mama," Serena says, "I wasn't even tired!"

"That's great, sweetie," bubbles Evangelina. "Maybe we can go out running this weekend. I think I've got a little of the old spark left."

"But the only time you run these days," Grace adds, "is when a man comes calling."

"Mama, that's not fair."

"So, how many dates you got lined up for this weekend?"

"Mama," Evangelina glares, "I'm just not into that right now."

"Right now is stretching into years. You're a beautiful woman, you should get out there."

"Mama, let's not go there again, okay? I'm not a teenager, I can figure out my own life."

"I know you're not a teenager. That's why I'm concerned. You're twenty-five, you're not gonna have those looks forever." There's a familiar edge in her mother's voice now.

Evangelina looks down. "I've got plenty to keep me busy—" Just then the phone rings, and everyone looks relieved for the interruption.

"That'll be Reynaldo," says Grace, "probably calling from some pay phone along the interstate." She leaves the table to get the phone in the kitchen.

When Grace is gone, Esteban leans forward and rests his fingers on Evangelina's arm. "Your mother worries that you work all the time. She just wants you to be happy."

"I know, Papa. It's okay. I just wish she wouldn't always—"

Grace returns to the table. "So what does that no-good brother of yours want?" Esteban asks with a wink of his eye.

"It wasn't Rey." Grace pauses for a moment. "It was some man asking if you live here, Vangie." There's a breathlessness to her voice that conveys fear. "He sounded suspicious. I asked him who he was and—"

"What did he say?" Esteban asks.

Grace's lower lip trembles. "I didn't get his name, but he said he's from the FBI."

Evangelina goes rigid. They all look at Serena.

ॐॐ

At midnight, Josh stands at the window in his studio apartment in Los Alamos, just a mile from the Lab, looking out at the Conoco station across the street. The storm has moved in fast, and the red and white lights of the station reflect off the rain-soaked street, nearly deserted. Unlike down in Santa Fe, they roll up the streets here at nine. At least that's the local joke.

Geez, he shouldn't have had that second margarita. Josh rubs his pounding temples and relives the Santa Fe trip again. He probably shouldn't have gone. He was still in a funk about the seminar, and he's never felt comfortable trying to pick up women in bars anyway. Sure, he wants to meet someone, and that's probably what got him to say yes to Hal in the first place. That and the fact that he had nothing else going on tonight, or the upcoming weekend for that matter.

The bar at Casa Bonita had certainly lived up to its reputation, with its classy pueblo-chic ambiance. The walls, a warm gold accented by that pale blue Santa Fe is famous for, were covered with brightly colored local art. The large ceiling timbers, called vigas, gave the place an ancient look, and the dim lanterns created the feel of candle light. In spite of this beauty, Josh's first comment after they had entered was, "Let's not stay too late. We've got to work tomorrow."

Hal had rolled his eyes. Despite the leather vest he probably just picked up at the western wear store in the mall and the way he left the top buttons of his shirt unbuttoned to reveal a tuft of chest hair, Hal looked like a deli owner from Brooklyn. Josh still wore the clothes he had on at work, a simple plaid sport shirt over a white crew neck tee shirt and khaki chinos.

It wasn't long before two women took seats at the bar, not far from their table, and Hal, trying to be subtle but not succeeding, gave Josh a head nod in their direction. "Check those babes out, Bro," Hal whispered with excitement, like he'd just discovered life on another planet.

Josh had his mouth full of nachos at the time, and it took a few moments before he could say, "Good grief, Hal, you know I'm not really looking to pick up women."

"Let's not go through that again, okay, stud?" 'Stud' irritates Josh even more than 'Bro.' "Look I know one thing about you, you're interested in the female of the species. What about that chick at work that you've got the hots for, huh?" He waited for a reply.

Josh turned his gaze toward the colorful paintings, like he'd just found an appreciation for southwestern art. He wished he'd never told Hal about the girl in Building 28. Cripes, it's not like he's actually gone out with her, or even had a conversation with her. He doesn't even know her name. "I've got to use the bathroom," he said.

When he returned, he saw that Hal hadn't wasted a minute. The women had already pulled up chairs around the table. "Hey, ladies, this is Josh. That limp is from the Gulf War. The guy's practically a hero. Josh, this is Bree and Laney. We were just getting acquainted."

Laney took a gulp from her tall drink, then shook her head, Jennifer Anniston style, to move her long red hair away from her face, and said to Josh. "So you guys are scientists? Wow."

"That's right, ladies," Hal added, "Josh here is a physicist at the Lab, like me. Pretty fancy stuff he works on. Hey, Josh, tell our friends about parallel universes."

Josh shot Hal an irritated look and said, "Actually, I don't work on—"

Bree interrupted, "I heard Letterman mention parallel universes the other night. Does this mean there's another universe besides ours?" Bree gave Josh her best 'I-think-I'll-sign-up-for-graduate-school-next-week' look.

Laney and Bree weren't bad looking, but flirtatious banter is just plain awkward for Josh. He took a deep breath, then let it out slow. Josh actually knows little more about parallel universes than what he'd gleaned from his father's lectures years ago. "Well, nobody knows for sure. It's just that some of the math from quantum mechanics and string theory suggests there could be other universes, and—"

"So what's it like in this other universe? Will there be another Bree there?" She giggled, flashing wide-open blue eyes at Josh.

"Who knows? Scientists are uncertain about—"

Hal interrupted, "I'm sure there's only room for one Bree, no matter how many universes there are!" Everyone let out a big laugh, except Josh who didn't know what was so funny.

"So do you think they really exist?" Laney asked breathlessly, shaking her red hair again, as if this was really important to her.

"Well, I won't believe it unless I see some experimental evidence, and that's unlikely until we have a whole new generation of observational technologies, and—"

"What our whiz kid is saying," Hal interjected, "is that if we ever find one, we'll come by in our spaceship and take you girls there for dinner." Again, the three of them bellowed.

"So ladies, I see the drinks are getting a little low," Hal observed, "What say we get out of here?" Bree and Laney exchanged questioning looks.

But Josh interjected, "I really need to be going. An early day at work tomorrow, you know." He shifted his chair as an indication that he was ready to leave.

"Hey, the night is young!" Hal was still trying to drum up a little enthusiasm. "I know a little place over by the plaza where they serve the best—"

"Yeah, maybe we need to be going too," said Bree, obviously realizing this wasn't going anywhere. "It's been great getting to know you guys and hearing about parallel universes. It's not every day we get to meet a famous scientist."

In the car, Hal was livid, "Well, that was a cool move, stud. Didn't you see that you really had a shot at old Laney? She was practically ready to hop in the sack. What's up with you, anyway? Maybe you're not interested after all."

"That's just not the way I want to meet women. It seems too …" Josh paused, searching for the right word. "Too superficial."

"So who gives a rip if it's superficial?" Hal's voice was now raised. "You're going back to that dreary little apartment of yours and spend the night alone, like some old maid."

Old maid? Josh shot Hal a menacing look, then bit his lip, and was silent, holding back any indication of emotion. He's good at that. Looking straight ahead into the night, he was silent the rest of the way home.

Now Josh turns from the studio window and shakes his head, as if trying to dispel the memory of the ill-fated evening. He scans his small living room that doubles as a dining room, with a kitchen nook in one corner, and concludes that Hal is right. His place is dreary. The flat white walls and the cheap popcorn-finish ceiling give it a bleak feel. His high-end home theatre system dominates the small living room area. Why did he buy this thing, anyway? He never watches movies. Maybe it's his obsession with high-tech gadgets. A futon is stacked with issues of *Sky and Telescope* and *Scientific American* and a mess of papers from work. The small dining room table is also piled with papers, with only a tiny area cleared for his cereal bowl.

He considers the only colorful thing on the dull walls, a small print of a painting from the National Gallery in Washington, a New England seascape by Winslow Homer. A windswept beach, a wild surf, a small whitewashed village. He wonders again if he should have been an art major, but a physics major was never in doubt. His father had been prepping him for that since the beginning. But there had been questions raised, as early as high school, like when his SAT scores revealed he had a greater aptitude for verbal topics than mathematical topics. His father had been disappointed, but that didn't stop him from using his prestige to help Josh get into Yale.

Josh traces a finger along the edge of the frame, gazing deeply into the print, as if it might be a window into another world. Sometimes the Homer print makes him feel free, transports him to that wild beach where the gulls screech and the surf roars in his ears. But tonight the deserted beach reminds him of his loneliness. He returns to the window and watches the rain. Yes, he is lonely. Maybe he should get a cat.

❧

Evangelina lies on her back, unable to sleep. On nights like this, the soft breathing of her daughter nearby is a source of comfort. Serena's getting old enough to have her own room, and this concerns Evangelina, but Esteban's hacienda only has two bedrooms. She needs to find a place of her own, if she can ever get enough money saved up.

In her troubled mind, the questions churn about the man on the phone. For the remainder of dinner, the family worked hard to keep the conversation cheery for Serena's sake, but she had not missed a thing. At her bedtime, she asked, "Mommy, who was that man who called?"

"Nobody, honey. Now let's go to—"

"But you seemed worried, Mommy."

"I'm sorry, sweetie. It isn't anything to worry about." Evangelina stroked her daughter's hair and sang her lullabies, some in English, some in Spanish, until her child drifted into sleep.

In the middle of the night Evangelina's familiar dream begins. She's trapped in claustrophobic darkness, trying in vain to escape. She can't breathe. Suddenly there are screams. The dream has several variants, but they always have the screams. Loud, desperate, agonizing.

She bolts upright in panic. In the darkness, her heart pounding, she listens to the rain washing against her window. She goes to Serena, sleeping on her single bed in the corner, and kneels down next to her daughter, down close where she can hear the comforting rhythm of her steady breathing. She hasn't had the dream in a long time, but she knows why she had it tonight.

Chapter Two

Friday, October 14

They're parked at a roadside rest off US 285 near Española, just after dawn. Stilwell curses under his breath, while fumbling with the road map. Jesse Smith gazes blankly at the trucks roaring by on the highway. Finally he taps the map gently with his forefinger and mutters, "Ah, home sweet home." An hour later, the gray Maxima makes its way down the gravel main road into Rinconada, passes through the small plaza, still asleep at this early hour, and slides in under the cottonwoods in front of Esteban Gomez's house.

Stilwell sits quietly for a few moments, looking around, getting the lay of the land. "We gonna take care of some business here?" Jesse asks.

Stilwell considers the Cro-Magnon features, the slack jaw, the vacant eyes, the slouching posture of Smith. "You go around the back, be ready at the back door, wait for my call."

Smith slips around the side of the house, while Stilwell strolls nonchalantly toward the front door. At the porch he stops to touch one of the several red chile ristras, hanging from the rustic timbers that support the roof of the porch. "Beautiful," he says out loud. At the front door, he pauses to admire its hand-carved detail, running his fingers across the rough contours.

The door opens and a small brown man peers out at him. "Yes?" He sounds suspicious.

"Mr. Gomez?"

"What do you want?"

"May I come in?"

"Who are you?"

"Agent Ferguson. FBI." Stilwell flips open a small leather wallet to reveal a picture ID.

Esteban Gomez leans close, studies the card, then stands back and holds the door open.

"Nice place you have here, Mr. Gomez."

The man says nothing.

"So, Mr. Gomez, we're looking for a Miss Evangelina Gomez. Is she around?"

Gomez looks hard into Stilwell's eyes. "Why would the FBI be looking for her?"

"We just want to speak with her. Can you tell me where she is?"

"And just why would I want to cooperate with some strange man I've never seen before?"

"Oh, I think you'll want to cooperate with me, Mr. Gomez." Stilwell's voice is calm. Over Esteban's shoulder, he sees Smith, poised, through the screen door at the back of the house.

"You'll need to tell me more about your business here, Mr. Ferguson, before I'm going to be willing to say anything about this woman you're looking for."

"I understand your concerns. We just need to speak with Miss Gomez as a part of an investigation that's going on at the Lab. I'm not permitted to say more than that, Mr. Gomez."

The small brown man looks down, apparently mulling this over. Then he looks back into Stilwell's eyes. Their eyes are locked for several moments, neither man looking away.

Then a small girl comes bounding in from another room.

"Go back in your room. Stay there," Gomez barks at the girl, who doesn't catch on.

"But Grampa, who's this man?"

"Nobody. He's leaving right now." Gomez's eyes return to Stilwell.

"My, my, Mr. Gomez. What a beautiful little girl. What's your name, honey?"

"Go back in your room right now and stay there," Gomez says again, more forcefully.

"I'm Serena."

"Ah, Serena. Such a lovely name. Mr. Gomez, I bet you have to watch her closely. Out here in the country, there are all kinds of bad things that can happen to a small child." Stilwell smiles. "Especially one so pretty."

≈≫

Josh needs more coffee. He's trying to watch his caffeine intake, but he couldn't get to sleep last night. Maybe it was the achy leg or maybe the letdown after his seminar. Maybe the trip to Santa Fe that left him pondering his life into the early morning hours. It's almost noon and he's made little progress on his calculations. He checks the inventory of Cup O Noodles on the shelf above his desk. He'll work through lunch again today.

He leans back in his computer chair and stares blankly at the array of numbers on the large monitor in front of him. He's been trying to catch up on work, after spending most of the week getting ready for yesterday's seminar. *Interesting that no one's even mentioned the seminar this morning. Geez, it must have been a real dog.* He's having a hard time getting his brain engaged with the calculations, and several times he's found himself daydreaming, his mind wandering, mainly to that girl in Building 28. In his fantasy, he creates their meeting:

"Hi, I'm Josh Waverly. I work in the building next door. I walk by here every day and wondered if you have time to grab some coffee at the cafeteria. If you're too busy, I certainly understand." Relaxed, casual. That's the way he'll be.

"I am pretty busy, but, it's my break time, so, sure, why not." He watches her slip out from behind her desk, slender and shapely. *"I have to be back in fifteen minutes."*

At the cafeteria, Josh pays for the coffees, and they find a quiet table. She sips her coffee, as they awkwardly break the ice. He asks her questions about herself, her family, her interests. Then she wants to know about him. He keeps it light and breezy. She's impressed with his education, asks him what it's like to grow up in the East. He tells her a little story about his time in graduate school, and she laughs at all his funny lines. She thinks he's funny.

He's confident. Girls are attracted to confidence. Finally he says, as their fifteen minutes are about up, "Hey, there's a restaurant down in Santa Fe I've been meaning to try out. Casa Bonita. Ever been there?"

"No, but I've heard it's very nice."

"So, why don't we go down there tonight and check it out?"

"Gee, sure, I mean, thank you. That would be fun."

He walks her back to her office and says goodbye, polite and gentlemanly. Women don't see enough of that these days.

She extends a hand. It's slender and her skin is smooth. It feels soft and fragile, encased in his. Protected. "Thank you, Mr. Josh Waverly, I look forward to seeing you tonight." She gives him a smile that causes his knees to go weak. He feels her eyes on him as he walks away.

The fantasy dissolves, and Josh silently chastises himself for his silly daydreams. He takes a deep breath, grabs his mug and heads down to the coffee room. On the way, he decides he'll go over to Building 28 this afternoon and talk to her. Sure, there have been several times in the last month when he's walked by her office door, determined to go in, but he's always chickened out. After all, he has no professional reason to speak with her, good grief, he doesn't even know what she does.

So, why does he always chicken out? Sure, he's not the greatest talker in the world. Just ask Bree and Laney. But neither is he a complete loser. He talks to other people all the time. So why is the girl in Building 28 different from other people? Why does the thought of her make his knees go weak and his mouth feel like it's full of cotton? There's no good reason for it.

Except that the girl in Building 28 is just about the most beautiful woman he's ever seen.

☙❧

Evangelina spots Quizzlen out of the corner of her eye and sits up straight at her workstation. Dr. Thomas Quizzlen, leader of the Industrial Relations group, is strolling through the front office, making small talk with the employees, wearing a pasted-on smile that doesn't match the darting eyes that say he'd rather be somewhere else. Most of the time he stays in his office upstairs. Evangelina's been in Dr. Quizzlen's office only once, for about fifteen minutes during the interview for her job. It had been a perfunctory ritual, during which Dr. Quizzlen seemed more interested in checking out her legs than in asking about her qualifications.

Apparently Dr. Quizzlen leaves the low-level hiring decisions to Della, who sits across from Evangelina in the front office. One thing that makes Evangelina's job bearable is Della Wright. She's not at the top of the org chart, doesn't have a big title, but she's the go-to gal in this office. Della's been around forever, a good ol' girl she calls herself, from Texas. Evangelina considers Della a real friend, who took her under her wings from day one, when she walked in, scared and inexperienced, a year ago.

Now Quizzlen has stopped at Evangelina's desk. "And how are you doing this fine day?" he beams, looking down at her. Evangelina slides closer into her desk, covering her bare knees.

"I'm fine, thank you." His grin is so over the top that it's hard to look right at him.

"Well, I hope you're keeping up the good work."

"I'm trying," she says with a peppy voice. She exhales a sigh of relief as he moves on, makes a few more obligatory stops, then heads back upstairs for the day. She exchanges a quick look with Della and they both giggle.

Evangelina returns her focus to the spreadsheet displayed on her computer monitor, working her way through a stack of reports, timesheets and invoices, carefully entering all the budget details into the data base. She's worked through lunch, while she munched on an apple and a cup of yogurt. The work is intense, repetitive and detailed, leaving little time for office banter, but Della's bubbly personality and laughter help create a warm family atmosphere.

In mid-afternoon, Della stretches and leans back in her chair, yawns and says, "Lordy, girl, don't you ever take a break? You been goin' at it like crazy since you walked in."

"Well, I've got a lot of work to do, Della. It seems like I never get caught up."

"I'm glad you work so hard, honey, but after all this is just data entry. You're not negotiating for world peace. You can take a break once in awhile."

"I just like to get my work done." What Evangelina doesn't say is that because she's a contract employee, not one of the regular staff, she could be the first to be let go in a layoff.

"That's good, girl, but you should get out and circulate once in awhile. You dress so snazzy. Sittin' in here all day, you're depriving the males around here big time."

Evangelina considers her clothing. Is Della criticizing her dress? Snazzy? Her skirt isn't too short is it? Just above the knees, that should be okay. She considers her white pumps, then looks over at Della's Nikes. Della's been here for years, so she can dress however she wants. But isn't it important to dress up for work? It shows you take your job seriously. Sure, it's just data entry, but it's important to get it done right. "Those males are just going to have to stay deprived." Evangelina laughs, raising her chin defiantly. "I've got work to do."

"Just don't overdo it, hon, you're too smart to be doin' data entry. You ought to be settin' your sights on something higher. When the time comes, I'll sure put in a good word for you."

"Thanks, Della. That's a very nice thing to say."

Just then a man steps into the office. Tall and distinguished looking. Self-confident.

"Can I help you?" Della asks.

"Agent Stilwell Ferguson, FBI. I'm looking for an Evangelina Gomez."

A sound from somewhere causes Josh to jump, and he realizes that he had nodded off at his workstation. With a long exhale, he turns in his chair and his sleepy eyes take in his familiar small office, the same one he's been in for seven years. He scans the file cabinets stuffed with technical papers and the tall bookcase crammed with physics books. He scrolls across some of the titles, hardly the stuff to ignite conversations with the Brees and Laneys of the world. And he has to admit, stuff that holds little excitement for him these days, subjects he slogged through in graduate school in the middle of the class. He recalls one professor telling him that he was "capable but not exceptional." In other words, mediocre. He sighs.

Maybe he needs a break from the same old routine day in and day out. He's got enough years in for a sabbatical, and Hal's been bugging him about it, dropping off flyers about research opportunities in all kinds of exotic places. Sometimes the flyers fuel Josh's fantasies about running away, but they usually go straight into the circular file because down deep Josh knows he doesn't want to change.

His eyes continue around the small room, across a white board filled with calculations and sketches of detector calibration set-ups, to a small photograph of his father, Jackson Waverly, lecturing before a large audience. Josh used to accompany his father to some of these lectures, back in high school, before his leg injury and his disappointing SAT scores. His father knew how to hold a crowd spellbound, raising provoking questions and laying out apparent paradoxes, keeping his listeners on the edges of their seats. Then, at a key moment, he would pause, then say with emphasis, "Which brings me to my point." Audiences had learned to wait for that moment, when Jackson Waverly would reveal some new truth about the laws of physics. Josh inevitably picked up the habit of saying, "Which brings me to my point," in his own talks, but it never has the same effect as when his father used it. In fact, he used it yesterday, but by then the room had already fallen into a glazed-over state of drowsiness. *So what's wrong with doing gamma ray detector calibrations, anyway?* Is it because Jackson Waverly had his sights on bigger things for his son? Because his dad, down deep, seemed to be ashamed of him?

Jackson Waverly died when Josh was twenty four, collapsing in the middle of one of those famous lectures from a burst aneurism in his brain, while Josh was just across campus, completing a thesis his father would never see. His father's collapse was big news around the university. He hung on for four days, unconscious in the Yale Memorial Hospital, while crowds gathered around his bed, and someone noted that at one point there were two Nobel Laureates in the room with him. What Josh remembers most is that he never got to speak to his father again.

Josh returns his attention to the computer monitor, groans, then looks at the clock. If he's going to make his big move, then this is the time. He decides to drive over to Building 28, though it's just a quarter mile away, because the ground is still muddy from last night's storm. He's been rehearsing all day how he'll segue from his opening words, to coffee, to dinner, but it's Friday and she probably has a date, might even be married — *Stop it, Josh, you'll chicken out again.*

Her office is on the way to the cafeteria, just around that next corner. The door is open, the light is on. He knows that her desk is tucked away to the right, amidst several other desks. He takes a deep breath and enters. But there's no one at her desk. Josh trembles with a rush of disappointment and, he has to admit, relief. A friendly woman asks, "May I help you?"

"Uh, no thanks," he says, backing out the door. The cafeteria is another twenty yards beyond her office. Josh grabs some coffee, still breathing hard from his near encounter, and sags into a seat at an empty table where he can be alone to recover.

Then he sees her at a table across the room. He could speak to her now, but she's talking to a man whose back is to him. She's sitting up straight, hands folded in front of her, listening intently, it appears. Her long black hair has a tousled look, the kind of tousling that is probably the result of intentional design. It falls onto her shoulders and a sizzling pink sleeveless blouse, buttoned up high in front. She has a light brown Hispanic complexion, and her lips are full and voluptuous, though the rest of her is petite. She is probably a native New Mexican, but her nose is slightly angled in a way that may suggest a native American ancestry. Or she could be from Central America. His eyes follow the shapely line of her body, down to the white skirt, which stops just above her knees, along bare brown calves to shapely ankles encased in white pumps. His mouth falls open. *Good grief, am I leering?* He forces his eyes away.

"Hey, Bro!" It's Hal. "Mind if I join you?" he asks, after he's already sat down. Josh is in no mood for Hal right now. Fortunately, Hal doesn't bring up last night, but instead starts talking about the Lab management, always a popular topic of discussion.

Josh could care less. He finishes his coffee while Hal drones on, then stands and says, "Well, Hal, better get back to work. Got a lot of catchin' up to do, you know."

"Q. E. D., Bro. Hey, seen that chick of yours? She's over here somewhere, isn't she?"

"Haven't seen her recently," Josh tries to say with nonchalance. He looks over to where she is sitting. But she and the man are gone. Maybe she's back in her office.

"No time like the present, stud! Like I've been sayin', walk right in and ask her out! Once she sees your handsome face, she'll be putty in your hands." Josh feels his face redden.

Josh could go back by her office, but doesn't. One try today is all he can handle. He slinks out to the Prius and slowly heads back toward his building. Then he sees her, standing next to a car with a man, apparently the man from the cafeteria. He slows to watch them, as the man opens the door of the car. Suddenly the man grabs her arm roughly and begins to push her into the car.

Disbelief, then horror, surges through Josh, and his instinct is to flee, but somehow he is able to turn his car toward them. Twisting frantically, the girl breaks free and starts to run, right toward Josh's car. She stumbles in her pumps, falls to the blacktop, hard. The man is nearly upon her, as she rips the pumps from her feet, then like a flash writhes out of his grasp and is on her feet again, sprinting toward Josh's car. The man is in pursuit, close behind her.

Josh is paralyzed, like his whole body is locking up, unable to push the passenger door open. He wants to shout, "Get in!" but no words come out. But she's already jumping into the car. Josh hits the gas, even before she has pulled the door fully closed. They leave the man standing in the parking lot.

"Oh God, please help me!" the woman shrieks. "You've got to take me to my house. My little girl, she's in danger."

Chapter Three

Josh peels out, to the extent a Prius can peel out, while his chest is about to explode and his brain is churning on overload. He heads toward the heart of the Lab site, with no particular destination in mind, just trying to escape the man in the parking lot, who might be hot on their heels right now.

"Rinconada. That's where I live. You know how to get there?" The girl is breathless.

So is Josh. "More or less. I may need some help."

"Do you have a phone? Mine's still back in the office." Josh fishes his iPhone from his pocket and hands it to her.

The girl begins to dial a number, while turned in her seat to look out the rear window, then stops. "Oh God, he's following us!" Josh checks the rearview mirror and sees a gray car gaining on them. He floors the gas pedal, but the Prius is no match. "Do something! He's getting closer."

Josh can't think. He knows at a gut level that he needs to steady himself, get control of the panic that is raging through him. He wants to cry, he wants to scream, he wants to hide. He doesn't know what to do, but he knows he must do something and do it now. There is no time for a physicist's evaluation of the options. Desperate, he turns sharply to the left, right in front of oncoming traffic. Brakes squeal, cars skid, horns blare, but they make it across the lane.

Josh pulls up to a guard shack at the entrance to a secured classified area. "Get your badge out," he says to the girl. "We should be safe behind the fence."

"I don't have a clearance ... I'm sorry."

Josh slams the car into reverse, then sees the gray car right behind them. He makes a hard right turn and heads up along the sidewalk. *Focus! Focus! Thank God, no pedestrians.* He swerves to avoid a tree, then a fire hydrant. *Is the car still back there? Can't look now.* There's a narrow alley that leads to the left between two large buildings. Josh remembers this route as leading to the other side of the laboratory grounds. He cuts hard into the alley and accelerates past the "Authorized Vehicles Only" sign and in a few seconds they are out onto another street.

Evangelina, up on her knees in the seat to watch out the rear window now turns to Josh. "He's not back there anymore," she says with a long exhale.

Josh, still shaking, says nothing. He merges into the commute traffic and heads through the heart of Los Alamos, toward the road which will lead them down to the valley and Rinconada.

They ride in silence for several minutes, both of them trying to pull themselves together. Then the girl tries the phone again. She hands it back to Josh with a desperate sigh. "My family's not there." She pauses and for a moment Josh thinks she's about to cry, but she doesn't. She continues, "I guess I owe you some explanation. I'm Evangelina Gomez. Thank you for helping me."

"I'm Josh Waverly."

Her words come out fast, in a breathless gush. "That man, I don't know who he is, came by my office … said he was with the FBI … asked me to come over to the cafeteria and talk with him. What choice did I have? I was scared. He said he was investigating the disappearance of some guy who works in my department. Then he asked me to come out to his car to look at some information about the investigation … that's when he grabbed me … I was so stupid."

"Shouldn't we go to the police?"

"No, please, just take me—"

"But they'll help, the station's not far from—"

"No!" she shrieks, then more softly says, "I mean, please let's just go to my house. There's no time to lose."

"Doesn't sound like that guy was really FBI. They wouldn't grab you like that."

"I don't know, I'm not sure. I'm really afraid. I think he called my house last night, so he probably knows where I live. My little girl is there." She gives him a desperate look. "Dear God," she stammers, "We've got get there before he does."

Josh says nothing. It takes everything he's got just to keep the car going straight.

≈≈

In an hour, they pull in under the cottonwoods of Evangelina's home. Even before the car has come to a full stop, she is out the door and bolting toward the house. Josh follows. As he enters the small adobe home, he hears her screams, "Serena! ... Mama! ... Papa!"

She emerges breathless from one of the back rooms. "They're gone."

"Maybe they just went to the store or—"

"No. This doesn't feel right." She darts to the kitchen, as Josh follows. "Look!" she gasps. A fire on the gas stove is on, under a blackened tea pot. She lifts the tea pot. Empty. They exchange a glance.

"Maybe they just forgot to turn off the—"

"No, they wouldn't do that. They left in a hurry. Or," she gasps, "They were taken."

Tears form in Evangelina's eyes. Josh doesn't know what to say.

"Let's go to my uncle's place, it's just up the road." She's already heading toward the front door. But then she freezes in her tracks. "He's here."

Josh is speechless. Through the open door they see the gray sedan has pulled in behind Josh's Prius. Two men are getting out. One has drawn a gun.

"Out the back!" Evangelina whispers with urgency, pushing Josh toward the back door. Quickly, they are out through the back door, then Evangelina grabs hold of Josh's hand and pulls. "To the acequia. We can hide there. Run!"

But Josh cannot keep up with Evangelina. With amazing speed, she sprints toward the back of the property, while Josh lopes along as best he can, his bad leg holding him back. In seconds Evangelina has reached her destination and dives out of sight into what appears to be a low ditch about fifty yards away.

He'll never get to the ditch before they catch him. Panicking, Josh makes it to the rear of a dilapidated garage and ducks in behind the sagging structure. Crouched low, Josh gasps for air, but can't catch his breath. He lays a hand against a pile of old lumber to steady himself, but lets go as it almost topples. Peeking out around the edge of the lumber pile, he sees one of the men, the one with the gun, appear around the side of the house. Shaggy blond hair, a filthy looking shirt hanging out over blue jeans. Definitely not FBI. But who are they, and why are they here?

The men will soon be coming his way, once they've discovered the house is empty. He's a sitting duck here. Can he make it to the ditch? Maybe if he keeps the garage between himself and the men, he can get there without being seen. But it's risky. If they come too quickly around the garage, they will see him. He has no choice. Rising unsteady on his shaking legs, Josh eases away from the garage, backing toward the ditch as quickly as he can, driven by a desperation that overcomes his fear.

His eyes locked on the corner of the garage, around which the men might appear at any moment, his heel catches on something hard, and he starts to go down. His arms flail wildly as he regains his balance. He looks down to see what tripped him, just a small stone, then resumes his awkward flight to where Evangelina has disappeared.

Somehow he makes it to the ditch, which he now sees is a shallow channel of water, probably for irrigation. He drops down into the water, his body sinking partially into the muddy bottom. His head is now below the lip of the embankment. Perhaps they will not see him here.

A tap on his shoulder causes him to jump. It's Evangelina, close beside him. "Stay low," she whispers. "Get down under the water."

They are crouched low in the ditch, up to their chins in the murk, peering through tall grass that lines the bank. The men have left the house and are now in the garage, thrashing around and cursing. Soon they may be heading their way. But there is no other place to run. Josh is breathing hard, but carefully controlling his gasps to keep them inaudible.

Now it's quiet for a moment. Then a voice, a calm voice. "Evangelina Gomez. Please come on out. We just want to talk to you."

More silence. Then the voice again. "Miss Gomez, I met your little daughter this morning. She sure is pretty. I hope she's doing alright." Another moment of silence. Josh feels Evangelina shaking next to him. "Serena. What a beautiful name. Why don't you come out and we can talk about her?"

Evangelina begins to rise from the acequia, perhaps considering going out to meet the men. But Josh pulls her back down into the water. "No!" he gasps, taking in a mouthful of muddy water which he quickly spits out. His voice shakes, but his 'No' comes across as a command. "I don't think they have her. They'd say so. They've got guns. They're not here to talk." Evangelina glares at Josh, shakes free of his grasp, but stays put, trembling.

They lie submerged in the ditch for what seems an eternity. Silence. Then a crashing sound. Then another crash, like breaking glass. Then more silence.

Finally, Evangelina pronounces, "I'm going up. I can't stay here forever."

"But they might still be there." His voice cracks.

"I don't care. I've had enough." She slowly climbs out of the acequia, briefly examines her body, soaked and muddy, and shudders, then heads toward the house. Josh ponders what to do. The men could still be there. They are armed. For a moment, indecisive, he watches Evangelina striding defiantly toward the house. Then he too climbs out of the irrigation ditch, but his soaked loafers slip on the muddy edge, sending him splashing back into the water. On all fours, he makes it out and follows her toward the house.

The men are gone. Inside they find the house has been ransacked. Every drawer has been pulled open, their contents emptied on the floor. Evangelina is frantic, her arms raised high, palms upward, as if she is imploring some deity for help as she surveys her home, now trashed.

Josh is scanning the windows, expecting their sudden appearance. "We've got to get out of here. They could come back."

Evangelina is still doing a slow three-sixty, taking in the mess, but she nods in agreement. "I know. I've got to find Serena. You don't have to come if you don't want to."

Josh opens his mouth as if to say something, but doesn't. He's in over his head. What should he do? What's going on? Who are these men? And why is this woman afraid to go to the police? Maybe he should get out while he can. After all, they don't know him. He can slip away unscathed. Maybe call the police anonymously. Tomorrow it would be like this never happened. A dozen urgent thoughts are doing battle in his brain, and he's unable to sort them out, unable to make a decision.

"Wait a second." Evangelina runs into one bedroom, then the other, and is back in seconds. "Here are some dry clothes for us. We can change later."

"Where are we going?" This is moving way too fast for Josh.

"I've got to get to my Uncle Rey's house. Maybe Serena's there. But the men may still be watching, and we can't risk them following us there. I'm thinking we head out of town, and if they're not following, we can double back. I know some back roads—"

"Hold on, wait a minute," Josh interrupts, putting up both hands, palms forward as if stopping traffic. "It's time to call the police. I insist—"

"No," she shrieks, crossing her arms across her chest. "We need to go now. We can't wait here."

Josh softens his voice. "Can't you just call your uncle?"

Evangelina gives Josh a helpless look. "He doesn't have a phone. We've got one of the few phones in Rinconada."

Out front, from behind a tall bushy juniper, they look up and down the gravel road, scanning for any sign of the gray car, but apparently the men have gone. Turning toward the Prius, they stop in their tracks. Josh gasps. The windows have been smashed, and its tires are slashed. They stand in silence for a moment.

Evangelina grabs Josh's arm and pulls. "There's a truck in the garage. It may still run. Let's go."

It may still run? Josh shakes his head, mouth open, wondering what this woman now has in mind, but follows her back to the old garage he had recently hid behind. The doors are still half open from the men's intrusion, and they step into the darkness inside. There's an ancient Chevy pickup. Must be from the fifties, thinks Josh. A piece of rusted junk. In the dim light, Evangelina finds her way to the rear of the garage and reaches up behind a stud. "Yes! The key's here. Let's go. I'll drive." They have to move a set of saw horses, an old plow, and several large bags of seed to clear a way for the truck. Clearly this thing hasn't been driven in ages.

Evangelina has jumped into the driver's seat and found the ignition. The passenger door creaks as it opens, and Josh has to avoid a sharp spring poking up through the ripped vinyl seat covering, as he slides in.

Amazingly the truck starts, but then it sputters. Evangelina pumps the gas pedal to rev the engine, which coughs a few times then hits a steady stride. Josh also coughs, as the cabin is filled with the odor of gasoline mixed with wet rust.

"Has it got any gas?" he asks.

"Umm, a little. It'll have to be enough." Evangelina has to stretch out her legs, her feet still bare, to reach the brake and clutch, then expertly throws the floor shifter into reverse and eases the truck back into the yard.

Even in his terror, Josh is impressed how she handles the truck. He doesn't know how to drive a stick.

They edge carefully out onto the gravel road, looking for any sign of the gray car. But it's not in sight. "They could be hiding anywhere, waiting for us. We can't risk them finding Uncle Rey's place. Let's head north a few miles, then we'll double back."

As the old truck lumbers along, Josh keeps a keen lookout. They follow a gravel country road out of Rinconada, through broad fields backed by high mesas, now turning a deep pink in the fading sunlight. Piñon pines dot the arid landscape. A few miles north, the road winds into a rugged canyon, sharing the gorge with a river, and Evangelina turns on the headlights, as the sun is lost behind the canyon rim. Along the river and the walls of the canyon are aspens, with just a few golden leaves still clinging this late into the fall. This is country Josh has never seen. *Where is she going?* "Look, there's no sign of them, shouldn't we be cutting back? I'm worried about the gas."

"Would you please stop it? Your worrying isn't helping." She glares at him and he sees fire in her eyes. Then she says, her voice turning soft, "I'm sorry. I think there's enough gas. Let's just get to the top of the canyon, that's where the farm road cuts back."

They ride in silence for awhile. Josh's right hand grips the arm rest, his left is braced against the rusted dashboard. The truck has no seat belts. Evangelina is going too fast, Josh thinks, for the winding road.

As the road begins to climb up the left wall of the canyon, Josh hangs on for dear life, while Evangelina downshifts to keep her speed up. Josh's eyes are glued on the hairpin curves ahead, while risking frequent darting glances back through the rear window.

Then Josh sees them. The gray car is gaining on them. "Oh no, they're back there!"

"How far?" Evangelina's eyes are focused on the challenging driving.

"Maybe half a mile, but they're coming fast. Can't you go faster?"

Evangelina works the shifter again, jamming the clutch and flooring the gas pedal. Josh can detect no increase in speed.

"How did they find us?" Evangelina almost screams.

"How far to the top of the canyon? They're almost here."

"It's still a ways."

The gray car is now just a few feet off their rear bumper. There is no escape. High beams flash, the car's horn blares. "What do they want?" Evangelina shrieks, darting her eyes back and forth between the rearview mirror and the steep, winding road.

Then it happens. The worst thing imaginable happens.

Evangelina, keeping too close an eye on the gray car, misses the next hairpin turn, a sharp curve to the left. She tries to regain control, but it's too late. She cuts the wheel hard to the left while hitting the brakes, causing the rear end to spin out onto the gravel shoulder. The old truck goes over the edge, careening rear first into the canyon.

❦

Stilwell Ferguson and Jesse Smith stand by the roadside, looking down into the canyon at the lights, still on, of the truck far below.

Jesse is elated. "That was cool! You think they're dead?"

Stilwell is thinking it over. "Probably, but we've got to assume they're alive."

"We goin' down to finish business?" Jesse rubs his hands together in anticipation.

Stilwell considers the steep terrain. Darkness has fallen in the canyon interior, and this would be a dangerous descent in the poor light. He glances down at his Ferragamo loafers, hardly the shoes for boulder hopping. Twenty years ago he might have gone for it. "No, we'll wait til morning. The map shows a small town over on the far side of the river. If they're alive, that's where they'll be heading. They'll be afraid to come back up here. We'll be waiting for them on the other side."

"I say let's just go get them now, finish it off."

"It's nice of you to voice your opinion, Jesse," Stilwell says calmly. He turns slowly toward Jesse, then suddenly unleashes a brutal punch to the face that sends Jesse to the ground. "But one more thing. Don't ever, I mean ever, second guess my decisions again. Got it, Jesse?" Stilwell smiles.

Jesse can only nod obediently, as he lies on the ground, holding his bloody face with both hands.

࿇

Josh moves his head slowly. His neck hurts. *Am I alive? Have I been unconscious?* Time seems to have stopped. Through the windshield, surprisingly still intact, all he sees are tree branches and the shafts of light from the headlights shooting off into the darkness. He looks over at the driver's seat. The girl is gone!

Josh tries to move but his body feels like lead, like he weighs a ton. He remains still for a moment. Maybe his back is broken. Then he realizes the truck is in an almost vertical position, pointed upward, at an angle that presses him against the seat back.

He tentatively flexes each arm and leg, testing for injury. They seem okay. He runs his hands over his chest and stomach, down his legs, feels no blood, nothing that seems out of place. The crash plays back in his mind. The truck sliding backward over the edge, then accelerating downward, slowed momentarily as it slammed through a small tree or brush, something, before accelerating again. Bumping, pounding but remaining upright. He remembers looking straight ahead, out the windshield up to the sky. It all seemed to unfold in slow motion, his mind calmly analyzing what was happening, as if he were a detached spectator. He remembers thinking, oddly without a trace of fear, that this might be the moment when he dies.

But he is not dead. And as the adrenalin surge begins to subside, his objective calmness is displaced by a now-familiar terror.

He slides toward the driver's side. The door is unlatched but leaning against the body of the truck. He carefully pushes it open and looks out. Ten feet below him in the dark is Evangelina's body, draped across a thick tree limb. She is not moving.

Josh leans out of the cab and reaches down toward Evangelina, but then the truck lurches, causing him to recoil in panic back into the cab. Instinctively he grabs the steering wheel to hang on, as the hair on the back of his neck stands up, then quickly realizes this provides no real security. As best he can tell, the truck has come to rest in a tree and is teetering above the ground, but how high it's impossible to know. What does he do now?

His heart feels like it might explode, but even in his terror, he knows he can't stay where he is. The truck could fall at any second. And what about the men? They are undoubtedly on their way to investigate. And what about Evangelina? Is she alive? A brief pang of shame washes through Josh as he realizes that he's more concerned with his own safety at this moment than the girl.

He pulls out his cell phone to see if he has a signal down in this canyon, but the phone won't even come on. Of course, it was submerged in that muddy ditch.

He tries the passenger door. It won't budge. A huge tree limb has pinned it closed. Again he slides toward the driver's door. In the dim light he sees another thick limb just a few feet away. He realizes it's the upper reach of the same limb upon which Evangelina's motionless body lies below. If he can make it out onto that limb, he might be able to escape to safety. But it will require a leap out into the darkness. He swallows hard as he looks down again into the darkness, beyond Evangelina's body, but cannot see the ground. He's not sure he can make it to the tree limb, and even if he does, he would have to climb down the tall tree. But he has no choice. It's the only way out. But he cannot make his body, trembling and immobilized by fear, move from the temporary safety of the cab.

Then the truck shifts again. Josh gasps and leaps into the darkness. He grabs the tree limb and holds on with everything he's got, as the truck shakes loose of the tree and crashes downward, the headlights bobbing and bouncing in the dark, before disappearing out of sight.

Josh hugs the tree tight, his arms and legs circling the large limb. Frozen in place, afraid to move, eyes closed, he whimpers.

ༀ

A sound from below jolts him. How long has he been in this tree? Hours? Or just seconds? Did he black out? He's not sure. Nothing makes sense now, nothing fits together. There's only darkness around him, and the tree limb firmly in his grasp. The smooth bark of the tree is damp and slippery, and the air is pungent with the smell of wet leaves.

The panic that overwhelmed him earlier has now subsided somewhat. His mind begins to ponder what to do next. But there is no logical path to follow, no clearly delineated set of options to which a physicist's mind might be applied.

He is beginning to get cold in the late autumn chill of night, and he understands, at least at an intellectual level, the dangers of hypothermia. His clothes are still damp from the irrigation ditch, and this doesn't help. He knows that he must climb down the tree. Now. Even though that means encountering the girl's dead body and whoever else might be waiting for him at the base of the tree. Whoever it was who made that sound a moment ago.

Slowly he begins to inch along the large limb he is on, toward the trunk of the tree. Slivers of faint light from a full moon, filtered through the aspen branches, provide ghostly glimpses of his surroundings. The smooth-bottomed loafers he wore to work this morning are lousy for gripping the slippery bark, and he slips over and over again. He knows that one misstep here could be fatal. As meager as his plan -- getting down the tree -- is, it helps focus his mind onto the work at hand, diverting his thoughts and emotions enough to stave off the panic attack or sobbing fit to which he could easily succumb.

After a few minutes he has made it down to where Evangelina's body had been. But she is not there. Maybe her body fell to the ground when the truck broke loose from the tree. He exhales a deep sob, as the reality of this beautiful woman, now dead, begins to sink in.

The going gets easier when he makes it to the main trunk, much thicker and easier to wrap his arms and legs around. In the darkness he cannot see the limbs below, and each step lower involves dangling a foot and probing the darkness for a new foot hold. So far, so good. He even begins to experience a small level of satisfaction at his accomplishment. An unwelcomed memory returns: his father, hanging his head in shame, when Josh had dropped out of Boy Scouts because he could not shinny up a pole like the other boys. But that was just after the injury to his leg, when he could barely walk. He imagines his father watching him now, gimpy leg and all, descending a tall tree on the side of a cliff in the dark of the night.

Moments later he drops to the ground at the base of the tree and sinks, up to his knees, into a deep pile of leaves. He still holds tightly to the trunk, knowing he is on steep terrain. But there seems to be a level spot here. Exhausted, he collapses at the base of the tree, almost up to his neck now in the leaves. They are still damp from last night's rain, and already he is shaking in a chill. But soon the insulating quality of the leaves begins to warm him, like the slowly growing warmth after crawling in between cold sheets on a chilly night.

He checks his cell phone again. Dead. Then from nearby, a soft rustling sound, then silence. His heart jumps. He thinks about rattlesnakes. They're nocturnal, aren't they? Josh turns his head, trying to identify the location. Then he hears it again, but now something more. It is the sound of sobbing. It's Evangelina. *She's alive!*

"Evangelina!" he calls out. She's not far away, in fact just around the other side of the tree trunk. "I ... I thought ... you were dead," the words coming in emotional bursts.

But her sobbing continues and she does not reply.

"Are you okay? Are you injured?"

No response, just more sobbing. Josh isn't sure what to do. He slithers through the leaves closer to her. Again he asks, "Are you injured?"

"I'm okay," she says through the sobs. Josh moves next to her, both of them buried in leaves. Immediately, Evangelina moves close to him, puts her arms around him and lays her head on his chest. Her sobbing continues, as she trembles. Josh is not sure if her trembling is from the crying or from the cold. He tentatively puts his arm around her, his hand lying as gentle on her back as if he were touching expensive china.

His face in her hair, as her body snuggles close to him, he is almost overcome by how good she smells, even after the horrible day she has been through. Oddly, a fleeting image of long ago flashes in his mind. He's at a high school dance, and he's finally gotten up the courage to ask Megan to dance. He remembers holding her, the feel of the muscles in her back, beneath her smooth cashmere sweater. He was unable to speak. But he still recalls, fifteen years later, the little squeeze she had given his left hand as they danced.

"I think we'll be safe here until morning, but then we'll have to leave quickly," he says, sounding like he has some plan of what to do next.

"I know." Her crying is subsiding.

"I thought you were dead. You're sure you're not hurt?"

"I'm okay, a little sore, that's all." Her voice is now a soft whisper.

For a long time they lie there, not talking, until Evangelina falls asleep.

But Josh can't sleep. Through a thick maze of aspen branches overhead, he watches the moon, crystalline on this clear, still night far from city lights. The serene scene gives little evidence of the jarring reality that they are stranded in rugged wilderness, stalked by killers.

There is much they need to talk about. Topics upon which their survival will depend. Many questions that need to be answered. And he hates unanswered questions. But for now they are safe under this huge aspen midway down a canyon wall, and warm under this blanket of newly-fallen leaves. He's holding a beautiful woman. The only sound is her breathing against his chest. For now, this is enough.

Chapter Four

Saturday, October 15

A shuffling sound nearby brings Evangelina to her feet. Goose bumps pop up on her arms, and she feels the hair on the back of her neck rise as she quickly scans around her. Quiet. Then behind her, the shuffling sound again. She spins. A red squirrel darts from the back side of a tree, then gives her a quick look before dashing up the trunk, as Evangelina sighs relief.

In this cold first faint light of dawn, Evangelina begins to shiver, and she wraps her arms around herself. But her thoughts are not about the cold. They are about Serena. Where is she? Is she okay? She cannot allow herself to imagine that she is anywhere but safe at Uncle Rey's. This was her first night ever away from her daughter. Was Serena able to sleep? Oh God, she must have been afraid, not having her mother nearby or even knowing where her mother was. What will happen when Serena awakens this morning and her mother is not there?

It is only now that Evangelina becomes aware of the terrain where she stands. She is on a level spot at the base of a huge aspen, knee deep in leaves, but just a few feet away the ground falls away steeply, through a dense aspen forest, to the canyon bottom. She cannot see the canyon bottom through the dense maze of tree trunks, or the truck that must lie somewhere below. She shudders and lets out a soft cry, knowing that she must somehow make her way down this canyon wall if she wants to see her daughter again.

Only now does she become aware of a stiffness in her arm, bruised in her fall from the truck. She flexes her elbow several times and concludes that nothing is broken. She also takes inventory of the several scrapes on her arms and legs, where the bleeding that had occurred has now stopped. It is a miracle, she thinks, that she is alive with such minor injuries.

Evangelina looks down at the man next to her, now stirring awake. Josh? Is that his name? What does she do about him? She's grateful he's here. But there's so much he doesn't know. It would be better if he left soon. She studies his face. His skin is pale and looks soft. His features are rather sharply chiseled, and she's surprised to see wire-frame glasses still straddling his thin nose. How had they survived the acequia and the crash? His hair is a light brown, almost blond, and straight. Not too long and not too short, a safe middle length. It's mussed up now, but she imagines that he keeps it neatly combed over to one side. He wears a conservative plaid short sleeve shirt over a white crewneck tee, khaki chinos with a shiny narrow black belt, and soft black loafers.

The Lab is full of guys that look like Josh, highly educated and serious. Her coworkers call them coneheads, with derogatory scorn, but she has always suspected a little jealousy was behind the name calling. She's never really known one of these guys very well. They seem different, come in from places like Boston or Los Angeles with their big fancy degrees. So different from the people she has grown up with, families going back many generations still living in the same community.

There's no question that he was a big help yesterday, but what does she do with him now?

Her thoughts return to her nonstop crying last night. She had plenty to cry about – her missing daughter, the pursuit of dangerous men, but Evangelina seldom cries, even in the worst of times. But it was something else that had shaken her so badly. It was the accident, those horrible first moments, which replay through her mind again, threatening to bring back the tears. The terrifying plunge into the canyon, her spontaneous panicked attempt to flee the truck and fall into the tree branches below, her climb down the tree as the truck crashed to the canyon floor, the horror that an innocent man was being carried to his death.

But worst of all were the memories, the awful memories, it triggered of an event long ago that occurred in the blink of an eye. An event that's haunted most of her life, has caused the terrifying nightmares, has changed her life forever. And Serena's, most importantly Serena's. An event that threatens their lives today.

She brushes damp aspen leaves from her body. Even with all the challenges she faces, she is aware of how disheveled she must look. She notices the glances from Josh, now rising from the deep bed of leaves. *Don't you have something else to look at?* She runs a hand through her long black hair, but it feels tangled and matted. Lordy, what she'd give for a shower and fresh clothes right now, but their change of clothes went down to the canyon bottom with the truck.

Josh is now standing, shivering in the cool dawn, and looking around with a grimace. He's rather tall, maybe six feet. "Geez, we're still here," he says. "I thought maybe this was all just a bad dream."

"Like a nightmare, yes," she says, then pauses. In spite of their awful situation, she is struck by the amazing fact that they are both still alive, in fact uninjured. She also realizes that they are never going to make it out of here unless they can put a positive spin on their circumstances. "But consider this," she says, "We are still here. Doesn't that strike you as amazing? I'm just thinking, if we hadn't gone off the road backwards, so that the seat back cushioned our fall, we'd probably be dead. And if that huge tree hadn't caught the truck, we could have wound up smashing into the rocks and killed, and if the leaves hadn't just fallen from the trees we probably would have frozen to death. Look, I'm really scared right now, but this gives me hope. Maybe someone's watching out for us." For the first time since she climbed into his car yesterday, she smiles.

But Josh frowns. "I think it's time to go to the police. Does your cell phone work? Mine died in that ditch."

"No, I can't do that. Not yet. And anyway, my phone's still in my office back at the Lab. Look, you don't have to stay if you don't want to—" Josh looks down the steep canyon wall into the thick aspen stand. "Okay," she adds, "maybe you don't have any place else to go right at this moment, but when we get—"

"Why won't you call the police? We're in great danger. You don't know where your daughter is. What are you waiting for? You're not wanted for something, are you?"

"No, I'm not, I mean—"

"So why are those guys following you? You must have a clue about that. Or don't you?" He sounds exasperated and his face is reddening, maybe from the cold or maybe from his anger.

"Look, I can't talk about it now. You'll just have to trust me." She looks down, biting her lip.

"Trust you? Look, I've known you for what? Twelve hours, and most of that time we were fighting to survive, I mean—"

"Like I said," she snaps, raising the volume on the word 'said', "You don't have to stay. I appreciate all you've done, but you have no responsibility for me. When we get up to Santuario, you should split ..." Her voice trails off, as tears well up in her eyes.

Josh looks around like he's hoping to find a doorway out of this situation. He opens his mouth to speak but says nothing. Now he's studying her face. *Geez, don't look at me like that. What is that look, anyway? Pity? Contempt?* She looks away.

Then his features soften, as he says, "You say there's a town around here?"

"Santuario."

"Like a sanctuary? That sounds pretty appealing right about now." He smiles.

"Well, Santuario is not much of a town. I think if we can make it across the river and up the other side, we should come out close to it."

"I guess we can figure out what to do when we get there." He shrugs, looks around at the wooded drop-off before them, then adds, "If we ever get there."

Evangelina is thirsty, and she hasn't eaten since lunch yesterday. Her stomach feels cramped and knotted up on itself from hunger. She hadn't noticed missing dinner last night, but that's understandable under the circumstances. But now the hunger pangs are strong. She's certain Josh is feeling them too, but since there's little likelihood of finding anything to eat until they get out of this canyon, she keeps quiet.

They are still wearing the clothes they had on yesterday, now dry but caked with mud and plastered with aspen leaves. Of most concern to her on this rocky terrain is that she is still barefooted.

Silently they begin to make their way toward the canyon bottom. The going is difficult and slow. The terrain is formidable, steep gravelly slopes that make traction nearly impossible, interrupted by sheer granite ledges that require finding handholds to support their descent. They need the thick stand of aspen trunks to hold onto as they work their way down. Evangelina had first noticed Josh's limp yesterday at the acequia, but now she is worried whether he can make it to the river. And her bare feet are beginning to throb.

After a rough half hour of inching their way downward, they hear the rushing sound of the river below, and a few minutes later they emerge from the trees into the narrow canyon bottom. Smooth water-polished stones frame the river. The water is fast, but the level is low. She feels like celebrating and looks over at Josh with a grin. But he is leaning against a tree, gasping for his breath and massaging his leg.

There on the rocks, just upstream from where they have emerged, upside down, its roof crushed, is the truck.

Obviously, the men could be prowling around this area, especially near the truck and especially since the truck does not contain their bodies. Josh's voice is full of caution, "I'm not sure we should we go over there. They could be around here."

"Or watching from the canyon rim."

Josh looks down at Evangelina's feet. They're bleeding. "Oh my God, your feet."

"Yeah, they hurt. I wonder if any of the clothes are still in the cab or if they got thrown out in the fall. My runners were in there with them."

"It's too risky to go over there." Josh pauses. "But I'm not sure you'll make it out of this canyon without shoes."

"You stay here and watch. I'll go check the truck."

Josh runs his hand through his hair, licks his lips like he's about to say something, but then looks down as Evangelina edges out from the security of the trees and hobbles toward the truck. It takes her several minutes, carefully stepping over the smooth river rocks to reach the truck. Down on all fours, she peers into the upside-down flattened cab. Her heart sinks. The clothes, which had been piled on the seat between them, are gone. No doubt lost in the tumbling fall to the canyon floor. But wait. There, wedged between the seat and the floor, the toe of one of her running shoes pokes out. There's barely enough room for Evangelina to extend her arm into the flattened cab, but she's able to grab one of the shoes, and yes! The other shoe is right behind it, tucked under the seat. In moments she has the shoes on and is quickly back to where Josh is waiting in the trees.

"Geez," he says, head cast down, "I shouldn't have let you go out there. That was dangerous."

It sounds like an apology, but Evangelina brushes it off. "No problem," she says, almost jubilant, "I've got my shoes! But I'm afraid the clothes are gone." Then casting a glance toward the canyon wall across the river, she says, "Let's go."

At the river's edge, Evangelina kneels and splashes water on her face and over her bare arms, then drinks from cupped hands. Then she gives Josh a questioning look, as he holds back. "What's wrong?" she asks.

"Don't you know about giardia?" he asks. "I think you can get it from a river." His lips are pursed in a worried frown.

She shoots him a look of exasperation. "Yes, Josh, I have heard of giardia, and no, I don't want to get it." She takes another drink and splashes her face again, then adds,

"But I also don't want to die of thirst. In case you forgot, we haven't had anything to drink since yesterday." She takes another drink. Josh drops to one knee beside her and takes a tentative sip from one cupped hand. Then after a pause he falls to both knees and begins slurping with both his cupped hands.

෯෯

Wiping his face dry with the back of his hand, Josh squints toward the high rugged canyon wall, now washed in the early morning sun, searching for a route up. "I don't see an easy way," he says, "Maybe we should just follow the river back down the canyon."

"We could. But it's going to be miles before we get out of the canyon. There's a town up there somewhere, if we can get up to the top."

Josh marvels at the beauty of the canyon. Sunlight sparkles on the crystalline water, washing smooth polished stones. Tall aspens, white and ghostly, nearly devoid of their golden leaves, are like a silent army guarding the river. It's like a scene from a national park calendar. He and Evangelina should be carrying a picnic basket, looking for a romantic spot next to the river for their lunch, instead of fighting for their lives.

The canyon walls loom high above them, their nearly-vertical slabs of ochre-colored rock jutting up through the clusters of aspens that cling somehow to the steep terrain. Josh estimates the vertical to be at least four hundred feet. He can see no gullies or chutes up which one might climb.

"This looks impossible, unless you're a rock climber," he says.

Evangelina nods her head in agreement, as she continues to scan the foreboding landscape. "I say let's just head up river. At some point, there's got to be a way up."

"How far does this river go?"

"I think it comes out of the Rio Chama, so probably this water comes all the way down from Colorado."

"I hope we don't have to go that far," says Josh, trying to lighten the mood.

But Evangelina doesn't laugh. "Let's stay close to the trees on this side," she says. "If those men are still up by the road, maybe they won't see us. Anyway, this'll give us a better view of that canyon wall."

They continue along the river bottom for another hour. Josh follows Evangelina, who is adroit and nimble at maneuvering across the small boulders and fallen tree limbs, almost catlike. But the round washed river rock does not provide sure footing, and for Josh each step requires watching carefully where his foot is placed, causing him to take his eyes off the cliffs, where the men could be lurking. A breeze whispering through the trees and the sound of the rushing river completely mask any other sound, making them even more vulnerable to a stalker's approach.

Out of the corner of his eye, Josh sees something that doesn't fit. Something metallic and shiny. Something man-made. A surge of panic grips him. He grasps Evangelina's arm. "Get down!"

"What is it?" she gasps, after they've dropped onto the rocks.

Josh points upstream. "I saw something. A reflection in the sun. It might be them. Over there across the river."

Evangelina squints. "I see it too," she whispers.

Josh scans around frantically for a place to hide. Maybe they should crawl back into the cover of the trees. He rejects this idea. It would require too much motion, too much risk of being spotted. Better to stay still.

Moments pass. Evangelina rises to her knees. "It's not moving. Let's check it out."

They remove their shoes to cross the river, which is no more than a foot deep this late in the Fall. Even so, the water is cold and fast flowing and their footing is unsteady. Several times Evangelina reaches out to take Josh's hand for balance.

A few minutes later they stand at the base of a weathered metal sign, punctured with rust-rimmed bullet holes. The letters are barely legible. *Santuario Canyon Trail,* and in smaller letters below, *City Park 2.0 miles.*

"Thank God," says Evangelina. "Way to go, Josh."

"So we don't have to climb the canyon wall after all," grins Josh. But then he realizes something else. "But if those men are coming down here, wouldn't this be the way they'd come?"

"I don't really see an alternative, do you?" She looks at him with wide eyes and raised eyebrows that say this should be obvious to him.

Josh is silent. He casts an anxious glance up the trail, half expecting to see them appear now. "Let's just be careful. That's all I'm saying."

"Sure, but I need to get up there as fast as I can. I've got to get to Uncle Rey's."

The going is slow. The trail evidently has not had maintenance in years. It's littered with fallen trees, which they must climb over. At each switchback they have to navigate narrow stretches where erosion has all but washed away the path, and crossing is precarious.

Josh stops and leans against a tree. His leg is stiffening up. It's been awhile since he's exercised it this much. Evangelina stands in the middle of the trail, waiting for him. She's not breathing hard at all. She says, "We've got to keep going. I've got to find my daughter."

"I know. Just need a moment."

"What happened to your leg?"

"I injured it when I was a kid."

"A sports injury?"

"No."

"So what happened?"

"It was an accident."

"Tell me about it."

Josh looks around at the rugged canyon scenery. He doesn't like talking about this. He feels her eyes on him, but he can't meet her gaze. *Cheesh, does she think I'm some kind of invalid? It isn't even noticeable most of the time. Is it?* Looking down, he says, "It was just some accident. I'll fill you in some other time. Okay?"

"Sorry, I didn't mean to pry. You're a scientist or something?"

"Yeah, a physicist."

"Wow."

"It's not that big of a deal."

"It is to me. I've never known a physicist before."

He shifts the conversation. "So, what do you do at the Lab?"

"I'm just a contract worker. Data entry." Evangelina runs her hand through her long black hair, looking self-conscious. She looks up the trail. "Ready to go?"

"Yes, but first I need some more answers. I think it's time you told me everything you know about these men. I'm not exactly getting a coherent story here, you know. You're being chased by men claiming to be FBI, but they obviously are not. So, who are they? You won't go to the police, even though your life is in danger. What gives?"

Evangelina steps closer to Josh and looks him squarely in the eye. "I swear I do not know who these men are. One of them came into my office yesterday. I already told you that. Flashed a badge that looked official. Started asking me about a man who works in my department. Louis, Louis something. I don't know him. Asked me a bunch of questions about my department, but I didn't know the answers. I was scared. I only do data entry, type in numbers into a spreadsheet. But he wouldn't take my word for it, kept grilling me. Then he asked me to come outside." She pauses and looks down, then back into his eyes. "You know the rest."

"And the police?"

Her large brown eyes are warm and watery. She looks like she might cry. But then they glaze over, as if she has suddenly claimed an inner strength, attained a resolve. "I can't talk about that. Not yet. Just please trust me." They stand in silence for a few moments, eye to eye. Then she says, "Can we go now?"

Josh nods and steps out with his good leg. They continue in silence up the trail, struggling to maintain their footing on the steep stretches. Josh's smooth bottom loafers are nearly useless. But Evangelina isn't doing much better with her running shoes.

Evangelina's focus has apparently returned to her daughter. "Dear God, I hope I can find a pay phone there," she says, as they walk. She seems to be talking to herself as much as to Josh. Thinking it through.

"Thought you said your uncle doesn't have a phone." He's trying to fit together pieces of a puzzle, but things are not adding up.

"I'm going to call Della, she's the woman I work with, maybe she can go over to Uncle Rey's house and see if my family's there." After a few moments she adds, "Or maybe I can find someone to drive me there."

"I hope you find them," he says, then silently censures himself. *What a lame comment.*

He thinks back to her comments about how lucky they were to be alive. The truck going down backwards, the tree, the leaves. About how maybe something or someone was looking out for them. He hadn't responded. Hadn't known what to say. He usually avoids any kind of spiritual issues, doesn't see how it makes sense rationally, and such talk makes him uncomfortable. He had thought about saying, "Yeah, and if those killers hadn't been after you in the first place, none of this would have happened!" He's glad he hadn't. But now, following Evangelina up the trail, despite all the unanswered questions, he cannot help but appreciate her shapely and agile body beneath the white but now filthy skirt, her smooth brown muscled calves working on the steep grade. And what he might say now, if he had another chance, would be, "Yeah, and if those killers hadn't been after you in the first place, I wouldn't have had you in my arms all night." Maybe he would say that, but probably not.

They pause for another breather. The sun is now high in the cloudless sky. It feels about ten. Like his cell, his watch stopped working after its plunge into the ditch. They stand side by side, gazing out over the deep canyon. She comes up to about his chin, must be about five-six. He notes the fine patina of perspiration on her forehead.

"Where is your husband?" Then he adds, "I'm sorry, I don't mean to pry."

"You're full of questions, Josh. I don't have a husband. Single mom." She says this matter-of-factly.

"Oh." Then he adds, "I mean that's okay."

"So what about you? You have a family?"

"No. Just me."

"No sisters or brothers?"

"Nope."

"Not even some parents somewhere?"

"My mother lives in California. My father is dead."

"Do you see your mother often?"

"Not often. We weren't close."

Evangelina seems puzzled and curious about this. "I'm sorry. You mean you don't ever talk to your own mother? That must be—" Suddenly she's pointing up the trail. "Hey look!" Through the trees, the canyon wall is now being replaced by blue sky. They are near the top.

❧

The blue sky, peaking through the aspens above them, has renewed their energy, and minutes later they emerge onto a level mesa top. Josh leans over, hands on knees, breathing hard, while his eyes scan the surroundings. No sign of the men. After several moments, when his breathing has eased, Josh turns and looks back into the deep canyon. From here he cannot see the canyon floor, the river or the wrecked truck. A good thing, he thinks, imagining that the men had probably stood right here peering down into the canyon.

They are in the midst of what apparently was once a park. Small broadleaf trees, most of them dead, dot a brown field of dead grass, overgrown in weeds. No cars or people in sight.

They follow a gravel road that leads them out of the park into what appears to have at one time been a new housing subdivision. One that never got started. A large weathered sign reads, *Welcome to Azurite Acres, Santuario's newest residential community. Now building. Select your canyon home now.*

"Azurite is a copper mineral," notes Josh.

"I know that," says Evangelina, with an edge that suggests his comment had been condescending.

Two boarded-up structures look like they had been model homes. A sign in front of one of them, now barely legible after enduring years of the New Mexico sun, shows a map of the development and the available lots.

"This is depressing," says Josh.

"Welcome to Santuario."

"It looks like no one lives here."

"Well, that's almost true. Gee, this place looks just as bleak as I remember."

"You've been here before?"

"Just once, a few years ago. I don't think very many people come here."

"Looks like there were big plans for this place at one time."

"Yep. Santuario used to be a little village, like Rinconada. It's been here for centuries. Farming and weaving. Maybe you've seen some of the famous Santuario rugs?"

Josh gives her a blank look.

"Or maybe not," she adds.

"What happened? This place looks like a bad dream."

"They found copper in the hills over there." Evangelina is pointing toward a rugged barren ridge in the distance. "My father told me that a mining company moved in and started buying up land, said they were going to make Santuario a modern American city, with all the conveniences the thousands of employees would need."

"Let me guess. It didn't work out."

"You noticed." Evangelina laughs, the first time Josh has seen her laugh. He likes it. She continues, "So the mining company started pouring a lot of money into

Santuario. A few stores, you'll see them. Modern streets. And I guess this housing development was part of it."

"What happened?"

"There was no copper. As quickly as the mining company moved in, they moved out."

"So now it's a small village again?"

"With these ugly scars they left behind. That's one reason nobody ever comes to Santuario."

The terrifying events of the past twenty four hours flash through his mind. "Well, if the Chamber of Commerce wants a testimonial, I've gotta say, I'm awfully glad to be in Santuario." He smiles at Evangelina, who returns his smile.

"Me too. Now let's find a telephone."

The road from Azurite Acres feeds into a broad two lane paved street that appears to be the main drag. It's empty. They walk past a supermarket, now closed and boarded up. Across the street, a modern brick building sits at the rear of a paved parking lot. An expensive bronze sign, set upon a large stone base, says *Santuario City Hall*. The building is empty and a forest of tall weeds rises from cracks in the parking lot. Shaking his head, Josh says, "I feel like I'm in one of those day-after-the-nuclear-war movies."

They pass several more abandoned buildings, separated by vacant lots, with sun-bleached signs bearing messages like *Excellent Commercial Opportunity*.

Evangelina stops in the middle of the road, her forefinger on her chin. "This is the new section, I think. Hmm, let's go that way." She points off to the right, apparently knowing where she's going. Down a narrower gravel road, they come to several older buildings that appear to be occupied. The old town. Evangelina picks up her pace, apparently seeing what's she's after. A small convenience store sits midblock a hundred yards away.

The store occupies an old adobe building and looks like it's been there for years, certainly predating the copper boom. *El Mercado de Santuario*, reads a painted sign over the door. Merchandise lines the front of the building. Bundles of firewood, a couple of faded wheelbarrows, a rack holding shovels, rakes and hoes. An old Coke machine. And a telephone booth.

"I don't imagine you've got change?"

"You kidding?" Josh laughs. "Let's see if we can place a collect call on it."

They both see it at the same time. A few blocks away, the gray car has turned onto their street. For an instant, they freeze in place, as the car speeds up. They've been spotted.

Josh feels the now familiar surge of panic return. Looking left and right, he cannot see a way to go. Through the store. That's the only way. "In here," he gasps, grabbing Evangelina's hand and pulling her into the store. The interior of the store is dark, and Josh's eyes, conditioned by the bright sun, cannot see how to navigate through the aisles. He crashes into a counter, sending dozens of small plastic items rattling to the floor. He can't tell what they are in the dim light. Turning, he stumbles over a large burlap bag of seed, or something.

Evangelina follows behind him, clutching his hand, as they fumble their way to the rear of the store. An old woman watches in silence as they race through. In the back, past a sink and a mop, which Josh knocks over, they come to a screen door. Beyond they find themselves in sunlight again. They pause for just a moment, looking around for an escape route. They're standing in a dirt alley. Beyond them is a small storage shed, then another dirt road, lined with small adobe homes. No sign of the car yet.

"This way." Josh points to the houses a hundred yards away. "You run. I'll get there as fast as I can."

Evangelina releases his hand, shoots him a look of appreciation, and sprints off toward the houses. Josh follows, running with only a little pain in his leg. Apparently the hike has limbered him up. Across the dirt road, he plunges into a thicket of tall junipers. There, Evangelina waits.

"They'll be down this road in a second. Let's keep going out the back." They climb a low wooden fence into someone's yard, which starts a dog barking. On the far side of the yard, a large mangy dog, teeth bared, snarls and lunges toward them. They make it over a second low fence, just as the dog is upon them. Now they are in a vegetable garden. Making their way through vines of squash, they come to the edge of a sparse forest of plump piñons, head high. This should give them a little cover. They stop for a second to catch their breath.

"I say let's keep going," Evangelina says. Josh nods and continues. In fifty yards, they come to another dirt road. Fewer houses on this street. And beyond, nothing but barren landscape, dotted with piñons and yellow chamisa. To the right, a quarter of a mile away, sits a sprawling, one-story brick building. It's not clear if the building is occupied, but it could be a place to hide. They exchange a glance and nod, and without words begin running toward the building, checking frequently over their shoulders for the car.

They make it to the front of the building and push against a glass entrance door. "Cripes, it's locked," Josh gasps, as the door does not budge. He looks over his shoulder again, then pushes harder and the sticky doors swing in. Inside, they both stop to catch their breath again.

"Do you think they saw us come in here?" wonders Josh, still gulping for air.

"I don't think so." As they back into the interior of the building, away from the doors where they could be spotted, they see the gray car drive by slowly. But it doesn't stop.

They turn to see a young receptionist behind a low counter.

"Who are you?" the woman demands. "You can't stay here unless you have a family member here. You'll have to leave now."

They don't know what to say.

Then, from behind them a voice, loud and unsettling, "There you are!"

Chapter Five

Evangelina turns quickly toward the voice. A small white-haired woman is bent over a walker.

"My kids! I knew you'd come!"

The receptionist interrupts. "Maggie, these aren't your kids. These people just wandered in off the road. Look how dirty they are. They're homeless, I suspect." The woman glares at Josh and Evangelina. "Now you must leave. Only residents and their families are allowed here."

Josh whispers to Evangelina, "What is this place?"

Evangelina looks toward the glass doors. No sign of the gray car, but there's no way they're going back out there. "I'm not sure," she whispers back. Then she says to the receptionist, "I just want to use your telephone, please."

"The telephone is for residents and their families only. State regulations. Now I must ask you to leave."

"But they're Gwen and Roger, my kids." There's now a high-pitched sound of desperation in the old woman's voice. "Gwen, you bring Roger on down to my place. You can stay with me. I'll fix us a nice—"

"Maggie, these people are not your children. Now you go back to your room."

Now a third woman has joined them. She's tall and slender, elegant in stature, her hair is a metallic silver, tied back in a bun, and she must be at least eighty. "What's all the commotion?" she asks with a gentle but firm voice.

"Esther, my kids are here! Gwen and Roger, this is Esther."

The woman at the desk intrudes again. "Listen, I've told you to leave. If you do not leave, I'll have to call the authorities. Do you understand?" The woman's voice has become loud and shrill.

"Now, Olive," Esther says, "take a deep breath. You're not going to call anybody. These folks don't seem to be hurting anyone." Turning to Josh and Evangelina, she extends her hand and says, "I'm Esther. Welcome to Copper Point. So you're Maggie's kids, huh?" She gives them a wink. "Maggie's been waiting for you for a long time." She turns back toward the woman at the desk. "Olive," she says with a firmness that indicates there will be no negotiation about this, "we need to make a place for Gwen and Roger to stay. Isn't there an empty room near Maggie's place?"

"You know I'll have to check with Mrs. Harshburn first."

"Olive, this is family. You don't have to check with Mrs. Harshburn or anybody else."

"But Esther, these people just wandered in off the—"

"Olive, we need to find Maggie's kids a room. Her apartment is too small. Now, why don't you give me the key . to that place that just opened up?"

Esther has taken control of the situation. Grimacing, Olive reaches under the counter, fiddles in a drawer, and brings out a key, which she hands to Esther.

"Thank you, dear," Esther says to Olive, who is now silent. Then she turns to Josh and Evangelina. "Kids, why don't you follow me?" Another wink.

Josh and Evangelina exchange puzzled looks, glance once more out the door toward the road, then dutifully follow Esther down the hall.

"So, just what is Copper Point?" asks Josh.

"Copper Point Senior Living Center. That's nice talk for old folks home."

Evangelina takes in the scene. The hallway of Copper Point is depressing. The walls are concrete blocks, painted a dirty tan. There are no pictures, probably because of the impenetrable concrete surfaces. The ceiling is cheap acoustic tiles, and quite a few of the tiles are missing. Others are stained brown from water leaks. There is a faint smell of urine. "Look, Esther, it's kind of you to offer us a room, but we don't need to stay. We just need to use a phone."

Esther stops and faces them. "Suit yourself. But I take one look at you two and I see a couple who are down on their luck. Doesn't take Einstein to figure that out. You're filthy. Have you had anything to eat today?"

Evangelina gives Josh a quick look, then says to Esther, "Well, no we haven't. We are hungry."

"And you two sure look like you could use a shower. I figure you don't have a car, otherwise you wouldn't have stopped here. I'd like to hear how you got here, bet you've quite a story. After you get cleaned up and we get some food in you, of course."

Quite a story indeed, thinks Evangelina. She studies Esther's face. It's smooth and amazingly wrinkle free, but her skin has that translucent porcelain look that many elderly have. She is very thin and there's a hollowness under her cheekbones. More delicate than frail. Her eyes, a very pale blue, are deep set and have a piercing quality that makes you want to look away, as if somehow she might be able to see right through you.

Esther unlocks a door and stands aside. "It's not much," she says, "but there's a shower and a bed. I'm guessing you two didn't bring a couple big Samsonite roller bags full of fresh clothes, right?" She pauses and smiles. "Figured as much. I have to think about how we're gonna get you some fresh clothes."

Evangelina takes in the room. A double bed against the far wall. A sagging sofa near the door, covered in torn rust-colored vinyl. A small writing table and chair. The gray concrete walls are stark in the harsh fluorescent light, and they are bare, except for a simple cross hanging above the bed. A small window with drawn venetian blinds, several of the slats broken. Most importantly, there's a phone by the bed.

"Lunch is served at eleven thirty. I'll be back to escort you down to the dining hall."

"What time is it now?" asks Josh.

"Why, hon, it's eleven. So if you're going to get a shower, you'd better hurry." Esther gives them a gentle smile and leaves.

"One more thing," Evangelina calls after Esther. "May I use the phone?"

"Of course, dear."

Without hesitation, Evangelina lunges for the phone and starts to dial her work number, then stops, remembering it's Saturday. She lets out a soft whimper, then dials information, praying that Della's got a listed number. She does and in a moment the phone rings. Della picks up on the second ring, bringing a great sigh from Evangelina.

"Della, am I glad to hear your voice."

"Evangelina! Where are you? Are you okay?"

Josh is standing in the doorway, watching her, and she gives him an I'd-like-some-privacy look. He backs out the door, while saying, "I think I'll just take a little walk."

Returning her attention to the phone, Evangelina says, "I'm okay." Of course this isn't true, but it seems best to sound calm at this point. Then she says, "Della, I need your help."

"Anything, girl, you got it. But I gotta tell you, there's been a lot of commotion around here. Quizzlen even called me to—"

"I want to hear about it. But right now I need you to go down to Rinconada, where I live, and check on my family. Okay?"

"Sure, but why can't you go?" There's an edge of concern in Della's voice. "Are you in some kind of trouble?"

"I'm fine," she lies. Can't risk Della calling the police. Not yet. "But I just can't go right now, and Della, I need to know that they're okay. They don't have a phone."

"Tell me how to get there."

Evangelina gives Della the directions to Uncle Reynaldo's house. "I'm not sure of my number here, and I don't know how long I'll be here, so can I call you back in a little while? You have a cell?"

Della gives her the number and says, "I'll go right away. Now look here, Evangelina, I don't know what's going on with you. When you didn't come back yesterday, I got worried but just figured you left early. But then a little later I decided to check the parking lot and your car was still there. And then I checked your desk and saw your purse was still there. Evangelina, what's going on? Did that FBI man take you away?"

A long silence. "Della, first of all, he's not an FBI man, and second, well I just can't tell you about it right now. I ask you to trust me—"

Della cuts her off. "Evangelina, you need to know that after you left yesterday, we heard from the police about Louis Wessel. I don't think you knew him, but he's dead. They found his body out in the boonies by some campground. And word is he may have been murdered."

A chill grips Evangelina's spine, but a steely determination keeps her going. "Dear God, that's awful. But right now, just please check on my family. Tell them I'm okay. I'll call you back in a couple of hours. Okay?"

"You take care of yourself. I'll wait for your call."

"Della, if I don't make it in on Monday, can you cover for me with Dr. Quizzlen?"

"You got it. But he's so wrapped up with the big wigs, he probably won't notice."

Evangelina replaces the handset and looks around the room. She feels better, knowing she can count on Della. But then she sags, staring at the blank wall. What does she do now? The last year has gone so well. It seemed like things were finally turning around. Then this. Just the latest reminder of the disastrous choices she has made.

While Evangelina makes her call, Josh wanders down the hallway toward the rear of the building. He holds his hands to his head like he's got some terrible migraine, but it's just because his mind is still racing with all the events of the past twenty-four hours. In a life that has been so predictable, so humdrum, so safe, how did he wind up in this mess? He's not even completely sure what the mess is. There are too many questions to sort out. He needs to prioritize. Right now he cannot think about questions like why Evangelina is afraid of the police or even why these men are after her. There are more urgent issues to worry about. Like where are these men right now? They are cruising this small town, he knows that much. Had they been spotted entering this building? Probably. Will they soon be storming in? A new surge of fear courses through Josh's body as he considers this threat.

Oddly he remembers an old TV show that Hal made him watch. MacGyver. MacGyver was a secret agent who always wound up in a dangerous situation, usually accompanied by a beautiful woman, and used his knowledge of physics to outwit the villains and save the girl and himself. MacGyver always knew how to improvise with a Swiss Army knife, a roll of duct tape, or whatever happened to be lying around to create a way to defeat the bad guys. Josh has got the dangerous situation and the beautiful girl, for sure, but as he considers his own physics knowledge he comes up short. Theoretical subjects. Advanced math. Microelectronics. They all seem pretty useless right now. This evokes an audible chuckle from Josh. He has no clue at all about what to do next.

Maybe he should call the police, even if Evangelina disapproves. But no, that doesn't feel right. He doesn't know all the facts, but he feels like he needs to trust the girl right now. He realizes, of course, that this feeling may stem largely from the effect of her beauty on him. He sees no alternative for the time being to staying put here in this strange depressing place.

With a huge sigh, Josh stops in the hallway and considers his surroundings. The place is deserted. *Where are all the residents?* He's never been in an old folks home before, never wanted to visit one, always thought they'd be too depressing. But though he's heard some awful stories about such places in his life, this place is even more depressing than he could have imagined. The floor is covered with the kind of cheap carpeting you'd see in a garage or workshop, a tough outdoor grade obviously designed for abuse and not good looks. The carpet is heavily stained, and Josh wonders about the origin of the stains.

The fluorescent lights give the hallway a cold institutional feel, rather dark because perhaps half the tubes are out. *Do they have any maintenance around here?*

There's a small name-card holder on each door along the hallway, but only a few of them have name cards. The few doors that have name cards are also decorated with festive decorations that make Josh sad. A birthday card or a brightly-printed little saying: "The loveliest flower in God's garden," "Laughter is the best medicine" and "World's Best Mom." Some of the doors are adorned with a few artificial flowers and one still has a Christmas wreath. It all strikes Josh as pathetic attempts to brighten up this gloomy place.

He comes to where the hallway branches into two other hallways. At the junction, he briefly considers if he wants to explore farther. Evangelina should be done with her call by now. He starts to turn around, but just then something catches his eye. A motion, a shadow, maybe nothing at all, maybe just his imagination. Get a hold of yourself, Josh, he almost says out loud. He shakes his head slowly and silently chides himself about how jumpy he is right now.

He turns and his heart almost explodes. Out of nowhere, a hulk, a giant, is blocking his way. A dark ominous presence looming over him, nearly reaching the ceiling, blocking the light from the fluorescents. A tiny squeal is the only sound that comes out of Josh, and he feels his knees buckle. Large hands grab him by the shoulders, strong hands that hold him fast.

"Are you okay?" comes from a deep voice.

For a moment Josh is silent, then quickly recovering and now somewhat embarrassed, he says, "Yeah, I'm fine. You scared me, that's all." Standing before him and above him is the largest and blackest man he's ever seen in his life.

"Sorry about that," the man says in a deep, clear voice, "I was just on my way down to the laundry room. Didn't mean to startle you. I'm Hollister Williams."

Breathing easier now, Josh says, "Josh Waverly," and reaches out to shake the huge hand that is extended towards him.

"You visiting someone here?"

"Not really, we're just here for a little bit. Had to use the phone. Esther said it would be okay."

"Esther, huh? Now there's a character. She'll take care of you, all right."

"Seems like a nice lady."

"Oh yeah, she's nice all right. In fact, I'm not sure this place wouldn't fall apart if Esther wasn't around." Casting a glance at the walls, he laughs, "Anymore than it's already falling apart, that is."

"You live here?"

"Well, temporarily I guess. I'm staying with my grandmother, Rosey Williams, who's a resident here."

Josh looks up into the face of the huge man. High chiseled cheek bones, a wide nose, and large brown eyes, warm and gentle, that cause his fear to dissolve. Braided black dreadlocks down to his shoulders. "May I ask how tall you are?"

"Six nine."

"You must be a basketball player. Sorry, I guess you get asked that a lot."

"It's okay. Yeah, I played at Creighton a couple years back."

Now self-conscious, Josh puts his hands on his hips, stretches his six-foot frame and sucks in his gut, like he's ready for a little one-on-one. He's not sure what to say next. "Well," he says, but then has nothing to add. Neither, apparently, does Hollister.

After another awkward moment, Hollister says, "So I'll see you around, Josh," and heads off down the hall.

Josh returns to the room to find Evangelina sitting on the bed, holding the phone in her lap. She extends it toward Josh and asks, "You need to use the phone?"

He ponders this question for a moment, realizing that there is not one person who will be worrying about where he is today. He has absolutely no one to call.

❧❧

A poke on his shoulder causes Josh to jump. Esther is standing behind him with an armload of clothes. "These ought to be about the right size for you two."

"Where did you find clothes for us?" Josh asks.

"They belonged to some of the residents."

"Won't they mind?"

"Oh," she says with a smile, "they won't be needing them anymore."

"You mean…?" Josh starts to ask, but Evangelina, now standing beside him, gently rests her hand on his arm and he stops.

"Thank you, Esther. These look great," she says.

"You better shower pretty fast, kids. Lunch is in fifteen minutes. I'll be back to walk you down. And we'll get your clothes washed too."

"Oh, you don't need to—" Evangelina says, but Esther has already left.

Josh and Evangelina look at each other and laugh. Josh almost melts at her beauty, even in her disheveled condition, even with all the fear and worry that must fill her. He has the urge to put his arms around her, but holds back.

"Let's see what we got," she says, flopping the clothes out on the bed.

"Almost anything would be better than what I've got on," says Josh, looking down at his muddy clothes.

"You might want to rethink that," Evangelina says, laying out a pair of maroon wool pants, a white dress shirt and a button-up green wool sweater. She then spreads out a long white dress. "But this isn't too bad," she adds.

She scoops up the dress and the underthings that Esther has brought and darts into the bathroom. "I call first shower," she laughs over her shoulder.

Josh watches the bathroom door close behind Evangelina, amazed at how easily this woman can warm his frightened empty heart.

❧❧

Stilwell Ferguson stands beside the Maxima at the only gas pump in Santuario, while Jesse fills the tank. He thinks through the situation carefully. Analysis has always been his strength. The ability to coldly assess all the possibilities, weigh all the odds, determine the best course of action. He's seldom been wrong. After Louie's stupidity, it was necessary to do something about the girl, quickly before she learned of Louie's death and could take flight. After their talk, and her obvious evasiveness, it was clear she was hiding something. He could not just walk away. Closing out this deal means elimination of all the dangerous loose ends. It means killing the girl. But this has been frustrating. More difficult than he had anticipated.

He paces the area around the pumps, brooding. Just then his cell rings. Only one person ever calls this number, so Stilwell knows who it is. The Contact. He checks caller ID, always a different number, apparently from an untraceable no-contract phone. He groans, knowing he'll have some explaining to do, before clicking the talk button.

"So the trail on Wessel was not clean," the voice says, "the cops are looking into it. This was supposed to look like an accident. Are you slipping, Stilwell?"

"The cops won't be able to tie it to anything. I'm not worried."

"When you took out Tucker two years ago, everyone thought he'd just left town. No investigation, clean. I don't like it when the cops are snooping into things."

"You know as well as I do, they'll never make a connection to anyone. Not me, certainly not you." No one knows the name of the Contact other than the Client. Not

Stilwell, certainly not the lowlife gofers like Wessel and Tucker.

"Maybe you're right. But involving the girl was a stupid move, Stilwell. Not like you."

Stilwell wonders how the Contact already knows about the girl. "I got her name from Wessel. So she was already involved. I figured I had to move fast."

"I don't have to tell you that you are to never appear on Lab property. That is too risky. How could you—"

"Look, we tried her home first. It was seven in the morning. She should have been there, but she had already left for work. Going to the office was safe, I cased it out. Do you think I'm some kind of an idiot? I don't like your insinuations that I don't know what I'm doing. She was alone in the office, just her and some dumb broad, who didn't seem to notice anything. I talked with the girl, seemed like some ignorant Mexican bimbo, but she was evasive, scared—"

"But that doesn't mean you should—"

"I think she knows something, maybe something big." Stilwell isn't sure any of this is true, but he savors making the Contact squirm, sitting there in some air-conditioned office while he's out here in this hole of a town.

"What indication other than Wessel's BS do you have that she knows anything?"

Stilwell considers what he is about to say next, enjoying the moment. "For one, I see no indication that she's called the police. They'd be swarming around here if she had. That alone tells me she knows something, she's got something to hide."

"Like?"

"I think she may have pieced together the chain of operations, or at least the Weasel did and he let the bimbo know. And then her getaway. Not normal. A car waiting to whisk her away. Think about that. Could she have signaled a getaway car when I asked her to go outside? And she hasn't called the cops, like I said, it all fits together." He pauses another moment to let the Contact stew. "Yes, there's something fishy going on here."

The Contact is silent.

He adds, matter-of-factly, "I'm thinking she may be a danger to you." Stilwell grins as he paces in circles around the pump, while there is another moment of silence on the other end.

Then the Contact speaks. "Either way, she's involved now, now that you botched your hit. We've got no choice but to take her out. Think you can handle that Stilwell?"

"Of course." Stilwell stiffens at the Contact's questioning of his proficiency. Though they've never met, he has a mental picture of the Contact's face. And right now he'd like to be mashing his fist into it. Yet, the Contact is his anonymous connection with the Client, the top rungs of this business, and Stilwell wisely knows his boundaries. He has his suspicions about who the Contact might be, but he's a veteran and knows to keep such ideas to himself. His job is to be the link to the lowest operatives like Wessel and, of course, he's the one on whom falls the responsibility for the really dirty work, at which he excels. "And there's one more thing," Stilwell adds, "There's a guy, a Josh Waverly, who's with her. We've got to assume he knows whatever she knows."

The Contact shouts out a string of obscenities, then pauses. "So you need to deal with him too. But I don't have to tell you, Stilwell, this has got to be clean. No trail. You're the professional, I shouldn't have to tell you that either."

Stilwell's face flushes, as his temper flares, but he keeps himself under control. "It might not be easy getting to them."

Another silence on the other end. "So, Stilwell, do I need to come up there and show you how to do your job?"

Seething, Stilwell answers, "It'll be taken care of soon."

"That's not an option." There is a click on the other end.

Stilwell pockets his cell, then suddenly unleashes his fury by kicking a plastic tank containing window cleaner and long windshield cleaning brushes, sending water and brushes flying.

This brings an attendant running out from the office. "Hey, what do you think you're doing, pal?"

Stilwell shoots the attendant a glare so menacing that he stops midway between the office and the pumps, puts his head down and returns to the office.

He's gotta think this through carefully. *We've got to get the girl.* Despite his big talk to the Contact, he's still not sure what she knows. Maybe nothing, but maybe she knows enough to do some real damage. Maybe they could have ignored her, no harm done. Maybe. But that's not the way a thorough practitioner like Stillwell Ferguson operates. Of course, ever since the incident in the parking lot yesterday, ignoring her is not an option. He feels the rage surging in his chest. He kicks the window washer container again. How could he have anticipated her speed and strength when she so quickly squirmed out of his grasp? And how did they survive that crash into the canyon?

And this guy. Josh Waverly. That's the name on the Prius registration. How is he involved? The situation has gotten more complicated.

But it's about to get a lot less complicated. Gomez and Waverly are here in this cesspool of a town, that much he knows. And they're on foot. He saw them this morning darting into that store. But where did they go after that? *Maybe you're getting old, Stilwell.* One thing for sure, he'll make them pay for this, make them suffer extra for this humiliation. No one does this to Stilwell Ferguson.

Jesse has finished filling the tank. "What are we gonna do now?" he asks. Apparently the Cro-Magnon has regained a little respect after shooting his mouth off yesterday.

"We know they're here, probably not far away. We know they went out the back of that convenience store. Wherever they're holed up right now, we know it's a place they got to from the back of that store. It's just a matter of time before we get them, and when we do …" Stilwell doesn't finish the sentence.

"Take care of business?" the submissive Jesse asks.

"Oh yes, we're definitely going to take care of business."

"Where do you think they are now?"

"Close by. Get in the car. I want to check out that brick building two streets over from the convenience store. They could've made it that far."

Jesse licks his lips in anticipation. He's never even bothered to wipe the blood, now crusted, from his filthy face.

Chapter Six

An old man's clothes. Josh groans as he studies the stiffly starched white shirt with a monogram, DS, over the pocket. DS, whoever that is. Was. The maroon wool pants, good grief, is he actually supposed to wear these? But they are neatly ironed and creased, and they're clean. He appreciates Esther's kindness.

The bathroom door opens and Evangelina steps out into the room, nearly taking Josh's breath away. The long white gossamer dress reaches almost to the floor. She looks ethereal, angelic. The neckline, rimmed in a delicate lace, comes up high around her neck and the sleeves, with puffy frilly cuffs, reach to the wrist. She is stunning.

"Ready to escort me to the ball, Mr. Darcy?" she asks with an affected British voice, then giggles, while extending one hand delicately toward him.

Yes, she does look like one of those beauties from a Jane Austen novel, but then he glances at his new duds and pictures himself as an old geezer preparing for the seniors golf classic. "My pleasure, my dear, as long as you don't mind going with Grandpa Jones." They both laugh as he heads in for his shower.

No sooner does Josh emerge from his shower, but there is a knock at the door, which causes both of them to jump.

It's Esther. "Ready for lunch?" she asks, then says, "My, aren't you two the smashing couple, if I don't mind saying so myself."

"Thank you, Esther," says Evangelina. "You really shouldn't have gone to all this—"

"Of course I should," Esther interrupts. "You're guests. Now, are you ready for lunch?"

"Yes we are," Josh is quick to say.

Evangelina says, "By the way, I'm Evangelina Gomez, and this is Josh, uh, Waverly," apparently stumbling to recall his last name for just a second. "I'm not sure we ever really got introduced."

They follow Esther, who moves with a brisk purposeful stride, to the dining room, just off the lobby area. It's a large room, obviously designed to accommodate a hundred or more, but there are just five round tables set up in one corner of the room. About twenty five people. The walls are concrete like the rest of the place and are painted a flat gray, probably a primer coat still waiting after all these years for a colorful finish coat. No pictures on the walls. Same industrial carpeting and garish fluorescent lighting as in the hallways.

"You'll be at my table," she says to them. Evangelina and Josh take their seats in folding metal chairs. The table is covered with a cheap plastic table cloth, worn through in several places. Two others are already seated. One is Maggie, who had earlier thought they were her children. The other is an elderly man, hunched and shriveled. He wears thick glasses and a well-worn cap with the letters USMC. "Where's Rosey today?" Esther asks the others.

"She's having lunch in her room with her grandson," says the old man.

"Rosey is our other table mate," Esther explains to Evangelina and Josh. "Her grandson Hollister is here visiting, a rather extended visit, you might say."

"Hollister Williams. I met him a little earlier," Josh says.

Esther does introductions. "Josh and Evangelina, this is Maggie, who you already met."

"Who are these people?" Maggie asks, confused, obviously forgetting their earlier meeting.

"Just visiting us, dear. And this is Bud."

"Bud Ewing," the old man growls and extends a hand. His eyes look huge, magnified through the thick glasses. His head sits low on his shoulders, like a tortoise whose head is partially retracted into its shell.

The food has not yet been served. While they wait, Josh tries to make conversation with Bud. "So you were in the Marines?"

The old man immediately perks up. "Sure was, young man. Korea for two years. Fifth Regiment, First Division. We were there in '50 at Chosin, you've probably heard about it."

Josh feels a bit ashamed that he knows very little about the Korean War. "Afraid I don't know a lot about that, sir, but I'd like to—"

"Chosin. Thanksgiving it was. Thirty below zero. We were freezing our tails off, but—"

"Bud," interjects Esther diplomatically, "I'm sure Josh is very interested in hearing about the war, but maybe now's not the—"

Josh politely interrupts, "Oh that's okay, really I don't—"

"The commies were pouring down on us hard. If we don't hold them, there's no stopping them anywhere. There I was, just a wet-behind-the-ears kid, no good sense at all, but there I was—"

Maggie speaks up. "I don't think you ever were in the war, Bud. You just make all that stuff up."

"Now Maggie," Esther says softly.

Bud goes quiet.

"Who are these people?" Maggie is now looking hard at Evangelina and Josh again.

"They're our guests, Maggie," Esther says again.

"How come no one introduced them to me?"

Just then a woman appears through a swinging door pushing a cart of food. She's a young Hispanic woman, no more than twenty, wearing a drab beige uniform with her hair tightly bound in a white scarf. Her face is expressionless, as she wordlessly delivers a plate of food to each person, making no eye contact with anyone. A Melmac plate with green peas that look more gray than green, obviously from a can, sauerkraut and sausages. It looks greasy and not very appetizing, but Josh is starved. He's ready to dig in, but Esther says, "Well, shall we say grace?" Josh quickly sets his fork down as Esther says a short prayer.

Josh goes for the sausages, as Evangelina, obviously much more comfortable than Josh in this social setting, says, "So Esther, tell us about Copper Point. Why is there such a place as this in a little town like Santuario?"

Esther laughs. "You're very diplomatic, my dear. Well, when the boom hit Santuario back in the seventies, folks had some big dreams. The copper company built this place, or mostly built it, but it never got finished. They had the idea that with all the executives and engineers moving in, they'd need a senior facility for their parents and grandparents. Copper Point was going to be a fancy place, not some low budget dump, like you think of when you think of your typical old folk's home."

"But the place never got finished?"

"Nope. When they realized there was no copper here, or at least not enough to make them billionaires, the big boys pulled out real quick. And so did almost everybody else, except the few native families that had always lived here."

"So how did you all get here?"

"Well that's a good one. There's a big home down in Santa Fe that was overflowing. Too many folks getting old." She laughs, then continues. "They needed more space for the old people. There was talk about a new facility, but then some genius found out about this place, which was just an abandoned shell at the time, and they bought it for a song.

They finished it off, on the cheap, as you can see. Saved 'em a bundle. That's why you don't see fancy furniture and Michelangelos hanging in the hallways. They decided to use it for the overflow."

"Overflow?"

"Yep. We're the overflow. The ones that don't have any family raising a big stink about being stuck out here in the middle of nowhere. Most of us don't have any family at all, or at least that ever come to visit. And no money, for that matter." She laughs. "You think we'd be here if we did? That's why we're in this dump, at the end of the line. Not your fancy senior living here, like you see in the ads, with the well-tanned, good-looking couple sipping margaritas and getting ready for an afternoon of golf, followed by a gourmet supper. At Copper Point you won't find any shuttles taking us down to Saks and Bloomingdales for shopping sprees, no group outings to the opera here. Here, you're just darn lucky to be in out of the cold." Esther's eyes sparkle. She is clearly an accomplished story teller.

Bud chimes in. "Well said, Esther. Sometimes I think I'd rather be back freezing my tail off in Korea."

Josh notices that everyone seems to ignore Bud.

Evangelina asks Esther, "So who's this Mrs. Harshburn I heard the woman out front mention?"

"Harshburn. Don't you just love that name? Tells you everything you need to know. She's the facility supervisor, I think that's what her title is. She lives down in Santa Fe, comes up here once a week to check on things. Stays no longer than she needs to."

"So there's no on-site care?"

"Ha, you've seen it, dear. Olive out front at the desk from nine to five. And Yolanda. You just saw her. Our cook and dishwasher. She's responsible for our gourmet fare." She raises an eyebrow as she glances down at her unappetizing plate. "Oh yeah, we have a guy comes through once a week to sweep and vacuum. But other than that, we're pretty much on our own."

"No nurse or doctor? What if somebody gets sick?"

"A nurse sometimes comes along with Harshburn, but other than that she's on-call. Then there's Lauren over at the clinic. She's a nurse practitioner who's here when she's not at the hospital down in Santa Fe. She's good about coming over when we call, if she's in town. If something real bad happens, we have to call 911 and hope an ambulance makes it up here from Española or Santa Fe in time."

Josh asks, "What about police protection in Santuario?"

This draws a dirty look from Evangelina and a big laugh from Esther. "You heard me say 'out in the middle of nowhere.' There's no police department here. A state trooper cruises through about once a week, Fridays I think. That's it. And just between us, ever since Reies Tijerina and some of his kind, I don't think they want to hang around up here very much."

"Tijerina?"

"That's right. It means tiger. Names say a lot about a person, if you ask me. Tijerina was a local tough guy. In trouble with the law back in the sixties over land rights or something like that. It was basically a small war. Shootouts and everything. Pretty bloody."

"I've heard of him," Evangelina says.

"Yep, the feds even came in. They arrested some of Tijerina's gang. Tried 'em in the courthouse over in Tierra Amarilla. But he came in, guns ablazin' and they shot their way out of there. He never did spend much time in jail. Kind of a folk hero around these parts. The cops don't want to spend much time around here with good reason. If we have problems, the cops figure we'll just take care of them ourselves."

"You mean—" Josh begins, but Bud starts in again.

"That's right son, we get used to taking care of ourselves here. Back in Korea, we were outmanned and out flanked. We were out of food and almost out of ammo. Couldn't get any airstrikes called in, the weather was too miserable—"

Maggie interrupts. "Bud, stop it! You're just a silly old man."

Bud looks down, then turns his attention to his peas.

Esther says, "Now Maggie—"

But Maggie cuts her off, looking again at Evangelina and Josh. "Who are these people?"

❧❧

Eric Sandoval follows the power mower around his backyard. On this beautiful Saturday afternoon, after a long week in the office, this is all he wants to do. Mindlessly working his way around the outer perimeter and converging inward with each successive lap toward the center, he works on creating the perfect pattern of cuts. A red UNM Lobos tee shirt, blue jean cutoffs and Chaco flip flops feel good after the coat and tie he's had on all week. This just might be the way he chooses to dress for the rest of his life. And his wife Sally promised that she'll be waiting for him on the porch with a cold beer when he's done. A perfect day.

But now he spots Sally standing on the patio, waving to him, with the cordless phone handset in her hand. "Oh man," groans Eric to himself, "this had better not be the office."

Eric sinks into a webbed patio chair with the phone. It is the office. A voice on the other end says, "Eric, sorry to bust up your weekend. You didn't have any special things going on, did you?"

Sandoval looks over at the lawnmower. "Well that depends on what you call special," he says to Erica Wang, the Special Agent in Charge of the Albuquerque office of the FBI. "Doesn't she ever take a day off?" he wonders.

"Look, Eric," says Wang, "we're gonna need you to get up to Santa Fe this afternoon. Take Carol Shepherd with you. We've got something going on up at the Lab – maybe it's something important, maybe not – but we've gotta be on top of it."

"Don't suppose you could get somebody else to handle—"

"I would if I could Eric, but you're the guy today I'm afraid. Can you get over here in an hour? I've already called Carol. There'll be a briefing at two, then you can be on the road by three and up at the Santa Fe office by four."

"I'll be there, boss." Eric sighs and gives Sally, who's watching from the back door, a sad look.

༄༅

The sausages from lunch were too greasy. This and the faint urine smell in the hallway are causing his stomach to audibly churn. And the old man's trousers he's had on for the past hour or so are too small and are beginning to bind. But these are not the life-threatening issues that plague Josh's mind. While some of the residents remain in the dining area after lunch for a game of Crazy Eights, Josh wanders toward the lobby area, headed nowhere in particular, trying to put the pieces together. The lobby area of Copper Point, where they entered just a couple of hours ago, is the only half-way attractive area he's seen. There's nice carpeting, worn but with an attractive flowered pattern. A large fireplace, with brick all the way to the ceiling, adorns one wall. It looks seldom used, but there's a fireplace screen and hardware in front of the hearth. Off to the right are two large sofas.

Behind the counter, Olive stares into space, looking bored. She averts her eyes when he looks at her. Josh edges up to the glass entry doors and looks out. No sign of the gray car. When and how will he know when it's safe to venture outside?

As he turns back from the door, he spots Hollister sitting on one of the worn sofas, working on a laptop.

"Hey, Josh," says Hollister, looking up from his work. "Nice duds."

Josh sits down on the other sofa, adjacent to Hollister. "Yeah, really. What are you working on?"

"My resume. It sucks."

"Looking for work?"

"Yeah, guess you could say that. What about you? What are you doing here?"

Josh tries to formulate an answer, but all he can say is, "It's a long story."

"That's okay. I don't mean to meddle."

"You're not meddling. Why are you looking for a job? Surely a Creighton grad wouldn't have any trouble at all."

"It's a long story." They both laugh. Hollister continues. "I went to Creighton on a basketball scholarship, which covered about half my tuition. My grandmother covered the rest."

"Where were your parents?"

"My dad split when I was three and my mom died of cancer when I was in high school. All our money went to medical bills. So, my grandmother covered the other half of my tuition, spent all her savings in fact. I didn't realize that at the time." He gives a sad shrug. "Now she lives here. For me college was all about basketball, every minute of the day. Now I wish I'd spent more time hitting the books."

"Were you a good ball player?"

"That's my problem. I was very good. But not quite good enough. Made all-conference twice, but I wasn't good enough to make the pros. So here I am, working on my resume." Hollister sighs, then asks, "So what kind of work do you do?"

"I'm a physicist."

"Physicist? Dude, you must be smart. How'd you get into that line of work?"

"Well, my dad was a physicist, quite a famous one. They considered him for the Nobel Prize once. So, I guess I had to follow in his footsteps."

"Nobel Prize? What did he do?"

"He studied parallel universes."

"You mean like there's other universes out there somewhere?"

"Something like that."

"So you started working on parallel universes too?"

"Not exactly. Guess you could say I was very good, but not good enough." They laugh again. Josh continues, "I got into Yale, probably on my father's reputation, and I did all right there. But it became clear I wasn't gonna shake the earth or anything like that. So now I calibrate detectors for cosmic ray studies. Kinda thing a lab tech with a junior college degree could probably do."

"Still sounds pretty impressive to me."

"Well, I like it. But it's not catchy like parallel universes."

"Parallel universes?" a voice asks from behind Josh.

"Esther, we were just talking about Josh's work. He's a physicist."

"Really. That must be interesting. So tell me about the parallel universes."

"Well, I don't really work on—"

"So what's a parallel universe anyway?"

Josh shifts his body on the sofa and sighs. "It's complicated."

"Humor an old lady." It's becoming clear that saying no to Esther is not an option.

Josh leans back in the sofa, gazes off toward the fireplace for a moment, sighs again, then says, "Okay, let's see." He pauses for another moment, picking the right words. "Everything we see and know about, all the stars, all the matter and even all the empty space, is part of our universe. It's huge, so huge that we'll probably never be able to explore much of it."

"So, what makes folks think there are other universes?"

Josh leans forward, pushes his glasses back up on the bridge of his nose with his forefinger, and says, "Well, a lot of the thinking began back in the seventies after the discovery of something called the anthropic principle."

"Now you're losing me," says Esther.

"Me too," adds Hollister.

"Well, the anthropic principle was just the realization that for life to have developed in our universe, or for that matter even for planets to have come into existence, many of the properties and laws of nature had to be finely tuned."

"What do you mean finely tuned?" asks Hollister.

"Okay, here's just one example. If the strength of the force that holds atoms together was just a little bit different from what it is, maybe even just one percent different, then carbon, which is the building block of life, wouldn't exist. There are dozens of other examples. Some people call them coincidences, but there's obviously more to it than that."

Esther and Hollister both shift forward in their seats, really getting into this. Which is exactly what Josh doesn't want, another teaching on his father's work. "So, let me get this straight," says Esther, "You're saying that the universe appears to be carefully designed just so life could exist?"

"Well, a carefully designed universe is one possibility," says Josh. "But the other possibility is that there's a very large, maybe infinite, number of universes, and we just happen to be in one where the conditions are right for life to exist. Obviously, we wouldn't exist in a universe where the conditions wouldn't allow life."

Hollister asks, "And so this suggests there may be other universes where the laws of nature are different?"

"That's correct."

Esther looks unconvinced. "But has anyone ever detected a parallel universe anywhere?"

"No. In fact, scientists believe they may be impossible to detect. It may be impossible for someone in this universe to communicate with someone in a parallel universe. The rationale is pretty complicated, but that's basically the bottom line." Josh leans back, hoping this is the end of the parallel universe conversation.

Esther sits up straight and puts an index finger on her chin, considering all this for a moment. Then she says, "I've got two things to say. First, I like the first possibility best, that God made the whole thing. And for what it's worth, a lot of us have experienced this God up close and personal, so I'd say that option is a lot more likely than one where it's impossible we'll ever prove it."

Hollister laughs. "I told you, Josh, this Esther is quite a package."

But Esther is not through yet. "And second," she says, "parallel universes do in fact exist. You say they're different worlds cut off from the other worlds? Well, that pretty well describes Copper Point, now doesn't it? So, how can you say parallel universes have never been detected? Son, you're sitting in one right now."

Josh's mouth falls open and he is at a loss for words. He looks into the eyes of the old woman, soft yet penetrating. Then over her shoulder, he notices that someone is approaching the front door. It's a man. It's the man from the gray car. He's struggling with the sticky glass door. Instinctively, Josh dives to the floor, as Esther and Hollister look on in astonishment.

"You can't let them find us," Josh blurts out, as he quickly crawls behind the couch, out of sight from the door.

Esther looks at Hollister, then over at Olive, now talking on the phone behind the desk. "I'll take care of this," she says.

ৎৎ৯

Stilwell curses under his breath as he finally is able to push the sticky glass door open. He glances over his shoulder at Jesse, waiting beside the car, ready if needed.

He heads over to the desk, where a young woman is talking on the phone, seemingly oblivious to his presence. Then an old woman approaches him. "May I help you, sir?"

Stilwell looks her over. "Yes ma'am," he says calmly. "Stilwell Ferguson, FBI." He flashes an ID, then continues. "We're looking for a couple who might have come this way a few hours ago, and we're wondering if anyone has seen them."

"I've been here all day. What did they do?"

"We just need to ask them some questions. Josh Waverly and Evangelina Gomez, that's their names. Have you seen them?"

The old woman ponders this for a moment, then says, "Well yes, I did see them. They came in a couple of hours ago, I think. Wanted to use the phone. But they didn't stay long. Left pretty much right away." She looks right into Stilwell's eyes.

"I see. And what about that guy over there?" He raises his voice, "Hey you, can we talk?" He gestures toward a black man, sitting on a sofa in the corner and begins to move in that direction, but the man stands and meets him halfway. *He's a giant.*

"Sure, what do you want?"

"Look LeBron, we're looking for a couple who came by here this morning. You see anybody?"

The black man scowls, then smiles broadly. "I ain't seen nobody, sir,"

Is he mocking me? thinks Stilwell. *I've got something in my pocket here that could level out the playing field real fast, jungle boy.* But he doesn't say anything.

"And what about the girl behind the desk?" Stilwell looks over at the girl, still on the phone, and begins to move toward the desk.

The old woman pipes up, "She just came on duty a few minutes ago. She wouldn't have seen anything. If I can get your phone number, I'll call if any of us see anything. We want to help."

Stilwell is silent, pondering his strategy. He scans the room again, looking for any tell-tale sign. "You know, lady, if you're not telling me the truth, you could be arrested for aiding and abetting a fugitive." He glares hard at the woman.

But she doesn't flinch. "Of course, sir. We wouldn't want to do anything illegal. We just want to help." She gives him a little smile that makes him want to slap her. He glances over at the big black man again, then quickly over to the girl at the desk.

Then he turns and leaves.

At the car, Jesse asks, "What happened? They in there?"

"I don't know. They may be. Seemed a little fishy to me."

"Why don't we just go back in there right now and take care of business?"

"You dumb slob. You wanna go in there with guns blazing and shoot your way through twenty old farts in the hopes we might find our target? That would be real smart now, wouldn't it? No, we're gonna wait awhile longer, and we're gonna be watching. They haven't gone anywhere very far from here. There's a cocky black dude in there. I want him too. When we get them, we're gonna have some real fun. I can assure you of that."

❧

The man knows my name. Josh has heard every word of the conversation, and he's still shaking, crouched behind the couch, just feet away from the man in the gray car.

"He's gone." There's a comforting tone in Hollister's voice. Josh peeks carefully over the couch before rising.

"I'm not sure he believed me," says Esther, looking worried.

"Thank you for helping. But I'm not sure why you're helping me."

"Give us a little credit, Josh," says Hollister, laughing. "Esther here trusts you, and that's good enough for me. She's never wrong about whom to trust."

"I guess I should tell you the whole story, at least as much as I know of it."

Esther rests a hand on Josh's shoulder. "You don't have to tell us anything, if you don't want to."

"Why don't you both sit down?" Josh takes his place back on the couch and begins, keeping an eye on the door.

≪ঙ৯

At one, Evangelina dials Della's cell phone.

"Evangelina, I'm glad you called now. I'm with your parents. Everybody's fine. You want to talk to them?"

"Oh yes."

"Vangie, where are you? Are you okay?"

"Yes, Mama, I'm okay. I'm in a safe place."

Grace Gomez is talking a mile a minute. "Vangie, that man who called the other night, he came to the house looking for you. Your father sensed danger and got us out of there fast. We're at Rey's. We tried to call you, but couldn't reach you. Oh, sweet Lord, I'm so glad to hear your voice. You're sure you're safe?"

"Yes, Mama, I am safe. Is Serena okay?"

"She's fine. Here she is."

Evangelina lets out a huge sob of relief and joy at the sound of her daughter's voice. "Mommy! When are you coming home?"

"Very soon, little angel cakes."

"I want to see you now."

"I love you, darling, and I'll be home very soon."

"Why can't you come now?"

"Mommy has to be away for a day or so, then I'll be home before you know it."

"But I need you here now."

Evangelina fights back sobs as Grace comes back on the phone. "Has that man been after you?"

"Yes, Mama, he has. But I got away from him, and like I said, I'm safe. Mama, he's very dangerous. You must stay at Uncle Rey's, don't even go outside."

"Okay, dear, so here's what I'm going to do. I'm calling the police and telling them where you are—"

"No, Mama, don't do that yet. You know what that'll mean."

Silence on the other end. Then Grace says, "But your safety's more important than anything that might happen."

"Mama, please, I beg you. Don't call them yet. Give me some time to figure this out."

"Okay, I guess. Can I send Rey up to get you?"

Evangelina ponders this for a moment. She hasn't considered this option before. "No, not yet. I'm pretty sure the man doesn't know we're here. I'm hoping he'll leave. Then Uncle Rey can come and get me."

Silence on the other end, which Evangelina doesn't know how to interpret.

Della comes back on the phone. "Evangelina, I don't mean to butt into your business, but I think we do need to call the law in on this."

"Please Della. I haven't done anything wrong, but if the police come in on this thing, my whole family will get hurt.

Real bad. So, Della, I'm begging you, please don't call them right now. Okay?"

She hears a sigh on the other end. "Look, Evangelina, I'm worried that this is tied up with Louie Wessel's death somehow, so this is deadly serious. But I'll hold off for just a little while. But I won't promise that I won't send them up there soon."

"Thank you."

"Look, Evangelina, I'm gonna leave my cell phone with your parents. I don't have a charger with me, but it ought to last for awhile. So you can call them at this number. Okay?"

When she is off the phone, Evangelina buries her head in her hands and sobs. Then she stands and paces the small room. Finally, she kneels by the bed and is quiet for a long time. Then out loud but very softly she says, "God, I know I've messed up in so many ways. I know you probably don't want to have anything to do with me, and I don't blame you. I'm really sorry. But I'm begging you right now, please God, protect Serena. And please protect my family. And please help me to know what you want me to do. Please, God." She makes a sign of the cross, then says, "Amen."

Evangelina turns and sits on the floor, leaning against the bed, staring at the wall. The image that comes to her mind is Serena, her big eyes full of life, safe at Uncle Rey's. This simple fact prevails over all the other concerns, even the worry about her own safety. She lets out a great sigh and adds one more line to her prayer. "Thank you, God."

❧

"Do you think they believed her?" Evangelina asks Josh, after he's told her about his encounter with Ferguson in the lobby. She sits on the bed, while Josh is on the couch.

"I don't know. Esther wasn't sure. What it means is we're not really safe here. If they ever talk to that girl at the desk, we're cooked. She hates us."

"What should we do?"

Josh looks into Evangelina's big brown eyes. *She's looking to me for guidance. This is a first.* Even with the grave nature of their situation, Josh is almost overcome by this woman's beauty. And, even more than his fear, this causes him to pause before answering. "Call the police?"

She doesn't answer the question. Instead, she says, "Because of me, you're in danger. And that's not fair. I think you should leave. It's me they're after."

"You want me to go?"

"No, I'm not saying that. I'm just saying that there's no reason for you to put your life in more danger for me."

"Look, as appealing as that idea may be, I suspect these guys plan to get me too. They know my name. Whatever it is they think you know or have done, I'm sure they now see me as your accomplice—"

"Don't say accomplice. That makes me sound like a criminal."

"Okay then, your partner. Anyway, I don't want to go out there. I think I'm better off here."

Evangelina stands up. "Enough of this scary talk." She's through talking about this for now. "I'm going down to the kitchen."

❧❧

Josh has no place to go. The small room is stifling and depressing. The lobby risks another encounter with Ferguson. Aimless, he wanders again to the rear of the building. The hallways are deserted. He comes to what appears to be a service entrance at the rear of the building, a metal door with a window opening out into a loading dock area. Josh peers cautiously through the glass, but the area appears to be deserted. He tests the door. It's unlocked, which bothers him, imagining the killers sneaking in through this entrance. He opens the door and steps outside.

Immediately he hears a thump. Then quiet. The hairs on his neck stand up. Another thump. Quickly he backs toward the door, then he hears a series of thumps. It's the unmistakable sound of a basketball. He peeks around the corner of the building and there's Hollister, with a basketball, standing beneath a backboard. He's wearing grey sweats and a deep-blue shirt with a big 'Creighton' across the chest.

He spots Josh and calls out, "Hey, Waverly, over here."

Josh is still surveying the area for safety. A blacktop pad that must be used as a loading area where vehicles can drop off deliveries to the rear of the home is enclosed by a tall brick wall, with access to the outside through a chain-link gate on rolling wheels. The chain link is covered with corrugated sheet metal. It's locked with a heavy chain and padlock. Apparently no significant deliveries have been made to Copper Point in a long time. More importantly, the gate provides privacy, a hiding place from eyes that may be looking for him.

As Josh looks up toward the backboard, mounted on the side of the building, Hollister says, "So, you've discovered Copper Point's best kept secret."

"Didn't expect to see a backboard around here." The net is long gone from the rusted rim.

"Me neither. Guess the builders put it in for the help to use on their breaks. Far as I can tell, I'm the only one who's used it in years. Here, take a shot."

The pass catches Josh off guard and the ball hits his chest hard, but he hangs on. Josh hasn't held a basketball in almost twenty years. But it feels good.

"So what's out there?" Josh motions his head toward the gate.

"Just a whole lot of desert, as far as I can tell. Haven't ever been out there. Not sure anyone has a key to that padlock. One thing for sure, you can hear the coyotes out there at night. Creepy things, must be a huge pack. Not far away either. They give me the willies."

Josh shudders. "For the record, I have no plan to go out there and meet them." He bounces the basketball a couple of times, then launches a shot from about fifteen feet. It bangs around the rim, then falls through.

"Way to go!" says Hollister, clapping his hands together. "You ever play any ball?"

"I may not look like it, but I loved basketball. Played on the JV team at my high school. That was before I hurt my leg."

"Yeah, I noticed you limpin' a bit. What happened?" Hollister tosses the ball back to Josh for another shot. Josh tosses up another shot from the same spot. Again he hits it.

"Well, it's a depressing story that I'd rather not talk about."

"That's okay by me, no problem." Hollister dribbles the ball once and makes a backwards slam dunk from underneath the basket, then tosses the ball back to Josh again. "So what are you and your friend going to do about these hoodlums who are after you?"

"Like I said, she doesn't want to call the police. I'm not sure why. Look, I just met her yesterday. But I'm gonna honor her wishes for awhile. But soon, I think we've got to get some help."

"Yeah, a lot of folks up here don't trust cops. They just handle things themselves."

"I think there's more to it than that though. Maybe I'm a fool to trust her, but that's what I'm going to do for the moment."

"You two an item?"

"Oh no." Josh feels his face redden, and he's sure Hollister hasn't missed it. "Like I said, we just met yesterday."

"Well, I haven't been around you two much, but I did see you two in the hall and I saw how you looked at her."

"Cheesh, was it that obvious?"

"I'd say pretty obvious. How about a game of HORSE?"

"Good grief, I haven't played HORSE since I was a kid. Let's see if I remember how it goes. I make a shot and then you have to make it too. If you miss, you get an 'H.' If I miss you can take any shot you want, and if you make it I have to make your shot or I get an 'H.'"

"You got it. You can go first." Hollister tosses the ball to Josh.

"You've gotta be kidding. Two times all-conference, I recall. That's Missouri Valley Conference, right?"

"Yeah, but I'm rusty. And besides, you got a better idea about how to kill some time on a pretty afternoon? Not figurin' you want to take a stroll down main street. Or …" He casts a sidelong glance toward the gate. "Or go visit the coyotes."

Josh looks around the area again, shakes his head and sighs, dribbles the ball a few times then fires up another fifteen footer.

"Dang, you got the hot hand, Waverly. I could be in trouble already." Hollister steps out to where Josh made his shot and launches a soft jumper that rattles the rim then bounces out. "H," he says.

Josh now has a grin on his face, although he's certain Hollister's going easy on him. He dribbles around awhile, thinking. "So, what kind of work are you looking for, Hollister?"

"Well, my major at Creighton was Communications. Look, I know everybody expects the jocks to be Communications majors, and a lot of them are. Supposed to be the easiest major at college. But the funny thing is, I really am interested in Communications."

"Like news broadcasting? I gotta say, you've got the voice for it. I can hear it now." He makes his voice go low. "From our newsroom in New York, here is Hollister Williams with the CBS Evening News."

Hollister laughs. "Yeah, that would be cool, but that takes more than a good voice. You've got to be an experienced journalist first. I'm thinking more along the lines of public relations or something in marketing. I love talking to people."

"Just the opposite of my line of work," laughs Josh. "I hate talking to people." Josh pops another fifteen footer.

"So speaking of talking to people, you told that girl how you feel yet?"

"I guess I'm a bit of a chicken. Ever time I'm close to her, my knees turn to jelly and I can barely open my mouth. What advice would a Communications major have for that?" He laughs nervously.

"Wo, you got it bad, son." Hollister misses the fifteen footer again. "H-O."

Josh is now certain that Hollister is cutting him a lot of slack. He stands, holding the ball, waiting for Hollister's reply.

"Well," says Hollister, obviously thinking this through, "First of all it's pretty normal to feel that way around a pretty girl like her. But what I've gotta say to you comes from basketball, not communications theory."

"Say more."

"So you're on the court. It's a big game. Final seconds of play. You're down by two. They pass you the ball. You have an opening for the basket, what do you do?"

"You go for it, I guess."

"Good guess, Sherlock. Of course you go for it. It's not the time for some interminable physics analysis, calculating all the probabilities, charting the process. No, you gotta do something, trust that the right thing to do is hard-wired into you somehow. It's risky. You may not make the bucket. You might double dribble. You might fumble the ball out of bounds and have everybody screaming at you. All kinds of bad stuff might happen. But you go for it, because if you don't go for it, you most certainly will lose the game. You go for it, because it's your only chance to win."

Josh says nothing, but fires up another fifteen footer, which misses everything. Air ball.

"So, you gonna go for it?"

Josh laughs. "I'm thinking it over."

"Well, don't think too long. The clock's running. But I'll be rooting for you." Hollister sinks a jumper from the corner, slinky and smooth, his dreadlocks swaying as he releases the ball.

Okay, so maybe he's not going easy on me. Josh chases the ball down and stops again. He takes a deep breath. "So, here's how my leg got hurt."

Hollister is giving Josh his full attention.

"When I was fourteen, my father had me help him move a refrigerator. We were moving it from the kitchen into the garage. It weighed a ton. My dad had it on a dolly, with one of those big canvas straps holding it in place. We had to go down three steps, this was the tricky part. My dad had the handles of the dolly and I was on the downhill side of the fridge, guiding the way. Well, apparently I wasn't guiding well enough. The fridge slipped and pinned my leg up against the wall."

"Man, that must have hurt."

"Yeah, it did. It smashed a bunch of cartilage and muscle below my knee. I was in the hospital for most of a week. It's the scar tissue from the surgery that causes me to limp some times. Worst of all, my dad blamed me for the accident."

"No way! No way was that your fault. Geez, you were what, fourteen?"

"I remember being in the hospital when my dad came in with the doctor. My dad says something to the doctor like, 'Wouldn't be here if he'd been able to follow directions. My son's a good kid, but he couldn't pour piss out of a boot if the directions were on the heel.'" Josh almost chokes on these last words. He's never told anyone this before.

"I'm sorry, Josh. That was terrible. It must have hurt real bad."

Josh winds up losing the game of HORSE, but it's close. He feels good. Walking back into the building with Hollister, a sense of peace comes over him. He's experiencing something he hasn't experienced in a long time. A friend.

He remembers to lock the deadbolt on the door behind him.

❦

He hasn't seen Evangelina all afternoon. She had said she was going down to the kitchen, but that was several hours ago. He's grown used to being near her in just twenty-four hours. He's a little worried about her, but doesn't want to hover, doesn't want to look needy. And now at five thirty, as Josh heads toward the dining hall, he's hoping she'll be there.

But she isn't. Josh takes the same seat he had at lunch. Esther, Maggie and Bud are already seated. A small black woman with delicate features and grey hair tied in a bun sits next to Hollister. She wears rimless glasses and bears the look of a woman of regal stature, like someone who'd teach poetry at the university. Not like a resident of Copper Point.

"Josh, this is my grandma, Rosey." He puts an arm lovingly around her as he speaks.

"Pleased to meet you, Rosey. I've heard a lot about you."

Rosey extends a slender hand and says, "Nice to meet you, Josh. Hollister already told me you are a pretty good ball player. Gave him a run for his money."

"I think he was going easy on me."

"Easy?" says Bud. "That's the problem with kids nowadays. They want it easy. I tell you when you're hunkered down in a trench at Chosin, you learn real quick that it ain't gonna be easy—"

"Josh, where's Evangelina?" asks Esther, interrupting Bud. She looks worried.

"I'm not sure. I hoped she'd be here."

Just then the swinging doors to the kitchen burst open and Yolanda enters the dining room, pushing the cart of dinner meals. Tonight a big smile has erased her sullen demeanor from lunch. Evangelina walks behind her.

"Hey everybody," says Yolanda. The room goes silent and everyone turns to look at the chef, apparently surprised to hear her speaking. Yolanda continues, talking fast.

"Tonight we've got a special treat. Vangie here has made us all some tacos, and you're going to love them. Plus she showed me how to cook all kinds of things, enchiladas, rellenos. I hope you love your dinner."

Evangelina helps Yolanda deliver the meals to each table. Their laughter indicates that they've hit it off during the afternoon. After everyone is served, she takes her seat next to Josh, and Esther says grace. Evangelina says, "After seeing how people didn't care for their lunches, I thought I'd offer to help a bit with supper. I hope people like them. We didn't have all the ingredients my mother would normally use."

Everyone is quiet for a few moments, as they dig into the tacos. Josh bites down through one of the crunchy tortilla shells and almost swoons. He's had Mexican food many times, but nothing like this. He can't identify the ingredients, but there's something almost miraculous about Evangelina's tacos. Even better than the expensive nachos at Casa Bonita, which now seems an eternity ago. How did she do this with just the ingredients available in the kitchen?

Bud speaks first. "God, these are good." Everyone else, with mouths full, make satisfied grunts and nod their agreement.

Rosey says, "The bible talks about all the blessings of our life and how he gives us grace upon grace." She glances over at Hollister as she says this, prompting a smile from him. "And your tacos, my dear, are certainly proof of God's grace. Thank you."

"That was a pretty wonderful thing you just did," Josh says to Evangelina. He continues to be in awe of this woman.

"I was just trying to help. I think Yolanda will now be able to cook some of these dishes after we leave." She touches Josh's arm as she speaks, then quickly pulls her hand away.

"Where are you going?" asks Maggie.

"We're just visiting, Maggie, so we'll be leaving pretty soon."

"Tomorrow?"

"I don't know yet," says Evangelina. She glances at Josh.

"Speaking of tomorrow," says Esther, "You're probably wondering where to go to church."

Actually Josh is not wondering about it at all. He's never been to church in his life, except for a couple of weddings. "I don't usually go to—"

"Service will be right here in the dining hall," says Esther. "Eight o'clock sharp."

"I'll be there," says Evangelina. "I haven't been to church in awhile, and I think I could really use it."

Josh says no more about the subject. He just nods. Sure, he'll go. He'd go anywhere with this woman. He already just about has.

∽৻৵৽

After dinner, a few of the residents remain at the tables, visiting. Most of them begin the difficult process of returning to their rooms, the awkward moments of trying to rise from their chairs. Several of them rock back and forth, attempting to get the forward momentum to stand. Rosey and Hollister help them, but many want to do it for themselves. Evangelina quickly joins in to help people get to their feet. She is surprised at how quickly she has come to feel she's a part of this scene. Josh had first begun to leave the room, but when he sees her helping, he joins in too. Many of the residents use walkers to head back to their rooms. A few have motorized scooters, which make a low humming sound as they zip in and out between the tables.

As they are leaving, Esther pulls Josh and Evangelina aside. "I think I may have made a bad assumption, and I'm worried about it."

"What's that?" Evangelina asks.

"Well, I got you both set up in one room, and I never stopped to think that maybe you're not married. My apologies." She looks from one to the other with expectant eyes, waiting for their response.

Evangelina sees Josh blush. What with everything else going on, she hadn't thought about it either. "Is there another room we can get? We can pay for it."

Esther looks deeply concerned. "That's the problem. We've got a lot of empty rooms here, but none of the others have a bed or any furniture at all, just bare floors. We only had this one because Mr. Neuman, he ..." She looks again from face to face. "Well, he died last week. The personal things have been removed, but the furniture's still there."

Evangelina looks at Josh, as she thinks this through. "Well, there's a couch in the room. I guess we could make do. What do you think?"

Josh seems embarrassed. "I don't mind sleeping on the couch."

Esther says, "Again, you two, I'm very sorry. I want to be a good hostess. I've already put some nightclothes out for you both, and your own clothes, they've been washed and pressed. Found some new toothbrushes too. I wish I could do more."

"You've done a lot already. And if this guy acts up, I'll make him move the couch out into the hall." Evangelina gives him a devilish little smile, the edges of her mouth curled upward. Josh blushes again.

❧

When they return to the room, they find that Esther has indeed left nightclothes on the bed for them, a long flannel nightgown for Evangelina and a pair of flannel pajamas that look like they'll be baggy on Josh.

They go through their preparations for sleep with obvious awkwardness and few words exchanged. Josh spreads a blanket over the hard cracked vinyl of the couch, and finds an extra pillow in the small closet, while Evangelina retreats into the bathroom. His face feels flushed and his hands shake in awkwardness. Sure they stayed together in the woods last night, but that was like camping. This is different. This is a bedroom.

Get a hold of yourself, Josh, you're acting like a silly fool.

In moments Evangelina emerges and Josh tries not to stare. The nightgown is very modest, comes down to her ankles and the neckline is cut high, but it's still a nightgown. He can't help but catch glimpses of her though, especially where the smooth brown of her arms emerges from the pink flannel sleeves, which somehow make her skin look even softer.

Josh groans as he studies his own bedclothes in the bathroom mirror. The pajamas are old and almost colorless, large and sagging on him in a way that emphasizes his thinness. Maybe if he tucked the pajama top in, it would be a little better. No, that was a bad idea. He shakes his head in hopelessness, then heads back into the bedroom to make his fashion debut and go through the ritual of saying goodnight, which he also had rehearsed in front of the mirror. Keep it light and casual, he had concluded. But Evangelina is already in bed, the covers pulled up high around her neck, her heavy slow breathing telling him that she is sound asleep.

Josh climbs onto the stiff plastic couch, and in exhaustion he also falls into a deep sleep that no hard vinyl surface can inhibit. In his dream he is standing in front of the physics auditorium, speaking about detector calibrations. Everyone is listening. In the front row sits his father, who is the most attentive of all, nodding proudly at each point Josh makes. As he continues with his lecture he becomes aware of a soft groaning sound from the audience. At first it's easy to ignore, but then the groaning becomes louder. Then he realizes that the groaning is coming from his father. His father is crumpled over in his chair. Josh comes awake immediately. Goosebumps rise on his arms as he realizes the groaning sound from the dream is in the room with him. It's coming from Evangelina.

In the pale stripes of light from the full moon coming in through the blinds, he can make out that she is writhing under her blankets. Josh rises on one elbow, squinting to see better, while he fishes for his glasses on the floor beside him. Then suddenly Evangelina screams and bolts upright in her bed, flailing and flinging away the blankets. Josh bolts up also, his heart in his throat.

"Are you alright?"

She continues thrashing wildly, apparently unaware of his presence.

"Are you alright?" he says louder. The thrashing has now stopped and Evangelina has wrapped her arms around herself, trembling as if she is cold. Her eyes are open, but it's unclear that she is conscious.

Josh considers turning on the lights, but this might startle her even more. He goes over to the bed and sits beside her. "Evangelina," he says firmly. "You're having a nightmare. Everything's okay."

He puts an arm gently around her, but this causes her to jump again and he quickly pulls his arm away. Then she looks at him, blinking her eyes as if trying to focus. She says nothing.

Again Josh tells her that it is only a bad dream. The trembling is now subsiding. Again she looks at him, and now there is recognition in her eyes.

She takes a deep breath and lets it out as a sigh. For awhile she is silent, then she begins. "When I was four years old," she says, "my parents brought me to this country." She's now looking straight ahead at the wall, as if talking to no one in particular. "They entered the country illegally. I'm not sure where they crossed the border from Mexico, but I know it was January. I'm not even sure what country we were coming from. We were riding with a lot of other people on the floor in the back of a van. I was in the very back, pressed up against the rear door. My mother and father were right next to me, and we were squeezed in so tight we could barely breathe. And it was completely dark." She glances quickly at Josh, who gives her a nod of reassurance.

Evangelina continues, again looking back at the far wall. "I learned later that it was near Albuquerque, in a mountain pass. There was ice on the road. I guess the driver lost control and the van rolled. Over and over. There was screaming. The back door flew open. That's all I remember." She pauses and takes several deep breaths like she is hyperventilating. "The next thing I remember is that I'm riding in the front seat of a big truck. I remember I was bleeding and hurting real bad." She glances at Josh again and her eyes are wide, filled with fear.

"You were injured?"

"Yes, I guess so, but apparently not seriously. The man driving the truck tried to help me, and he told me I would be okay. I didn't know who he was at the time, but it was my Uncle Rey. He's an OTR—"

"OTR?"

"Over-the-road trucker, drives big rigs. He drove a long way that night, all the way up to Rinconada. To Esteban Gomez's hacienda. It was several years later when they told me what happened that night. The van rolled on the ice and everyone was killed. Seventeen people. Everyone but me. I was thrown free from the van and into some bushes at the road side. Traffic was blocked on the highway, and all the other vehicles stopped. That's when Uncle Rey found me."

Josh is spellbound by the story. "And your parents? I thought they lived in Rinconada."

"Esteban and Grace are not my parents. My parents died that night on the highway. I don't even know their names. I don't even know what country they were coming from. Can you imagine that? I don't even know what country I was born in?"

"Can't you find that out? Surely there are records about the accident."

She gives out a sad laugh, then chokes back a sob. "The newspaper articles just reported them as illegals with no identification. Just illegals …" She stops talking and begins shaking again. Again Josh puts his arm around her, and this time her shaking subsides.

"So you don't even know what country you were born in?" Josh is aware of his arm around her, and he's working hard not to be swept away by how his fingers rest gently where her soft skin emerges from the short sleeve of the nightgown.

She nods her head sadly. "When I found out about the accident, I used to imagine about the country I had come from. Sometimes I'd wonder if I was born in Mexico, and I'd go to the bookmobile, when it came through Rinconada, and study about Mexico. Then later I'd get convinced somehow that I had been born in Nicaragua, and I'd study that for awhile. It was silly, I guess." She gives out a little self-deprecating laugh.

"I don't think it's silly at all." Josh wants to console Evangelina, wants to rescue her, wants to hold her and make things alright. Her story has brought him to the edge of tears, but he holds back. "So Esteban and Grace raised you as their child?"

"Yes. They had no children. So you can imagine that winter night when Uncle Rey brought me to their house. They've told me that story many times, how it was the happiest night of their lives."

"So, they really are your parents, I guess."

"I love them like they are my parents. When I came to them I knew my name was Evangelina, but I didn't know my last name, and I knew I was four. I knew nothing else about my identity. So I became Evangelina Gomez."

"And you're afraid of the police because of all this?"

"I have no proof of citizenship. If I'm found out, I will be deported, even though I have no place to be deported to. And my parents and Uncle Rey, they could go to prison for harboring an illegal. And Serena. That's the worst part." She stops and sobs again for a moment. "I don't know what would happen to her."

"Where is her father?"

"I don't know and I don't want to know. I met Billie at the junior college. Things were going so well then." She turns and looks Josh squarely in the eye. "Josh, I was valedictorian in my high school." She pauses, then looks down. "Now it's come to this."

"How come you went to junior college instead of the university?"

"People in Rinconada don't leave home, don't leave the village. It was expected of me to stay nearby. That was okay with me. But then I met Billie. I fell in love, or I thought I was in love." She gives out a little grunt of disgust. "He was kind. At least at the first. Full of big ideas and plans. I thought we were going to get married. I was so stupid. When I got pregnant, he split." She starts crying again. "You must think I'm the greatest loser of all time," she sobs.

"No, I don't. I think …" He trails off for a moment, his fingers now pressing ever so slightly harder on her arm. He is intoxicated by her scent, warm and soapy. "I think you're wonderful."

She looks at him, eyes full of questions. Their faces are just inches apart. "How can you think that?"

Though Josh is concentrating on her every word, he has not for a second been unaware that he is sitting in a bed with his arm around a beautiful woman in a nightgown. "Because when I look at you, I see someone who is kind and gentle, yet very brave and strong." He wants to say beautiful, but doesn't.

"But I'm ill. And so is Serena. That's what a woman in Rinconada told me, and I've never forgotten it."

"What do you mean 'ill'?" Josh is concerned.

"It's a sad joke. I'm il-legal and Serena is il-legitimate. We are both ill." She chuckles in a way that sounds like she might start crying again, but she doesn't. "It was a mean thing to say, but in a way it's true."

"Don't think things like that." Josh's voice now carries a tone of admonishment. He bristles at the injustice. "Look," he says, then pauses, waiting for her full attention. "You were brought into this country by someone else when you were very young. I'm not so sure they would deport you and your daughter. I think in your case—"

"Things get worse, I'm afraid." She's shaking her head sadly.

"How?"

"I dropped out of college when Serena was born. I had to find a way to support her. So I got a job cleaning houses, while my parents took care of Serena. When you don't have any papers, there's not much else you can do. One day a guy in the village told me about a place that could help me get a job at the Lab, a placement agency he called it. I went to see them and found out they were willing to fake my papers so I could pass as a US citizen. I knew it was illegal, but I needed money to help raise my child. It was just a contractor position, with no access to secret documents or anything." She looks at him again with pleading eyes, and he nods reassurance. "So I guess the Lab didn't look too close. I've worked real hard to do good in that job, and I thought if I worked hard enough, then after awhile it wouldn't matter if I ever had papers or not."

Josh nods but says nothing. His hand is now making a gentle rubbing motion on her shoulder, almost a caress.

She continues. "When that man, Mr. Ferguson, came by, I thought he was from the FBI, I thought that they had caught me, that it was all over. But when he grabbed me, I knew it was something else."

"So here we are." Josh smiles.

"Yes, here we are." Evangelina now smiles too. "Thank you for listening to me. You're the only person I've ever told this story to. I guess you could turn me in if you wanted."

Josh doesn't want to turn her in. What he wants to do is kiss her. Her face is so close that he already feels almost completely enveloped by her. He thinks about Hollister's advice. Go for it. But this isn't the time. Instead, he says, "We'll get out of this." He realizes immediately how empty this must sound.

"I need to see my daughter."

"I know. But we're going to need to get some help. I don't see how we can take these guys on by ourselves. I think they mean to kill us."

Evangelina says nothing. She looks deep into Josh's eyes, a look of complete helplessness.

Chapter Seven

Sunday, October 16

As the sun comes up over the barren ridge east of town, Stilwell stirs and then stretches. Jesse, in the seat next to him, is still snoring. Two nights of sleeping in the car has his muscles sore. He raises the front seat from its reclining position, then gets out of the car to relieve himself.

His cell rings. He screams out a string of curses into the sunrise. This job has already been a big enough pain. Just what he needs now, another call from the Contact.

"So the FBI are now on the case."

"So?"

"Stilwell, you've bungled this royally. They're now saying Wessel was murdered. And they know the girl has disappeared."

He hears panic in the Contact's voice, the first time he's heard that. He thinks about Montevideo. Hasn't been there in ten years. But he knows his way around there. He knows how to totally disappear into the woodwork there. This will be good. After the work is done here, and that will be soon, he can get there quick. He wonders if Maria still works at that club on the Boulevard Sarandi. He looks over at Jesse. Might be time to terminate their working relationship also. Let Jesse explore some new options, like what it feels like to be face down in an irrigation ditch. He can't be left to go free. No loose ends. Stilwell hates loose ends. Ah Jesse, that filthy slob. Never really cared for him. It's one thing to be a ruthless killer, that's really the only admirable thing about Jesse. It's another thing to be such a gross example of human existence. This is all coming together nicely.

"Are you listening to me, Stilwell?"

"Of course," he says with a nonchalance designed to drive the Contact nuts.

"If we have to, we can play our trump card."

"You mean the daughter?"

"I mean the daughter."

"I don't know where she is."

"That can be taken care of." There is a click on the other end.

Stilwell paces around the car, gazes out toward the sunrise. Hmm, the daughter. He smiles. Gratification on this operation has been delayed. But when it comes, it's shaping up to be one of pure delight.

৵৽

Josh follows several paces behind Evangelina down the hall toward church. She walks purposefully, as he trails reluctantly behind. He could use a cup of coffee and a few more hours sleep. The vinyl sofa had been like a rock, but it was the middle-of-the-night conversation that had done him in. Afterwards, he couldn't fall back to sleep, as a turbulence of worries and questions sloshed through his beleaguered brain.

In the dining hall, Hollister is just finishing the arrangement of the dining room chairs. They've been moved away from the tables and are now arranged in five rows facing a small table, covered with a sheet upon which a simple lighted candle sits.

Esther stands at the door, and Evangelina asks, "Where's the priest?"

"Well, we don't have a priest. Father Carlos used to come up every week from Española, but he died a couple years back. The new guy, don't remember his name, a young guy just out of seminary, came up once. Then after that he said he was too busy, and he never came again." She gives a coy knowing smile that says she'll say no more about that.

"So who leads the service?"

"'Fraid you're lookin' at her. I've got an old Book of Common Prayer I've had ever since my confirmation, and I've got my bible. Figure that's enough." Now there's a new twinkle in Esther's eyes.

By eight nearly all the chairs are filled. As best Josh can tell, everyone from supper is here this morning.

Esther stands before the congregation and smiles. "Good morning to you all."

"Good morning," everyone beams back.

Josh looks around at the small congregation. Nearly half of the people have walkers parked next to their chairs. Bud Ewing is wearing a coat and tie and takes his USMC cap off as Esther begins to speak. He watches her intently through his thick glasses. Maggie sits next to him, but she gazes absently off into space. Hollister and Rosey have been busy helping people get seated. Now they take seats at the edge of the seating area, obviously so that Hollister does not block the view of others. He's spiffed up this morning also, a dark blue polo over khaki chinos. He nods at Josh when their eyes meet.

Josh has not spoken to Evangelina since they entered the dining area, but he watches her out of the corner of his eye. They've said little to each other this morning, each taking their showers and dressing in the bathroom, quietly respecting each other's morning privacy. They are both wearing the clothes they'd worn into Copper Point, now washed and pressed. Evangelina's eyes are also focused on Esther, and he wonders what's going through her mind. She wears a gentle smile, but he senses an edginess, a discomfort in her. Maybe it's his imagination.

Esther has begun the service. She reads a few prayers, the words sailing past him as he is thinking again about his middle-of-the night discussion with Evangelina and his run-in yesterday afternoon with Ferguson. He has led a quiet life these past few years, a predictable, repetitive life. A safe life. All that has changed radically in the past two days. He thinks again about MacGyver, the clever agent, scientist and man of action. Shouldn't he, Josh Waverly, be taking some action? But he still has no idea, no plan for escaping the dangerous situation they are in. Yet he's pretty sure that about the last thing he needs to be doing right now is sitting through some church service, while mere feet away killers are plotting to take Evangelina and him down.

꧁꧂

Evangelina crosses herself and genuflects before taking her seat. She is unaware of the others who have gathered, her eyes glued on Esther. As much as she doesn't want to think about it, she cannot escape the memory that haunts her of the last time she went to church five years ago.

She had come to Our Lady of Mercy, the imposing adobe church on the plaza in Rinconada, as she had nearly every Sunday of her life. This Sunday seemed no different. She'd taken her regular seat with her parents and knelt to pray before the mass.

Then there had been a tap, a rather firm tap, on her shoulder. Evangelina had turned around to see Mrs. Maestas, who runs La Tienda on the plaza, glaring at her. Keeping silent, as she always did before the mass, she gave Mrs. Maestas a questioning look. Then Mrs. Maestas said, out loud so that everyone could hear, "I'm amazed you're here. If Father knew about your sins, I'm sure he wouldn't allow you to be in this holy place."

Evangelina was speechless and returned to her prayers, shaking. In fact she had talked with Father about her situation. She had made her confession just last week. Told him everything. She had asked forgiveness for her poor choices, for her lack of good judgment in getting involved with Billie, for letting her heart rule her mind. But then Father had asked her if there was more she wanted to confess, for example the baby growing inside her unmarried body.

Evangelina was twenty years old and had never questioned the judgment or authority of her priest, but she had bristled and had said something like, "I cannot think of what's growing inside my body as anything but beautiful and holy." She had left the confessional in silence.

With Mrs. Maestas' eyes no doubt glaring at her back, Evangelina braved it through the mass, until it was time to go forward for communion. She went to the altar rail for communion with her parents, as she did every Sunday, but on this Sunday when Father came to her, her hands outstretched to receive the Sacrament, he passed right by her. She was devastated. She did her best to return to her pew with her dignity intact.

She never returned to that church, or any other church, again.

This memory plagues her this morning, and she half expects a tap on her shoulder from Mrs. Maestas. But there's also a part of her that feels good about being here, like reconnecting with something she's deeply missed.

After Esther has read some prayers, Rosey stands to read a passage from Scripture, announcing the reading with that dignified voice of hers: "A reading from the Gospel of Saint Luke." Then she reads the story of the prodigal son, a story familiar to Evangelina, although she hasn't heard it in a long time. When Rosey sits down, Evangelina is shaking and looks around surreptitiously to see if anyone notices. Why has this familiar story shaken her so badly today? She glances at Josh, who is squirming uncomfortably.

Then Esther stands before the congregation to speak. She has no notes. She paces around a little, head down, obviously thinking. Then she stops, looks at the people and begins.

❦

Though Josh sits facing Esther, who has just begun to speak, his focus is on the doorway leading to the lobby, just at the edge of his field of view. There is no reason the men could not appear in that doorway at any moment. And here they are, sitting ducks. He feels a chill creep down his back, as he pictures them storming in with guns drawn, and has to fight off the urge to bolt from the room. Yet Evangelina doesn't seem to notice. She's caught up in Esther's words.

Esther is talking about the bible passage that Rosie just read, about some screwed-up kid who's left his family. "This kid was a real jerk, wasn't he? Rude to his father, demands all his inheritance. Dad shoulda put his foot down right there, but he doesn't. He coughs up the cash and allows the young man to go on his merry way. Oh, I sure would've told that young punk a thing or two." People laugh.

What is it with this Esther, Josh wonders. Speaking with such conviction, such confidence. She seems like she really believes this stuff. Not like the preachers he's seen on TV, who only seem to want your money. And she's so calm. Unlike … Josh quickly suppresses the memories of his disastrous seminar just a couple of days ago, now so distant in the past. So, what motivates this woman? Cripes, if he had to live in this place, he'd be fighting depression big time.

Josh fends off the anxiety about the men bursting in and tries to focus on what Esther is saying. "So the kid heads to the big city, where he blows the whole wad on wine, women, and song. Now he's broke. Has to get a job, but he can't find one. He's getting hungry. The nights are cold. All the good-timing friends who had flocked around him when he was buying drinks for the house, why they don't want to have anything to do with this loser. This guy is out of luck. Worse yet, he seems out of hope. He deserved it, right? Got his come-uppance, my daddy used to say. Right?"

Everyone chuckles and a few voices echo Esther's words, "Right!"

Josh squirms in the hard metal chair and looks over at Evangelina again. He takes in her gentle profile and weighs whether she is more beautiful in profile or face on. He cannot decide. She looks like she's about to cry. He wants to touch her, but holds back. She apparently senses his stare and glances briefly at him, her eyes questioning. Josh, caught in the act of leering, quickly returns his gaze back to Esther, feigning interest in the sermon.

"So the kid was out of hope," Esther says. "Have you ever felt like you were out of hope? Maybe you weren't a jerk like this young man. Fact is, you probably weren't. But I suspect you've felt pretty hopeless at times. Maybe you've screwed up, and there seems to be no way to make things right. Maybe you've never amounted to much, maybe you've fallen short of what somebody else expected and you don't know what to do about it. Maybe you're hurting real bad down inside, maybe you just never got a break in this world. Maybe you look around at this place and think, 'Is this how my life has turned out? Alone in the middle of nowhere?' Well, I can relate to all that. I'm here, just like you. Not the best place in the world. Seems hopeless."

Josh blows out a long impatient sigh, which prompts another glance, tinged with admonishment, from Evangelina. He's been slouching in the hard chair, trying to find a way to be comfortable, but now he sits up straight like a school kid who's just received a corrective glower from the teacher. Maybe it would be best for him to leave right now, slip out to a better vantage point, where he could keep watch on the front doors. He questions whether he could leave un-noticed and concludes it would make a scene, be taken as rude. Even in the face of killers, Josh is never rude.

Esther's just warming up. "Saddest word in the English language, if you ask me: hopeless. So, just what is hope anyway? Is it just wishful thinking? Is it clinging to some fairy tale you know down deep isn't really true?"

Well, yes, in fact that's just what it is, Josh reflects, as if silently debating Esther on the subject. Isn't hope just the unproductive alternative to actually taking action, doing something useful?

Esther has paused and looks out on the congregation, as if giving them all a moment to think it over, then she puts her hands on her hips, leans forward a bit and almost yells, "Nah, that's not what hope is."

Josh scans the room. Bud is glued to every word. Hollister has put his arm around his grandmother and gives her a gentle squeeze. They smile at each other and nod. Beyond the congregation, Josh notices Yolanda peering from the kitchen, over the swinging café doors, focused on Esther.

Esther continues, "So the young man comes to his senses, realizes what an idiot he's been. He knows he's burned all his bridges behind him. He has no hope." She purses her lips in pity and shakes her head sorrowfully.

"Then he decides, in desperation, to go back home. He's sure his father has disowned him by now. I mean, that's what any self-respecting father would do, right? Just wash his hands of this blight on the family's good name. The young man decides to go home, hoping that maybe, just maybe, dear old dad – who's already disowned him – will at least hire him to do menial labor around the farm."

Josh takes this in. Self-respecting fathers washing their hands of blights on the family name. Josh wants to blurt out, "Well, now we're onto something I know about," but of course he doesn't. He darts a quick sideways glance at Evangelina, just in case she can read his mind, but she's caught up in the story Esther is telling.

"Of course, you know how the story goes. When he gets close to home, while he's still rehearsing his speech to his father, dad comes running down the road and throws his arms around his son. Holds him. Welcomes him back. Puts a fancy robe on him. Plans a big party to celebrate his coming home."

Josh feels something in his throat and swallows hard. Images of his own father flood his mind. If he had lived, might things have worked out differently? If his dad had been able to see him get his Ph. D? Josh reflexively rubs his leg, sore from the rigid metal chair, and he's aware that he seems to notice his bum leg more when painful old thoughts about his father surface. A noise from Evangelina causes him to look over at her again. Was that a gulp? Or a sob? But Evangelina looks straight ahead, not taking her eyes off Esther. Josh sighs again. Surely this will be over soon.

"Of course the dad in this story is our heavenly father. He, my friends, is the source of our hope. No, hope is not wishful thinking. Here's what hope is, and you might want to write this down and hang it on your wall. Laminate it and put it in your wallet.

"Hope is confidence based on a promise.

"Because of the character of our God, who says he holds us in the palm of his hand, who says we're the apple of his eye. Because of these promises, I can be confident. That is the source of my hope."

She stops, faces the people and lowers her voice. "My friends, in the end the prodigal son wasn't a loser after all, because he had a father who never stopped loving him. He was a winner. And you too, no matter what you've done, no matter how much you've been hurt, no matter how much you may have hurt someone else, no matter how pathetic you think your situation is, you too are a winner. A winner, welcomed home and loved beyond all reason by your heavenly father. Amen."

When Esther finishes, she sits down and is silent. A hush falls over the room. Evangelina looks shaken. She looks at Josh, her eyes wide, her mouth open as if she needs air. Josh licks his lips, suddenly aware that his mouth is dry. Thank goodness this is over. That Esther can spin a good story, you've got to admit, thinks Josh. And it sure seems to be giving these sad people some encouragement. But what does any of it have to do with him?

��

A few more prayers and that's it. People rise and begin to navigate the few feet to the breakfast tables, while Hollister is hurrying to get their chairs in place. Josh and Evangelina pitch in to help. Breakfast is loud and full of laughter, joy produced no doubt by the inspiring service.

But Evangelina doesn't want to talk to anyone at breakfast. She wants to be quiet, to reflect. She does not want to lose one shred of connection to Esther's words. She has been cut to the heart.

��

After breakfast, Josh wanders the halls again. He is reminded of some old horror movie he once saw, where a man was buried alive, as the stark walls of this bleak hallway close in on him like a coffin lid. It's more than claustrophobia. It's a sense of hopelessness enhanced by the gray concrete. Some artwork would cheer up this place a lot. He thinks of his own apartment. Dreary. Isn't that what Hal called it? He pictures his one wall hanging, the Winslow print of the New England seascape. Thinking about it now -

- imagining the pungent salt air, the squawk of sea birds, the restful roar of surf – calms him a bit.

He passes a room with the door open. Inside, through a haze of smoke, he sees Bud Ewing watching a small TV, still wearing his suit from church. Josh intends to pass on by, but Bud has noticed him, waves a hand and hollers, "Hey, come on in."

Josh steps into the small room, identical to the one where he and Evangelina are staying. Bud, sitting on the only chair in the room, gestures for Josh to take a seat on the edge of the bed, neatly made.

"Didn't see Esther out there, did you?"

"No."

"Good. She gives me a raft of grief for leaving my door open when I'm smoking. Says it stinks up the place. You want one?" Bud extends a pack of Camels toward Josh.

"Oh, no thanks, I don't smoke." In fact, the thick smoke is already stinging his eyes, and his throat is feeling a bit raspy.

"Good for you. These things are coffin nails."

"What are you watching?" Josh gestures toward the TV.

"Not much on. Sunday morning. And I only get three channels."

"You don't have cable here?"

Bud raises one eyebrow, as if to say, "You've got to be kidding." But he just says, "Nope. The rabbit ears can only pull in three stations from Santa Fe, and one of them's pretty fuzzy."

The small 19 inch set causes Josh a pang of guilt, as the image of his seldom-used 52 inch flat screen and seven channel surround-sound flashes through his mind.

"Too bad. I bet you'd love the History Channel."

"Yeah, we had that in the last place I was in. That'd be great."

"How long you been here?"

"Let me see." He ponders this for awhile. "About four years."

"Do you have family?"

Bud turns off the TV, sets the remote on the small desk next to him and turns to face Josh. "Carol died six years ago." He stops for a moment, choking up a bit. "We were married fifty-five years. That's her." He points to an eight by ten on the wall.

"Fifty-five years. You're a lucky man, Bud."

"I sure am."

"Any kids?"

"I have a son, David."

"Where's he?"

"He has some big job out in California … no wait, maybe it's Oregon. Anyway, I haven't seen him since Carol died. But he sends me a Christmas card every year."

Josh looks away, hiding the mistiness he feels building in his eyes. "I'm sorry," he says.

"Oh, I'm doing okay. Truth is I wasn't the greatest dad. I was hard on David when he was growing up. Guess when his mother died, he just didn't see much reason to come around anymore." He says this matter-of-factly, but Josh wonders if there's regret buried down there somewhere.

Bud's admission stirs a brief flickering memory of Josh's own dad, who could hold his own in the hardass department.

Bud continues, "Yeah, there's some things you just can't change, but I can tell you that the little church service we just went to sure helps. Do you usually go to church?"

Josh has to admit that the church service did affect him in some way he doesn't fully understand, played with his emotions in some way that he's not used to, not comfortable with. But he says nothing about this. He says, "No."

Bud winces. "Do you believe in God?"

"You mean, do I think there's a creative force in the universe? Maybe, but I'd prefer to see some evidence."

"I'm not talking about what you call some creative force, I'm talking about a real God who cares about you, who hears your prayers, who gives you some comfort when things are tough."

"Well, then I probably don't."

"Well then, either you're a lucky man who has everything all lined up and doesn't need any help, either that or you're just a fool." Bud gives Josh a penetrating look.

Josh shifts on the bed, looks away from Bud for a moment. He takes in the room, though there's not much to take in. Bud has not done much to personalize the room, other than a small cork board and the several pictures above the desk. The photograph of Carol appears to be a professional portrait, but it's faded. Next to it is a picture of a middle aged couple, smiling in front of a docked cruise ship. Then another portrait that looks like a high school graduation picture. This is surely David. Another picture of a young Marine in dress uniform. A handsome young man, beaming a confident grin. He turns back to Bud. Even in his decrepit state, Bud Ewing still bears some of the confidence of that young Marine in the photo. Josh says, "Well, to be honest, maybe I haven't given it a lot of thought."

"Haven't given it a lot of thought, huh? Well, I hope sometime you do give it a lot of thought. I can tell you that this old Marine has seen some hard stuff in his life. I'm a tough old bird and I can take a lot, but there are some things you just can't face alone. I read that book every day and it sure helps a lot." He nods toward a worn bible on the desk. It lies next to a stack of Tom Clancy novels. *Red Storm Rising* lies open next to the bible.

"Doesn't that make God into a sort of crutch?"

Bud laughs. "God a crutch? You've got to be kidding—" He's interrupted by a throaty nicotine coughing jag. He comes out of it laughing. "Crutch, huh? He's a whole hospital!"

Josh looks down. He's never been confronted like this before about religion.

Then Bud blurts out a loud string of obscenities.

"What?" Josh looks up quickly.

"I just peed myself again." He's looking down at his lap.

"I'm sorry. Anything I can do?"

"No, I can take care of it. I should've changed out of my suit before. Just sit still for a bit." He rocks back and forth, getting momentum to rise. "One-two-three-up!" He's on his feet now and wobbles toward the bathroom.

While Bud is in the bathroom, Josh studies the cork board above Bud's desk. Almost empty except for a line of Christmas cards thumb-tacked along the top. He stands and peeks into them. Each one is signed simply, best regards, David.

Bud returns. He's in his underwear, but still wears his coat and tie. Josh has to stifle a laugh.

Bud lights another Camel. For a few moments they sit in awkward silence, then Bud says, "You and your lady friend. Are you in some kind of trouble?"

"Why would you think that?"

"Just a sense. Something doesn't seem quite right. Anything I can help with?"

"Well, we are in trouble, but I'm not sure what you can do to help."

"Creditors on your trail?"

"I think it's worse than that. There are some dangerous men after us. And we can't call the police."

"Why not?"

"We just can't. Please trust me about that."

"Okay. You're not running from the law, are you?"

"No. We've done nothing wrong."

With his forefinger, Bud pushes his thick glasses back up the chiseled ridge of his nose, then rubs his chin between his forefinger and thumb. "Dangerous men, you say?"

"I think they're armed and mean to do us harm."

"Well, if you're going to have to face them down, and you need someone by your side, then count me in."

Josh almost laughs, considering this frail old man in his underwear, but doesn't as he sees a steeliness in this ex-Marine's eyes. Solemnly, he says, "Thank you, Bud."

❧

Evangelina had hoped she could slink quietly back to the room after breakfast, but Esther's voice stops her. "Evangelina, can you spare a minute?"

"Yes, of course."

"Why don't we sit out in the lobby in one of those soft couches?"

When they are seated, side by side, Esther says, "You were awfully quiet at breakfast."

Evangelina smiles. "You gave me a lot to think about. And I hadn't been to church in years."

"Is that a fact? Why not?"

Evangelina tells her about Serena and her experience at the church in Rinconada.

"That makes me so mad," says Esther. "Nobody should be treated like that."

"That's what I thought with my head, but down in my heart I was crushed. I felt like maybe there really was something wrong with me."

"Well, it's a good thing the Blessed Virgin didn't go to that church, she would've been kicked out too."

This causes Evangelina to chuckle, but quickly her somber mood returns. "But there's more."

"I know about the men, Evangelina. Josh told me. And I met one of them yesterday. A bad hombre."

"Yes, I am very afraid. But I'm more afraid for my daughter."

"That's because you are a good mother."

"I should call the police, but ..." Evangelina sighs. Then the words come out in a gush. "I'm a criminal, Esther. I could go to prison or be deported. And my parents could go to jail too." She tells Esther the whole story.

Esther sits quiet for awhile after Evangelina is finished. Then she says, "I don't see that you have done anything really wrong, dear." Esther lays a hand softly on Evangelina's arm.

"But I've been a problem for everyone, Esther. My daughter will grow up without a father, because of my foolishness. My parents could go to jail because of me. This kind man Josh is now in trouble because of me. Oh God, I don't know where to turn."

"Oh, I think maybe you do. You said that church this morning gave you a lot to think about. Want to say more about that?"

"I don't know how to explain it. It just felt like when you talked about that young son who made so many bad mistakes, you were talking about me. I have felt out of hope."

"I'm sorry to hear that. You know the point of the story is that you can have hope. Because hope is a gift from God."

"A gift?"

"Absolutely. You don't have to do anything to earn it. In fact, you can't do anything to earn it. It's a free gift from God."

"Yeah, but why would God give me a free gift?"

"I sure don't know, dear. But that's what he does. I guess it's because that's the way he is. I see God as so full of love that he suffers when we suffer. He understands what we're going through. After all, he put up with that awful cross. I guess he knows what it's like to be hurting, don't you think?"

Evangelina nods.

Esther continues. "That's why the bible says 'God is love.' Everything he does, every motivation he has is out of love for us."

"So why don't I feel hopeful?"

"Maybe you just haven't opened the gift yet. I think a lot of people miss out on an awful lot because they haven't opened the gifts from God."

"So how do I do that? Open the gifts, I mean."

"Start praying. Read your bible. I mean study it hard, let it sink in. The Holy Spirit will make sure that happens, if you give it a chance. Go to church. Why, you've already started that today. Talk to friends about God. You've already started that too. And finally, start thinking about how you can help other people who are hurting. Our Lord says that when we help the folks who are down and out, that's when we're helping him."

Evangelina nods, then looks down. Her hands are clenched together, not as hands of prayer, but as hands that are hanging on for dear life.

Esther continues. "Evangelina. That's such a pretty name. Such a special name. Do you know what it means?"

Evangelina looks up. "I'm not sure."

"It comes from the word 'evangel.' The same word that the word 'evangelism' comes from. And do you know what that means?"

"Not really, I guess."

"It simply means 'good news.' Evangelina, your name means 'good news.' And dear girl, I think that's exactly what you are. You are good news. You are good news to that couple who never had a child. You are good news to that little girl, who so completely loves her mother. You're good news to that young man, Josh, who, in case you haven't noticed, can't keep his eyes off you. And, Evangelina, you're good news to me too."

Evangelina's mouth falls open. She releases her hands and touches one palm to each side of her cheeks, feeling her blush. "Esther, that is so wonderful, what you just said." She pauses, then adds, "But I'm an illegal immigrant. That's not good news."

"You're an illegal immigrant by the laws made by man, Evangelina. Not by the laws made by God. To God you are his precious child, who was lost but now is found." There is a twinkle in Esther's eyes as she says this. "When your uncle scooped you up off that icy highway all those years ago, do you think he said to himself, 'Oh, my, I've found myself an illegal immigrant?' Or do you think he said to himself, 'Why, look here at this beautiful little child of God. I'm gonna take her home to live with my sister'?"

Evangelina begins to cry. At first it is a gentle weeping, just a few tears trickling down her cheeks. She thinks of how she seldom cries, and yet she has cried several times the past two days. But those had been tears of terror, tears

of sadness. These tears are something different. Not
sadness. But release. Liberation. Then, the little weeping
sounds are replaced by sobs, loud sobs, and a flood of tears.
She moves closer to Esther, who gently cradles her, stroking
her long black hair with a gentle hand.

In the midst of her sobs, Evangelina lets out a small
giggle, a giggle of embarrassment, perhaps of joy.

"Let those tears flow," Esther says. "That's just you,
running into the arms of your Father."

❧

Josh sees Evangelina coming down the hall. She's been
talking to Esther since breakfast. She stops, and they stand
there facing each other in the hallway.

"Hey, Josh," she smiles. Her eyes are red.

"Are you okay?"

"Oh yes." A pause, then, "What did you think of
church?"

"It was fine. Not really my thing, though."

"Maybe you should talk to Esther. She has a lot of
wisdom."

With the memory of Bud's little lecture about God still
fresh in his mind, this is about the last thing he needs. But
he says, "Sure, I'll have to do that." Then he adds quickly, as
if moving on to more important things, "I've been doing a
lot of thinking, and it's time we talk this thing through, I
mean about the guys who are chasing you, I mean us."

"Yes, of course." Her smiling face has turned serious.
"It's not like I haven't already been thinking this thing
through like every minute."

"Look, hear me out on this. This guy Ferguson came to the Lab to find you. He knew where you worked. So I think this has to do with your work."

"I'm not sure about that. I only do data entry. I don't see how I could know or have anything that someone wanted."

"Hmm. So just what does data entry involve?"

She's looking impatient, but willing to humor him. "I use a data base program to enter information into a spreadsheet for the group. We handle lots of small contracts, and I enter stuff like hours worked in a given week on various program accounts, dollars spent for these accounts, and how the money was spent, whether on wages, or operating costs, or capital equipment. Just routine stuff like that. I don't know anything about the accounts or the people whose wage information I enter. I just type in numbers that I'm given."

"So what does your group, Industrial Relations, do?"

"What I know about it is that it keeps track of partnerships at the Lab between research groups and private companies. The company and the Lab sign a CRADA—"

"CRADA?"

"Stands for 'Cooperative Research and Development Agreement.' The company sends some money to the Lab, or it comes from the government, and the Lab works with the company to apply its technology to products the companies are working on. At least that's what I hear around the office."

"Yeah, I've heard about that too. What did the man who was murdered do?"

"I don't know. I never heard of him."

"Okay. So, the way I see it, this guy Ferguson lied about being with the FBI. I guess he could be with some other secret agency, but his violent action sure doesn't sound like someone working for the government. At least I hope not." He attempts a little laugh, but Evangelina's face remains serious. "So I say he's a criminal."

"Probably true."

"So he probably doesn't care about your immigration status. Maybe Homeland Security would, but I suspect this guy Ferguson doesn't."

"Look, Josh, I know where you're going with this. But what you don't realize is that I've lived my whole life with this hanging over my head. My parents had to go through these fears when I first went to school. They weren't sure they could get me in without showing my birth certificate, but somehow they did. I was shaking when I got my driver's license because I thought they would ask for my papers, but thank God they did not. I can't fly on an airplane out of fear they'll ask to see my passport, which of course I can't have. I can't drive across the state line out of fear someone will want to check me out. I have to live every day with this, so I don't need you telling me I have nothing to worry about." Her face has reddened and her eyes are flashing.

"I'm not saying you shouldn't worry. I'm just saying we need to figure out why these guys are after you. Probably now *us*. Evangelina, what do you think they want?"

"I don't know," she almost shrieks.

"Maybe you've been framed … or maybe they think you witnessed something."

"So you still want to call the police. Then what happens? They finally drive up, if they come at all. You heard what Esther said about the police out here. Then, if they show up, the gray car suddenly disappears, right? Until the cops leave. Then what do we do?"

"Look, I'm just trying to get us to think this thing through logically—"

Evangelina cuts him off. "You don't think I've thought this thing through logically already? You think I'm just some dumb Hispanic chick that can't figure anything out unless she's got Doctor Ph.D.-Know-It-All there to help her? Is that what you think?" Her eyes are on fire. She stands with clenched fists on her hips, leaning up toward his face.

Josh's mouth falls open. Then impulsively he takes her face in both hands and kisses her on the mouth. Her lips are warm and moist. She seems to respond, but only for a second.

She jerks back, pushing him away. Her eyes are wide in surprise, looking up at him.

"I'm sorry. I'm sorry. I'm—"

She shakes her head, then whispers, "Don't be sorry."

Chapter Eight

Sometimes a special moment becomes frozen in time, as if the laws of physics have been suspended. And for awhile there is no past or future, nor any need for such, just an all-encompassing present, where there is no recalling of the past, nor pondering of the future, just a need to be. In such a moment, Josh and Evangelina stand in the hallway at Copper Point. No words, no movement, frozen in time. Everything that is happening is taking place in their eyes.

Then a bouncing basketball announces the arrival of Hollister, who appears around the corner. He stops abruptly. "Oops, am I interrupting something?"

"No, no," says Evangelina quickly. "I need to go call my family." She backs away, shooting Josh one last look that he has a hard time deciphering.

"Looks like maybe you've been going for it, Josh. Hope you didn't called for a charging foul."

Josh is still shaking from the kiss, from his uncharacteristic impulsiveness. He grins at Hollister. "In fact, I guess I did go for it. Not sure how this will turn out. The game's not over yet. But I gotta say, that felt pretty good."

"Well, maybe this would be a good time for you to get your fanny kicked in a little HORSE."

"Good idea," he says, laughing, "Except I think you've got it wrong about which fanny is going to get kicked."

Out back, they shoot around for awhile. Josh notices that his leg is feeling quite good today, no doubt a result of the exercise he's been getting the past two days. Maybe the adrenaline surge that he just got from Evangelina is a factor too. As he sinks a ten-footer, he asks Hollister, "So, how's the resume coming along?"

"Well, I think I got it pretty well updated. I'll send it off to some places this week, when I go down to Santa Fe. No internet up here. Say, would you mind taking a look at the resume some time? I'd like your opinion about how I could improve the darn thing."

"Sure, I'd be happy to look it over. So, you have a car?"

Hollister banks in a twelve footer, gets the ball as it drops through the netless rim and tosses it out to Josh. "More or less. An old Escort with 200,000 miles, if you call that a car. But it's still running. The only car at Copper Point, I think. Sure not hard to find a parking place around here. So, what's the latest on the bad guys that are after you? You guys called the cops yet?"

Josh sighs. "Not yet. Haven't seen any sign of them since yesterday. I'm still trying to figure out what they want, but I know it's not good."

"Well, Josh, I saw that dude's eyes real good yesterday, and let me tell you, he's bad news. I'm worried for you guys."

"Thanks. Me too." Josh misses a fifteen footer and chases down the ball, hobbling slightly.

"What does Evangelina want to do?"

"She still wants to hold off on calling the cops for now."

"So I guess you guys need a plan B."

Josh can't betray what Evangelina shared with him in the middle of the night, so he says, "Got any ideas?"

"Well, I don't know what an over-the-hill power forward can do for you, but if there's any way I can help, I'm right here."

Josh is struck by the comment, recalling Bud's similar words this morning. It's been a long time, maybe not ever, since he's heard anyone caring about him this way.

"Thanks, Hollister. Now, are you ready for that major thrashing?"

≈≈

Evangelina calls Della's cell. It rings a long time, then Della's voicemail comes on. She feels a quick surge of fear, hangs up and tries again. This time Grace Gomez picks up on the second ring.

"I'm sorry, Vangie, I couldn't figure out how to turn the thing on."

"How are you, Mama?"

"We're doing fine."

"I'm worried about you."

"Needn't be, honey. Rey's got his shotgun and he knows how to use it. Della's been checking in on us too. When are you coming home?"

"Not quite yet, Mama. I'm safe here. But I think the men are still hanging around, and we're lying low."

"Can't you sneak out and come down here?"

"I will as soon as it's safe. There's a man with me, from the Lab. A real nice guy, named Josh. He helped me get away from the men."

"Can you trust him?"

"I think so, Mama. Can I talk to Serena?"

"She's right here." Evangelina hears Grace calling for Serena, then her daughter's voice comes on the phone.

"Mommy! When are you coming home?"

"Soon, angel cakes, very soon."

"Today?"

"I don't know, maybe if—"

"I want you to come home right now."

"I know, sweetie. I'll be there as soon as I—"

"I want you here now."

"I know, sweetie …" Evangelina feels tears welling up in her eyes. "But you've got your Nana and Grampa and Uncle Rey there. I bet they're taking real good care of—"

"They are, Mommy, but they're not you. I've only got one mommy."

Evangelina almost melts, but is also impressed at such words coming from a four-year-old. "And I've only got one angel cakes. I love you, sweetie."

"I love you too, Mommy. But I want you to come home right now."

"Soon as I can …" This is so difficult. *Dear God, help me to be with my daughter soon. Please God.* "Sweetie, I need to talk with your Nana now."

Grace comes back on the line. "Mama, I'm worried about the cell phone running low. So I'm going to go now. I'm doing fine, please know that. Tell Papa and Uncle Rey that I love them, okay?"

She sags on the bed after hanging up. She can wait no longer to leave.

❦

Josh is invigorated by the workout with Hollister and even more invigorated thinking about Evangelina's words following their kiss. He's looking for her now.

He finds her in the room, sitting on the bed. She looks like she's been crying.

"Are you alright? Okay, dumb question."

"I've got to see my daughter. She doesn't understand why I can't come to her."

"Thinking of maybe sneaking out of here?"

"I know that would be dangerous, but yeah, that's what I'm thinking."

"I'm not sure about that. Right now your daughter's safe at her uncle's place, right?"

"I think so. For now."

"And we're safe here. For now. Leaving might drag Ferguson right down on us, or it might lead him to your daughter. Anyway, Hollister's got the only car here."

Evangelina seems to take notice of this. After a moment, she says, "Josh, you've been very patient with me. I do appreciate it."

"Thank you. I still think we should call the police. In spite of everything we talked about last night, I think our life-and-death situation sort of trumps all that."

"Josh Waverly, you've lived here all these years, and there's still so much you don't know."

"What are you getting at?"

"Have you ever been to Taos?"

"Of course," he says quickly, trying to project confidence. The famous town is just an hour's drive north of Los Alamos, but he's only been there a couple of times. "Why?"

"Have you noticed that there are three towns of Taos?"

"Huh?"

"Three towns for three cultures. The one you probably know about is the main town, the Anglo town, the place with the plaza and the New Mexican restaurants and cute shops. That's probably where you've been. But there's also Rancho de Taos, the Hispanic Taos, a few miles south of the Anglo town."

"I guess I've driven through there. Didn't pay much attention, apparently."

"Then there's Taos Pueblo, the Native American Taos. Three towns for three cultures. In a way that indicates how things are in the rural parts of this state. The cultures are still pretty well separated."

"I can imagine that being true a hundred years ago, but not today—"

"The last century has broken down the divisions a lot, but they're still there. Did you ever hear of the Pueblo Revolt?"

"Uh, don't think so."

"Josh, you've got to read up on your New Mexican history a little more."

Josh looks sheepish, but keeps quiet as Evangelina continues.

"When Coronado and his men came into New Mexico in the 1500's, they showed little mercy for the native Americans, as they took over the area. Just look at every Native American pueblo around here today. They've been there a thousand years, yet right in the middle of every one of them is what?"

"A church?"

"Yes, a huge church, erected by the conquistadors like Coronado. Adopting the Spanish culture wasn't an option for many of these people.

"Then in 1680, the Native Americans revolted against the Mexican invaders and took back their land and towns. Threw them out. It was violent and a lot of people died. It wasn't until fifteen years later that De Vargas and his army came in and reclaimed the land for Mexico."

"I didn't know that."

"So the mistrust between Hispanics and native Americans ran deep for a long time, still does in some of the more rural areas. Then the Americans came along, with big plans for development and making money, and both the Hispanics and Native Americans mistrusted them. In some places like Rinconada, what you have is basically a traditional Hispanic village, where suspicion and fear still reside."

"How do you know all this?"

"I wanted to be a history major. Plus, I actually paid attention in high school, which it sounds like you didn't do." She gives Josh a coy smile, her head tilted to one side. "But here's where all this leads. So an Anglo crime is committed at an Anglo lab, and you want me to call in the Anglo authorities—"

"Evangelina, it's not that way. There are lots of Hispanic policemen. A lot of Hispanic politicians. This isn't just about Anglos who can't be trusted."

"But it's an Anglo system. Look at the national news. All the stories about illegal immigrants. People in places like my home town, people like me, are afraid. And whether it's justified or not, they may want to solve their problems with my Uncle Rey's shotgun and not trust them to the police. Does this make any sense?"

"I'm working on it, honest I am."

"I know you are."

She reaches out and lays her fingers on his arm. He feels his knees go weak as she looks deep into his eyes. Then she stretches up to him and kisses him. Softly and gently on the mouth, then pulls back. Josh takes her shoulders in his hands and pulls her back to him. This time the kiss is long and deep. When they pull away, they are both gasping for air.

Josh extends one finger and brushes her long wavy black hair back out of her face, but says nothing. He can't move his eyes from her face.

Evangelina looks down, then back up at Josh. "I don't know what this means. It's all too confusing. Too fast."

Josh smiles. "I'm not confused at all." Probably a lie, he realizes.

Evangelina begins to speak, but just then there is a scream. A loud scream just down the hall.

❧❧

Josh puts a hand up toward Evangelina. "Stay put," he says. "Let me check this out." Josh cracks the door and peeks out. There's no one in the hallway.

Then another scream, louder this time, then a shriek, "Oh, dear God, she's dead!"

Josh and Evangelina exchange glances. "Let's go," she says. They bolt through the door and down the hall toward the origin of the scream. Near the lobby a crowd of residents has already gathered, looking down. There is sobbing.

Evangelina makes her way through the crowd, while Josh stays back. It's Esther. On the floor. Still and unconscious. Evangelina kneels beside her, puts her face up close to her mouth, checking for breath.

"She's dead," someone says.

"No she's not. She's breathing." Evangelina looks around. "Has anybody called for help?"

Blank looks. "Who would we call?" someone finally says.

"The clinic," says Evangelina. "Call the clinic."

No one moves. Josh realizes it's up to him to get help. He races to the front desk, but Olive is gone. He finds the phone and calls information. "I need the number for the clinic in Santuario, New Mexico."

"Santuario Rural Clinic?"

"Yes, I'm sure that's it. This is an emergency."

As the phone rings, Josh realizes that this is Sunday, and it's unlikely anyone will answer. But on the third ring, someone picks up.

"Santuario Clinic. Lauren."

Thank God, Josh wants to say. "Lauren, a woman just collapsed here at Copper Point. She's unconscious, but she's breathing. She may have fallen." Josh is thorough in providing all the details.

"I'll be there in five minutes."

In moments a white Tundra screeches to a stop outside the front doors. Josh waits from well inside, out of sight, he hopes, from any watching eyes. A young woman jumps out, grabs a bag and an armload of supplies, then comes toward the doors. They stick, but before Josh can get there to help, she gives them an authoritative kick and they open inward. Lauren is tall and probably no more than thirty. She wears khaki cargo shorts and a black sleeveless fleece with a Mountain Hardwear logo, over a yellow tee shirt. Serious hiking boots. Her hair is cut short around a tanned, pretty face.

"Where is she?" she asks, as soon as she sees Josh.

"This way."

As they sprint down the hall, Lauren says, "Good thing I came up to clean up some paperwork this afternoon. Usually not here on Sundays."

The crowd parts for Lauren, who kneels next to Evangelina.

Evangelina says, "This is Esther. She was unconscious, but I think she's starting to come around."

Lauren is already pulling a small oxygen bottle from her case, and quickly puts a mask over Esther's face. Then she checks her pulse. "A little slow," she says. "Did anyone see her fall?"

"I don't think so."

"Esther," Lauren says, "This is Lauren from the clinic. You're going to be okay. Can you hear me?"

Esther stirs, eyes now open, but unfocused. She nods her head slowly, but still does not speak. Her eyelids now flutter. She tries to rise.

"Let's stay put, Esther," says Lauren. "We want to check for broken bones."

Starting at the knee and working up, Lauren gently moves her hands over Esther's body. "Can't find any breaks, but that doesn't mean there isn't one. We'll have to get her over to the clinic."

Esther's now coming to. "What happened?" she says.

"We think you had a little fall, Esther," says Evangelina. "Lauren's here. She's going to take good care of you."

Esther's eyes still look like she's trying to focus. She looks first at Evangelina, then at Lauren. "Oh good. Lauren, thanks for coming, it's good to – ouch, oh my hip. It hurts."

"You just lie still, dear," says Lauren. "We're going to immobilize your hip, then we're going to get you over to the clinic for an x ray. You breathing better now?"

"I'm fine." She tries to pull the little mask from her face, but Lauren stops her.

"We better keep this on for awhile longer."

Lauren busies herself attaching plastic braces to the sides of Esther's body to immobilize her legs and hips. Then she turns to Evangelina. "This is a bit of a risk. No guarantee we've got her perfectly immobilized, but we can't leave her here. I've got a gurney in the truck. Can somebody help me with it?"

Evangelina looks at Josh. Josh looks around to see if Hollister is nearby. He isn't. He nods to Evangelina and Lauren. He knows this means stepping outside the building, where Ferguson may be watching. But what choice does he have?

Josh helps Lauren get the gurney from the back of the Tundra. There is no sign of the men.

"Easy now," Lauren says, after she's instructed Josh and Evangelina how to help move Esther onto the gurney. Josh takes one end of the gurney, while Lauren takes the other. Evangelina follows close by. "We'll put her right in the rear of the truck," she says. "One of you should ride with her, keep her calm and still. I'll drive slow. It's just a couple minutes away."

Esther is now fully conscious. "Don't go to all this fuss over me. I'm fine."

Evangelina places a reassuring hand on Esther's shoulder. "We're just going to get you an x ray, Esther, to make sure you're okay. I'll be right there with you."

Esther looks up at Evangelina with appreciative eyes.

After they get Esther into the back of the truck, Evangelina hops up into the bed next to her. She looks at Josh and says, "I'm going with her. I'll be okay."

"I'll come with you."

"No, I'll be okay. I'll be careful. I'll be back soon. I owe Esther this much."

Josh does a three-sixty, scanning every detail, but sees no sign of the gray car. He sees no option to letting her go. "This is dangerous, you know. Please keep a look out. Lock the doors over there if you can."

"I'll be careful," she says again as the truck slowly pulls away.

Josh watches them disappear down the block. He does another careful three sixty, sees nothing suspicious, then hurries back inside.

❦

FBI Field Agent Eric Sandoval leans back in the office chair and puts his feet up on the gray metal desk. Both the chair and the desk are well worn and look like they're from some government surplus warehouse. The walls of the small square office are bare. There are no filing cabinets or bookshelves, just two plastic crates for hanging files sitting on the desk.

He scratches his thinning silver hair and says to his partner, Carol Shepherd, "So, what have we got?"

"A mess, Eric." Shepherd has been sitting in a straight-back chair, across the desk from Sandoval, but now she's up and pacing the room. She walks to the only window in the small room and gazes out at the bustling Sunday afternoon traffic on Cerrillos Road, toward a strip mall across the street, two miles south of the Santa Fe plaza. "Remind me again why we got dragged into this." She turns and faces him, shaking her head and suppressing a laugh.

"Yeah," says Sandoval. "We could be back home in Albuquerque, hanging out with our families, firing up the barbeque, watching the Broncos stomp the Raiders. But, no, this is how we get to spend our Sunday afternoon. If this guy Wessel hadn't worked for a government laboratory, that's where we'd be, while the local fuzz do their job."

He smiles at Shepherd, who's probably thirty-five. Long blond hair frames a pale, delicate face. Not a bad looker but not a head-turner either. Blends into the crowd well. She looks like any mother you might run into at the mall, wearing a pink turtleneck, blue jeans, and Keens. He chuckles to himself, thinking how this unlikely person is just about the best field agent the District Office has, and how she is about the last person you'd want to run into in a dark alley if she wasn't on your side. Sandoval has been with the Bureau for thirty years and has been thinking about early retirement for the last five. He's a different stripe from

Shepherd, a more analytical sort, good with investigations and putting the pieces together, but really an office type, not an action figure like Shepherd. Yet they've been a good team for three years, and he thinks the secret of their success is mutual respect.

Sandoval pulls his feet off the desk, then sits up straight. He's beginning to feel the claustrophobia induced by the room, not really a local office but just an unmarked rented space that the Albuquerque district folks use when work brings them to Santa Fe. "So let's go over what we've got," he says. "Hikers find Wessel's body in a canyon out in the boonies west of Los Alamos, next to his new Corvette. Blow to the back of the head. Could be from the accident, but everything says otherwise. Car going fast misses a turn and winds up in a gully. No news there. But what's he doing out there on some back road? And where does some peon like Wessel get the cash for a Vette? The guy works in Industrial Relations at the Lab. What do we know about that?"

"Yeah," Shepherd chimes in, "Industrial Relations is not exactly plutonium stewardship. They handle no classified work at all, no one even has a Q clearance in the whole place. No national security relevant work, nothing nuclear. Just industrial partnership stuff, lots of corporate agreements. Some of them are proprietary, not because of the Lab's technology but because of the corporate secret angle. Some of the workers sign nondisclosure agreements, and some stuff is treated very confidentially. Wessel was a tech who worked on some of those projects. He could have been slipping corporate secrets out of the Lab, I guess."

"That's why I wonder why we got dragged into this. If it's a spy trying to rip off the latest bomb code or walk away with a little plutonium, I'm all over it. But, business shenanigans … oh well. So how does the girl fit into all this?"

"That's the question alright. So we scan the offices last night. Good move, by the way, Eric, getting there on a Saturday evening when there are no employees around. Just us and the Lab security officer. Nice and quiet. Group leader's office, project leaders' offices, all clean. But the girl's desk. For heaven's sake Eric, she's just a contract data entry chick. Why would she have this?"

"Yeah, good question." He holds up the flash drive and studies it through the walls of the clear ziplock baggie. "Important little piece of evidence you found, Carol. Just a simple flashdrive. Everybody's got several of them. But only this one has a list of all the proprietary work in the office. And, only this one has Louis Wessel's fingerprints on it."

"Seems incriminating, but maybe it's a plant. She wouldn't leave this in an unlocked desk, where it would be easy to find."

"Or she didn't have a chance to hide it. Her purse was right there too, with her car keys and cell phone. Looks like the girl left in a hurry. Car still in the lot. Do we know when she left?"

"Tried reaching others in the office already. Talked to one or two, but none of them knew anything. But most of them I couldn't reach. It's the weekend, in case you hadn't noticed." She throws her hands in the air. "They're probably all out in the back yard firing up the barbeque." She laughs. "I'll work on that tomorrow."

"You check the call history on that cell?"

"Yeah, all the calls were to her home. No one else. Woman needs to get a life." She shakes her head, then laughs. "But, then of course, so do we."

Sandoval sighs. "So we go to the house. The place has been ransacked. But no signs of violence. Just like somebody was there looking for something. And the car out front. That's an odd one. Tires slashed, windows bashed in. Could just be vandalism, a coincidence I guess."

"But you and I know it probably isn't."

"So what do we know about this Joshua Waverly?"

"Not much. Physicist at the Lab. In Space Physics. Works in the next building over, that could be relevant or not. No ties to Industrial Relations or to the girl, as far as I can figure. And, of course, we can't reach him either."

"You've just been through his apartment. Nothing unusual there?"

"Nothing unusual."

"We've got the State Police in on this, now that we've got some missing persons?"

"Yep, as of two hours ago they're looking for Waverly and Gomez."

"Good, maybe we aren't the only ones missing the Broncos game. Lots of pieces to work with here. Lots of pieces that don't seem to fit."

"Especially Waverly."

"Yeah, he doesn't seem to fit at all."

৵৩

Back in the lobby, Josh is confronted by several residents, who look up at him as if he might have some crucial information about Esther. Josh sees the deep concern in their faces. He is peppered with questions.

"Is she going to live?"

"She's not dead, is she?"

"What happened?"

"Oh, poor Esther. What will we do without her?"

Josh is not used to being the person in charge, the person expected to know what to do next. But certainly the last two days have changed all that. He manages what he thinks is a calming smile and holds up his palms to quiet the throng. "Look, I think she's going to be okay. She's conscious and just seems to have some pain in her leg. The nurse practitioner has got her over at the clinic. Real close to here. I'm sure we'll see Esther again real soon, and she'll be fine."

One woman says to the others, "We've got to pray real hard for her to be okay." This is met by nods from several of the others.

Josh slowly backs away from the crowd and heads back down the hallway toward their room. About halfway he encounters Maggie, standing alone, leaning against her walker and gazing unfocused at the wall.

"Good afternoon, Maggie."

"Roger?" Maggie's pale eyes look into Josh's face, as if she's searching for some important clue there. Her white hair, hanging long around her face, gives her an almost ghostly appearance, enhanced by her drab housecoat.

"I'm sorry. I'm not Roger."

"Where is he?"

"I don't know."

"Roger's here to see me. He's my son." She perks up now, as she speaks with pride.

Josh doesn't know what to say.

"You're not Roger," she then says, her voice suddenly turning sad.

"No … I'm sorry. Can I—"

"Then who are you?" she interrupts. She now looks confused, then afraid.

"I'm Josh."

"I don't know what to do. I don't know where Roger is. He's my son, you know."

"Yes, I know." Josh begins to edge away, to disengage from Maggie. But then Maggie begins to weep. Silently, but tears are now flowing down her face.

Josh looks up and down the hall, hoping someone else will come to help with this situation. There is no one. Maggie's weeping continues.

Josh edges forward, reaches out and gently touches Maggie's arm. Her weeping now turns into sobs. Josh steps around the walker and puts an arm around her. Maggie buries her face in his chest, as her sobbing continues. This goes on for several minutes, then Josh asks her, "Do you want to go back to your room now?"

Her eyes are questioning, confused. "Yes, I think so."

"Do you know where your room is, Maggie?"

She bites her lip and slowly shakes her head.

"Why don't we just walk back down the hall until we find the room with your name on it?" Josh is trying his best to sound cheerful.

Together they make their way slowly back down the hall. It isn't long before Josh finds Maggie's room. The door stands open. Josh helps Maggie to a chair beside a small table. The room is plain, and few attempts have been made to liven up the place, unlike Esther's. It smells like an old closet, where musty linens have been long stored away with moth balls. "Why don't you sit here?" he asks, then helps her move from her walker to the chair.

Maggie looks up at Josh and says, "I have a son named Roger."

"Yes, I know." He's now backing toward the door.

"I don't know where he is."

"I'm sorry," he repeats.

She looks at him with new clarity. "He never comes," she says in a voice so soft it's almost inaudible.

It catches Josh by surprise, the sudden thoughts about his own mother. He wonders if she might be somewhere waiting for him. In some hopeless place, alone, saying to some stranger, "He never comes." He tries to remember when he saw her last. Instead, an image comes to mind of a seaside holiday when he must have been no more than four or five. His mother and father seemed happy then. But his mom had always been so quiet, so subservient, so always there in the background as a faithful supporter of her famous husband. Maybe she was just weak. But in the image that flashes through his mind now, they are happy.

That must have been, what, three years before that shocking day when she left his father and moved across town to live with her sister.

Joint custody was an agony for Josh, shuttling back and forth across New Haven – one month with dad and one month with mom. Josh swallows like something is caught in his throat, as for a moment the memory returns of those years of tearful monthly separations and awkward adjustments to a different house. Just when he was getting settled, just when he was re-establishing his connection to mom or dad, just when it was feeling like home, it was time to leave again and move to a place that now seemed unfamiliar.

That roller coaster life had gone on until Josh was fourteen, when he could legally decide where he would live. His father had pressed him for a decision, but he did not want to choose between them, afraid of hurting either parent. In the end he chose to live with his father, mainly because of his father's pressure and his mother's unwillingness or inability to challenge him.

Josh did not elect to live with his father because life would be better there. In fact the opposite was true. His dad was so consumed with his career that Josh rarely saw him. After school he was home alone until his dad got home, usually late. Then after supper, his dad retreated to his study to continue his work. But he piled the work and the expectations on Josh. Books and games about physics and math filled his room. Summer camps were not about hiking and campfires and roasting marshmallows. They were about preparation for a career in science. He didn't care for these camps, even though he was always somewhat of a celebrity, the son of the great Jackson Waverly.

His dad never talked about the divorce with Josh, seldom mentioned his mother at all. It was almost like she didn't exist. After Josh went to live with his dad, he only saw his mother a few more times before she met a man and moved to California. For awhile she wrote him letters, polite and non-newsy, never saying anything negative about his father. But in these sulky teen years he had been remiss about answering them.

He looks at Maggie now and sits down in a chair next to hers. He touches her gaunt hand and gazes into her desperate eyes. He thinks he might cry.

৵৵

Later, back in his room, Josh paces. He presses his palms to his head, like he's holding down the lid on a pressure cooker about to explode. Too much going on at once, too much chaos for his orderly mind. He needs to think things through. But fledgling thoughts are quickly crushed by waves of sheer emotion. This is stuff he doesn't trust, doesn't know how to process.

Dominant is the image of Evangelina, outside where Ferguson and the other guy are likely to be prowling around. They could be sitting ducks at the clinic. But he hadn't seen the car. Still, he also hadn't seen their car back in Rinconada, yet they had obviously seen Evangelina and him drive off in the old truck. What can he do? Nothing. Wait.

His mind turns to the kisses. He closes his eyes and relives them. What might they have led to if they hadn't been interrupted by the screams? A delicious thought. He sits on the bed and touches her night gown, folded neatly and lying atop the pillow. He lifts it to his face and breathes, inhaling her. He smiles with delight and anticipation, then forces himself to break the reverie. He returns the nightgown to its place atop the pillow, feeling a little ashamed, like he is invading her privacy somehow. She deserves more respect than this.

Amidst the terror that surrounds them, Josh has a deep sense that something important to his life is happening here. This woman and her effect on him defies his analysis. In just two days, is it possible to be breaking down years-old patterns of fear and caution?

And what about Bud's words to him? Words about faith. He doesn't understand this very well, but perhaps he has been missing something. He has so confidently built his understanding of life on scientific methods and rational analysis. So why did the words of this old man rattle him?

He remembers what Esther said about hope. Even though his mind was wandering throughout her sermon this morning, he recalls how she said that hope is more than wishful thinking. 'Wishful thinking' is exactly what he'd always thought hope was, and to Josh's orderly mind wishful thinking is a useless way to waste away a life. But Esther said hope is something else, confidence based on a promise. What does that really mean? Confidence, yes, he needs more of that for sure. But what is the promise, really? And how could he know he could trust it?

He presses down harder on his temples, uncertain what to do with these ideas. All these things are assaulting him now, frightening and overpowering him. Confusing him, challenging him, laying him bare and exposed and vulnerable. This is exactly the state that Josh has spent a lifetime avoiding. But he must confess that the past three days have also exhilarated him, made him feel alive. Like kissing a beautiful woman or sinking a fifteen-footer against a conference all-star. All these new things, new questions in his life about faith, hope, and, yes, perhaps even love.

But he is thirty two, has lived a life prepared in a certain way. Isn't it too late to change now?

❧❧

Evangelina kneels beside Esther in the back of the Tundra, one hand stabilizing the gurney against any motion, her other hand cradling Esther's head. She masks her own anxiety with soothing words. "We're almost there, Esther. Just another minute or so."

Lauren pulls into a deserted strip mall, with six small commercial units fronted by blacktop long overtaken by weeds. All the stores appear abandoned except the one on the end. A large faded sign that had been colorful in its day says Mario's Pizza Ristorante. In the window a simple printed sign says Santuario Rural Clinic, with a listing of hours underneath.

Evangelina helps Lauren get the gurney from the rear of the pickup and wheel Esther into the clinic. Inside, along one wall, a long glass counter that looks like it once held pastries, is empty except for several portable file boxes containing hanging files. A shelf along the other wall, framed by old Chianti bottles encased in straw, is lined with a row of red and blue medical books. In the center of the room, which had once been Mario's dining room, a row of molded plastic chairs share the décor with a few remaining fake Italian pillars. Plastic grape vines still hang down from the ceiling. The place doesn't look much like the waiting room for a clinic, but it's spotlessly clean.

Lauren laughs as they wheel Esther through toward the back. "Like the décor? Haven't had any time to change it. In the mean time, where else can you come and get your cholesterol checked and order a loaded sausage pizza at the same time?"

Evangelina smiles. "I think it's fine. Lauren, do you mind if we lock the door behind us?"

"Sure, we're not supposed to be open today any way. But why?"

Evangelina glances down at Esther, who seems alert and taking it all in. The answer to that question would take more time than anyone can afford right now. "I'd just prefer that, if you don't mind."

"No problem." Lauren returns to the front door and clicks a dead bolt. "That should take care of it."

They wheel Esther behind a partition, into an area that looks like a modern exam room in any doctor's office. Lauren flicks a switch and a bank of portable lights comes on, providing bright illumination. Then she removes her fleece and extends her arms into a white lab coat, while asking, "How are you feeling now, Esther?"

"I'm better. I don't want you making a big fuss over me. Just some Advil for this hip and I ought to be fine."

"We won't take long, but I do need to get some information from you." Lauren pulls out a laptop and enters a few characters, apparently pulling up a chart on Esther. "Okay, can you tell me what caused you to fall?"

"I'm not sure. One second I was fine, then next thing I know I'm on the floor. Could've just slipped."

"That's possible. Has this ever happened before?'

"Nope."

Lauren scrolls through information on her computer, then asks Esther what she has eaten today, how much liquid intake she's had, any previous symptoms, medications she's taking, activity level and so on.

Evangelina stands on the other side of the gurney, gently stroking Esther's shoulder.

"Okay, here's what we're going to do. I'm going to take a couple of x-rays of your hip area. We need to see if there are any broken or fractured bones. Then I'll need to get urine and blood specimens. This will help us to know if you have any infections, like a urinary tract infection, which could cause dizziness." She steps out of the cubicle for a moment, then returns, pushing a portable x-ray unit. "Evangelina, why don't you make yourself at home out front while I get the x ray and the tests." Straight-faced she adds, "If anyone calls in a pizza order, be sure to tell them we've got a special on garlic bread today."

"Evangelina, could you say a little prayer for me before you go?" Esther's eyes are expectant, as if this is something she truly needs.

Evangelina glances between Esther and Lauren. "Me?" She then clears her throat and says, keeping her hand on Esther's shoulder, "Dear God." There's a pause, as she struggles to compose this prayer. "Thank you for Esther and all the ways you love us through her. Thank you for Lauren and the wonderful skills she has for healing people. Bless Esther now. Make these tests come out okay. Amen." She looks up, apprehensively. Both Esther and Lauren are smiling.

"Thank you," says Esther.

"Yes, that was nice," adds Lauren.

Evangelina takes a seat in one of the molded plastic chairs out front. She remains seated for only a moment, as there is simply too much on her mind. She paces the waiting area, concerned about Esther, but soon thoughts of Serena flash in her mind. She wrings her hands, pacing faster now. Then an image of Josh pops up. What should she do about this man? How does she feel about him? Really. Isn't it normal to be attracted to someone during a time of emergency? How can she trust her feelings right now? He's from such a different background. Anglo. Ivy League education. In the long run, how much could he have in common with her?

She stops at the front window, behind a garland of plastic ivy, and stares out onto the deserted street. She thinks about her conversation with Esther this morning. Her connection with a faith she thought had been lost. Or maybe it's her who has been lost.

A motion off to the side catches her eye. She jumps away from the window, as the gray car pulls into the lot, parallel to the window. She is paralyzed with terror, unable to move as the heavily tinted window of the car is rolled down. He's seen her. Mr. Ferguson looks straight toward her, as she peeks from behind one of the Italian pillars. Then Ferguson points his index finger at her and makes a cocking motion with his thumb, accompanied by a big smile. He rolls up the window and speeds away.

Evangelina is gasping for breath, shaking. Her shaking hands fumble to check the deadbolt. Yes, it is locked. She turns quickly, half expecting him to be behind her, then races to the back door, past the examination room, and checks the back door. Locked. She peers through a small window next to the door onto a small area of blacktop behind the building. No gray car.

Breathing heavily, she staggers back toward the front, just as Lauren emerges from the examination room.

"Good news, Evangelina. No broken bones. Now I'll have to look at these …good Lord, you look like you've seen a ghost. You okay?"

Evangelina cannot speak. She nods okay.

"Maybe you'd better sit down. What happened?"

"It's too long of a story—"

"I've got time. Esther's very comfortable. I gave her a little something for the pain. She's taking a nap right now. I can look at the blood and urine tests while you talk at me."

"You probably wouldn't understand—"

"Yeah, maybe I won't understand. There's a lot I don't understand, but how are we ever gonna know if you don't try me?"

They move over to the other side of the room, where several benches are filled with chemicals, glassware, a microscope and several other pieces of sophisticated equipment that Evangelina cannot identify. Lauren sets about her work, as Evangelina begins. Tells her the whole story, which she's getting pretty good at by now. She exhales a deep sigh, then sits back, waiting for Lauren's response.

"Well, first of all," Lauren says with calmness, "It looks like Esther may have a urinary tract infection. I've got some antibiotic samples that will clear that up. Otherwise the tests look good. Rule out a lot of things. I can't rule out a TIA—"

"You mean like a mini-stroke?"

"Exactly. But she doesn't exhibit any weakness or speech impairment, so I think it's unlikely. We could get her in an ambulance down to St. Vincent's for an MRI, but I think the best thing now is to just get her back to her home, keep her in bed for a day or so and see how the antibiotics do. I'll stop by tomorrow to check on her." She pauses. "And the second thing is, Evangelina, that's about the most awful story I've ever heard. You say that jerk pulled up here a few minutes ago?"

"Yes."

"Wish I'd known. I've got a forty-five locked in my desk in the back. Could have given him something to think about. I'll have it in my belt when we take Esther back, that's for sure." She pauses. "Look, I don't know what to tell you. What do I know? I understand about not calling the cops in on this. They won't help much, not out here.

But, I guess, if I were you, I'd sure want to get close to my daughter right now."

Evangelina is nodding.

Chapter Nine

"You mean you went back out there after you saw them?" Josh is incredulous. He had not wanted Evangelina to go to the clinic in the first place.

"What else were we going to do? We couldn't stay there forever. We were careful when we left. And, frankly I felt pretty safe with Lauren. She knows how to take care of herself."

"I'm sure she does," Josh says with exasperation. "But against killers? C'mon, Evangelina, these guys— "

"You're not thinking about Esther." Evangelina's impatience appears to be matching his own. "She needed help. You have a better idea about what we should have done?"

Josh is silent for a moment. Yes, they had to get help for Esther. But … but what? Then in a soft voice he says, "You're right. I was just worried about you, I guess."

She smiles. "Thanks, Josh. I'm sorry I dragged you into all this." She lays her hand on his arm, causing a tingle to jolt up his arm.

He sighs. "I guess I am in it. And it's certainly not your fault. I'm thinking that they didn't attack you because they wanted us both. Ferguson asked about both of us when he came in yesterday, so I'm thinking he's waiting to get us both together—"

"I'm so sorry. I've caused you so much trouble, Josh. You should—"

"Look," he interrupts, "now they know where we are, but they haven't come after us yet. For some reason we're safe as long as we stay in here. Maybe there's too many other people around, safety in numbers, but for now they're unwilling to come in here and—"

"Josh, I can't stay here. I've got to go home. I belong with my daughter."

"Not yet, Evangelina, not yet."

She shakes her head, her lips pursed, her jaw set. She looks determined.

They've been walking through the hall at Copper Point and have now arrived at Esther's room. The door is opened a crack, and they can hear Rosey and Hollister's deep soothing voices inside. Evangelina knocks gently and then enters. Esther is in bed, her head propped up slightly with two large pillows, the lacy fringes of the pillow cases encasing her head like she is royalty. She's smiling and looking like her old self.

"I see you're all settled in, Esther." Evangelina goes to the bedside, next to Rosey and Hollister, then gently touches Esther's arm. Josh stays back a few steps from the bed. Don't want to overwhelm her with a crowd, Josh thinks, feeling awkward being here.

"I don't know what the big fuss is all about. But I gotta admit, I do kinda enjoy all this attention." She lets out a soft laugh.

"The big fuss is," Rosey says, "you're a very special person to all of us, Esther. And you got hurt today. So you gotta follow orders and take care of yourself for a few days, like Lauren said."

"I'm feeling just fine right now. I oughta—"

"You oughta be doing nothing," Hollister chimes in. "You're feeling fine because of the medicine Lauren gave you." He laughs. "Better living through chemistry."

"Lauren's coming back to see you tomorrow," says Evangelina.

"I know. She's a pretty reliable doc. I know she's not a doc, not quite, but she sure is the person I want in my corner when I get sick."

"What do you mean 'when'?" says Rosey. "You're not exactly ready to run a marathon right now."

"I know. Lauren doesn't pull any punches. She tells it like it is, and I like that. Says I've probably got a urinary tract infection, could have killed me if I hadn't gotten some help. I'm glad it didn't, but if it did that's okay."

"That's not okay with me," says Hollister.

"You know, I'm not afraid of dying, but I sure am scared about being in pain. Not too thrilled about that. But dying's okay. I feel totally okay about that. Whenever it comes, I'm ready."

They all smile at her but say nothing. It feels like Esther just may be the most confident person in the room.

Josh studies Esther's room. It's the same size as their room, the same worn industrial carpet, the same stained acoustic tile ceiling, the same dull concrete walls. But somehow, Esther has transformed her room into something else. In the place where the vinyl couch is in Josh's room, an elegant chest of drawer stands against the wall, backed by a mirror. It's a beautiful maple, looks hand-carved. No doubt a remnant of a former life, a better life, far from Copper Point. Attached around the perimeter of the mirror are a multitude of small photographs, some of them black and white and apparently very old. Josh squints to see them better, not wanting to go over and study them up close, obviously snooping. Photos of young couples, families, small children. He wonders if Esther has family. And if so, where are they? Atop the chest of drawers, on a white lacy runner, sit two jewelry boxes, and Josh wonders what might be inside.

Against another wall is a narrow bookcase, also crafted from a beautiful wood that Josh cannot identify. It's crammed with books, with many volumes stacked into the spaces above the shelved rows. Again Josh squints to scan the titles. Some literature, but mostly religious books, it seems. Next to Esther's bed is a small writing desk, an antique roll-top in dark wood. It's open. Neatly arranged stacks of papers, a tall cup holding pens and pencils. A logo on the side of the cup says St. Timothy's Episcopal Church, but the writing below, which probably says the city where the church is located, is too small for Josh to make out. A large bible lies open next to the stacks of papers. He notes how the pages look worn and some of the words seem to have been marked over with yellow highlighter.

Above Esther's bed is a small cross, just like the one in his room. He wonders who placed these crosses there. The windows have the same cheap, damaged blinds that are in his room, but here they are sided by white frilly curtains that add a cheery and inviting look to the room.

"I know you're ready to die, Esther," Rosey says, smiling. "I'm just not sure the rest of us are ready for you to go."

"Well, I'm not gone yet," Esther laughs, "so let's not start the mourning quite yet. I'm just saying that I know my Lord loves me and he's got me in his hand no matter what." She looks up at Evangelina. "I hope you all know that too."

"You are one amazing woman, Esther," Rosey says. "You're the person in bed and we're supposed to be looking after you. And here you are, all perky and sassy, looking after us." Everybody laughs. "As usual," she adds.

❧❧

Stilwell, pulled off on one of the gravel roads in Azurite Acres, leans against the hood of the Maxima, gazing off into the canyon.

This job will be done soon. And it will be done on his schedule. Let the Contact sweat a little. He has nothing but contempt for the Contact, that soft-palmed slime bucket. Their type makes Stilwell want to puke. Icons of the community. Fancy homes in the best part of town. Giving the after-dinner talks at the Chamber of Commerce, maybe considering a run for state office. They are all motivated by greed. At least he is a professional motivated by ethics. Sure, it's not the ethics that will be taught in a Sunday school class, but at least he has standards.

But soon he'll have the Contact off his back. There will be much to savor. Then maybe Montevideo. The night clubs, the casinos. He still knows a few people there. And after this job, he'll have enough cash to hold him for several years.

While Stilwell gazes into the canyon, Jesse's eyes are on him. "Hey, I'm not sayin' we shoulda done anything different back there, I'm just sayin' I don't understand why we didn't go in right there and take care of business."

"You're right, Jesse, we could have. But you're forgetting two things. We'd have had to take out two other people too. Not that I mind, but if the carnage gets too great, then that's just more trouble for us. We're under directions to keep it clean. And we still wouldn't have had Waverly. No, we have another plan."

"What?"

"Now we know they're in the old folk's home. We're going in there tonight. Late, after all the old goats have finished Lawrence Welk and turned off their hearing aids. We'll have the place to ourselves. Maybe we'll shoot 'em in bed."

Jesse rubs his hands together, smiling and nodding with enthusiasm.

"Yep, you're gonna love it." Stilwell laughs. "You sadistic monster, you're really going to love this."

❧❧

Even for a depressing place like Copper Point, the mood has taken an unusually somber turn with Esther's fall. At dinner, Yolanda brought out yet another wonderful New Mexican dish inspired by Evangelina. They were enchiladas, but she called them Evangelados, which got a laugh from several of the residents. Josh was amazed to see how Evangelina's help in the kitchen had somehow kindled a spark in Yolanda and transformed her from a sour and distant employee, plodding through her work, into a laughing part of the family. But without Esther the sparkplug, the dinner conversation is muted and several of the diners struggle off early to their rooms after eating, amidst a clatter of walkers and groans. The usual evening time of visiting and games of Crazy Eights and Hearts has never materialized tonight.

The diners at Esther's table are still seated, when Bud groans, "Well, isn't this just what we needed tonight?"

"What?" asks Josh.

Bud rolls his eyes toward the doorway, without turning his head. "Harshburn," he says. "Can't she have the decency to stay away on a Sunday night?"

"And without Esther here. Lordy, we don't need this," Rosey says, a grimace on her face.

"Well, good evening, everybody," a loud boisterous voice announces. The room goes silent. The residents look frozen in place, like children caught in the act by a scolding parent.

Mrs. Harshburn strolls between the tables. "I hope everybody's had a great day," she bubbles loudly to downcast heads. "Well, dear me, it seems like a month of Sundays since I saw you all last. Everybody doing okay?"

There is silence in the room. Again she says, even louder this time, "Everybody doing okay?"

She continues to stroll between the tables like a commandant inspecting the prisoners. All that's missing, thinks Josh, is a riding crop to whack against her hip. Mrs. Harshburn is well dressed in expensive looking slacks and what looks like a pricy cashmere sweater. Her red hair is piled high and pinned on her head, giving the illusion of considerable height. Her face is heavily made-up, and Josh wonders how old she might be.

Harshburn pauses at Esther's table. She looks directly at Hollister. "So, you," she says in an accusatory tone. She apparently doesn't know his name. "You're still here."

"I'll be heading out soon."

"That's good," says Harshburn. "We're not operating a homeless mission here, you know. I'll count on seeing you gone next time I visit."

Hollister says nothing. Rosey is visibly shaken by Harshburn's words, but says nothing.

Harshburn scans the rest of the table and her eyes settle on Josh and Evangelina. "And just who might you be?" she queries with a light tone.

Josh speaks up. "Uh, we're just here briefly, we'll be—"

"And eating our food, I see. It must be wonderful to get a free meal."

Maggie looks up at Harshburn. "Why don't you just go away and leave us alone?"

Harshburn turns toward Maggie. "Oh, don't we have a bit of an attitude tonight? I'll remind you, whoever you are, that I'm the facility supervisor here, and you will not speak to me that—"

Evangelina cuts in. "You leave Maggie alone. She hasn't hurt anyone."

Harshburn turns back toward Evangelina, her jaw dropping open. For a moment there is a complete hush in the room as all eyes are on Evangelina and Harshburn.

"Ah, you know I think I might just call the police right now and have you arrested for being on private property illegally, making a disturbance among these fine—"

But Josh jumps to his feet. "Mrs. Harshburn, I don't think you, I don't think you …" He flushes, aware of his stammering. He looks down at Evangelina for a moment, then back at Harshburn. "I don't think you want to do that. We're ready to report you to the State inspectors for gross violation of …" He pauses, thinking what to say next. "Well, it would be a list of violations." He looks down at Maggie and smiles. "And that list would include abuse of residents."

Out of the corner of his eye he can see Bud clenching his fists, as if silently saying, 'Yes!'

Harshburn is silent, her mouth hanging open. She bristles and stomps out of the room.

Josh is still standing, and as he looks around, the silence persists until someone laughs. Then someone else laughs, and soon the room is filled with laughter.

Hollister beams, "Dang, if you didn't tell her off, Josh. Way to go."

"Well," says Josh, suddenly feeling self-conscious, "I couldn't let her talk that way to Maggie and Evangelina."

"Josh, that was awesome," says Evangelina.

"You were awesome yourself," beams Josh.

"Thank you both," says Rosey. "When Esther's here, she can handle Mrs. Harshburn, she's able to keep her from going overboard. So you really helped tonight. Still I worry that she might cause you both trouble."

Josh looks at Evangelina and almost laughs. She smiles. How could someone like Mrs. Harshburn cause them more trouble than they are already in?

❧❧

Josh and Evangelina stroll quietly back to the room. This is the first time they've been alone together since the afternoon kisses, and that dominant memory causes Josh to feel awkward and tentative. Maybe she's feeling it too.

In the room, Evangelina sits on the bed and stares at Josh, who sits on the couch. For a minute or two they are silent, then Josh says, "Some day, huh?"

"Really." She smiles, then her face turns somber. "Too much if you ask me." Her shoulders slump, as if she is carrying a heavy burden.

Josh is not sure exactly what she means. Certainly too much of some things, Esther's fall and the run-in with Ferguson, but not enough of other things. He just nods.

"Today gave me a lot to think about," she says.

"Well, running into Ferguson would—"

"Yes, but I'm not talking about that."

Josh is quiet. Of course the day has given him a lot to think about too. Especially the possibility of a future with this beautiful woman. After a moment he says, "Well, there certainly were a few very pleasant moments."

Evangelina blushes, the first time Josh has seen her blush, the flush causing her brown face to absolutely glow. "Well, yes," she giggles, "that. That was nice." She looks down, suddenly shy, but then quickly looks back up. "But I'm thinking about this morning. About church and the talk I had with Esther afterwards. That really helped me."

Josh nods thoughtfully, as if that was also what he'd been thinking about all along too.

" Josh, you should talk to her. I think you would find it helpful."

Josh nods and purses his lips as if he's thinking about it.

Evangelina continues. "Remember what I told you last night about being ill?"

He nods.

"Well, Esther helped me to see beyond that. She told me that I am not ill, but that I am 'good news.'"

"I could have told you that."

"I know, thank you." She smiles at him. "But she helped me to see that just because my past was so full of problems, that doesn't mean my future has to be that way. I think she helped reconnect me with God."

Josh nods knowingly, although he doesn't understand where this is going.

"I want my future to not be based on my past. I want a clean start. I think maybe that can happen, if I ever get out of this mess we're in. Esther helped me to see that." She pauses for a few moments, looks down, then looks Josh directly in the eyes. "Josh, do you believe in God?"

Josh immediately thinks about his morning talk with Bud. *What's going on here?* She continues to look directly at him, obviously expecting a serious answer. He clears his throat. "Well, I guess I haven't given it a great deal of thought." He immediately realizes how lame this sounds, so he quickly adds, "I was raised by my father, who I guess you'd say was an atheist, but, in fact, he never talked about God. He drilled into me the importance of thinking scientifically. Rationally. He criticized people who talked about spiritual things, about feelings, said it was immature thinking." He pauses for a moment, thinking through what to say next.

"You think that a rational person can't believe in God?"

"I'm not saying that." *So just what am I saying?*

"Are you saying your father never had any feelings?"

"Oh, I know he had feelings. But he was critical of them. Thought of them as somehow being inferior, weak. He had feelings, but I think he tried to deny them."

"And you have feelings too. I know that."

"Yes." He swallows hard. Yes I do, he thinks. *And I wish I had the courage to tell you about them.* "Yes," he says again.

"So do you think believing in God is about feelings and not thought, that it's, what did your father call it, immature thinking?" Her voice is still soft, her curiosity genuine it seems.

"No, no." He's not sure exactly what he does think. "I'm not saying I don't believe in God." *Good grief, did I just say that?* "I'm saying I just haven't thought about it very much."

"I guess physicists work with equations and data and stuff like that. That's how they figure things out."

"Well, yes, that's true," he says. He realizes though that there are a lot of things he doesn't have 'figured out.' His life is certainly a testimony to that.

"But aren't there some things that you can't figure out with equations and experiments?"

"Like?"

"Well, like maybe the most important things. Like, um, the meaning of life."

Josh nods. *Does my life have meaning?* It takes mere seconds to conclude that nothing meaningful has happened to him in the last seven years, the last three days not included. No trajectory of events by which he might forecast that he is actually headed somewhere. Words pop through his mind. Routine. Monotony. Boredom. Isolation. Loneliness. Then defensively, he says, "I'm not exactly sure how you define the meaning of life anyway. Isn't life just the flow from one day to the next, and then you die?"

"Josh, you don't really believe that, do you?"

He squirms. No, of course he doesn't believe that, even if it has been a pretty good description of his existence so far. "I'm not sure what I believe right now."

They are again silent for a few awkward moments. Then Evangelina says, "I want to go to Uncle Rey's tomorrow."

"I know. But it would be so dangerous right now. And how would you get there?"

"Maybe Hollister could take me. I know it's dangerous. But once I get there, I'd be okay. I need to be with my daughter. Josh, she doesn't understand my being gone. I've never been away from her before. I can't do this to her."

"I know," he concedes. There is something very appealing about this young mother, so passionate about her daughter. Something glorious in fact. Something that a scientific explanation based on biology falls short of describing. He cannot explain it. But it is luminous. And it only adds to the growing feelings he has for her.

He rises and crosses the room toward her. She remains motionless on the bed, as he sits down beside her, her big brown eyes following his face. He cradles her face in his hands and kisses her. She responds, leaning into him, the softness of her body against him now. He pulls back and looks into her eyes, then kisses her again. But this time she pushes him away, gently.

"Not now." Her voice is soft but firm.

He backs away from her. "I didn't mean to—"

"It's okay. You did nothing wrong. It's just that ... it's just that ... I don't know. There's too much going on. I'm not sure this can go anywhere."

"Why not ... I mean ... okay, I guess." He is flushed with a mixture of desire, embarrassment, and great disappointment. His hands are now shaking and he hopes she doesn't notice. He wants to ask her why it cannot go anywhere. *What does she mean? Is this it?* He wants to know. But he cannot bring himself to ask.

Josh rises and begins to arrange his pillow and blanket on the couch, as Evangelina watches him.

"One more thing. I think we ought to push that couch out into the hallway for tonight."

He gives her a crushed look.

She continues. "Last night we were just roommates." She looks down, then back up at him with a tender smile. "Tonight, well, we're not just roommates anymore."

❧

Josh's first problem in sleeping in the hallway are the garish overhead lights, which apparently are left on all night. He wanders down the hallway looking for a switch, first one way, then the other. Finally he finds a bank of switches, then begins flipping them until he finds the one that cuts the overheads in his part of the hallway. There is still a wisp of light around his couch, streaming in from the lights in the next hallway down.

He stretches out on the stiff vinyl of the couch, still in his clothes. He's not expecting to get a lot of sleep tonight anyway. Lying on his back, with his hands cradling the back of his head, he stares at the brown stains, barely visible in the dim light, on the ceiling tiles. His mind is awash with problems, the foremost being the way the evening with Evangelina has just ended. What does this mean? Is it over? He is amazed that with killers circling in for the kill, the dominant thought in his mind is Evangelina. This makes no sense. It isn't logical. She hardly knows him. Why should he be expecting anything to come from their little weekend adventure together. Maybe that's all it will be -- if they get out of this alive -- a little weekend adventure. Maybe that's all it is for her, but he knows that for him it is more.

Somehow, he falls into a deep sleep.

જીજી

The full moon makes their approach easy, and Stilwell is able to turn off the headlights as they approach the rear entrance to Copper Point. A heavy rolling gate is secured with a chain and padlock, but Jesse is always ready for such occasions. A bolt cutter he produces from the trunk snaps the chain with a crisp thunk, and the chain rattles to the pavement as he pushes the gate open. Moonlight streaming onto the loading dock area makes a flashlight unnecessary, and they quickly find a door leading into the building, but it's locked. Jesse now produces the shovel from the rear of the Maxima, and with a quick downward blow sheers the handle from the door.

"I must say," whispers Stilwell, "you sure know how to make good use of that shovel." Stilwell's always in a good mood when the juices are flowing just before a hit.

They easily work the shattered deadbolt mechanism and are now inside the building. Stretching before them is a short hallway leading to a tee, where it branches into two other hallways. Some of the fluorescent lights are still on, but the place looks deserted just as they had expected. It's two AM.

There are doors along each side of the hallway. They stop at the first and test the handle. It's unlocked and opens easily. A storage room. They try the next door, also unlocked. It appears to be a resident's room, but it's empty.

"Where do you think they are?" whispers Jesse.

"They'll be in one of these rooms. We'll just keep going down the line until we find them." His fingers slide over the sleek barrel of the Glock 22 in his pocket, almost a caress.

The next room is also unlocked, but it's occupied. An old man snores softly on a bed in the corner. Stilwell quietly closes the door. "If all these rooms are unlocked, this is going to be a piece of cake."

They open every door along the short stretch of hallway leading up to the tee. Many of the rooms are empty, a few have sleeping residents. They come to the tee and make a left turn. Immediately they are face to face with an old woman, leaning over her walker.

At first she doesn't seem to notice them. Stilwell puts a finger to his lips and whispers, "Let's be quiet and just go around her, Jesse. I think the old bag's asleep."

Then the old woman seems to come to. She looks up and sees them. "Roger?" she asks in a soft voice.

"You just go back to sleep, ma'am," Stilwell says in his soothing tone.

"Roger?" she says again, a little louder this time.

"Let's just ignore her and move on," Stilwell whispers to Jesse.

"Is that you, Roger?" Her voice is now quite loud.

Stilwell's had enough. "Shut up, you old broad, or I'll shut you up for good."

"You're not Roger!" The woman then let's out a piercing scream. Stilwell quickly scans the hallway, but apparently she hasn't aroused any attention.

For a moment Stilwell recalls his own mother, loud and ugly. "Take her out, Jesse. I don't care what you do with her."

"You want me to kill her here?"

The woman lets out another piercing scream.

"Just be quiet and quick."

Jesse slips around the woman as he removes a slender leather cord from his pocket and stretches it tight between strong clenched fists. He's behind her now, the cord raised for the garroting. It will be swift and violent. Stilwell, calm, watches Jesse's face, the wide grin and the eyes bulging with anticipation.

༺༻

In his dream Josh sits in a great auditorium while his father lectures. There must be two hundred people in the auditorium. All eyes, including his, are on the great physicist. With his customary mastery he lays out the modern history of our understanding of the universe, beginning with Hubble's discovery of the Big Bang in 1927. Quickly he brings everyone up to date, up to the controversies about the anthropic principle, about the tantalizing controversies about parallel universes, touching on all the ideas and mysteries posed by quantum mechanics and string theory. Josh is very proud of his father.

And then the moment comes, the moment they've all been waiting for. Professor Waverly pauses, walks back and forth across the stage a couple of times, then stops and says, with a grand gesture, "Which brings me to my point." Everyone in the hall shifts forward in their seats. Many listeners open their notebooks to a clean page and prepare to write.

Then suddenly, Professor Waverly stumbles forward onto his knees, one hand pressed against his head. There is a collective gasp from the audience. The professor opens his mouth to speak. "This lecture must be finished."

Josh slides up from his seat, prepared to take over. In his dream he somehow knows what he will say. He knows what the point is that his father is trying to make. Confidently he begins his walk forward. This lecture must be finished.

But then his father, still on his knees, raises a hand and says, "The physics committee ... you will finish the lecture." He does not see, or chooses to ignore, his son, prepared to take the stage. As several men step forward to finish the lecture, the professor collapses face forward.

There is a scream.

Josh bolts upright, breathing hard. *Where am I?* It takes a few moments to get his bearings, the reality of the dream still throbbing throughout his brain. *Did I hear a scream? Or was it the dream?*

He is covered in sweat. He looks up and down the hall, but it appears deserted. He sits on the edge of the sofa, rubbing the sleepiness from his eyes, pondering what to do. He'd better check this out.

❧

Jesse's arms are raised, ready to slip the cord over the woman's head, but then a door next to them opens and an old man steps out. "What's up, Maggie?" he calls.

Responding to Stilwell's quick head nod, Jesse pulls the cord away. Then another door opens and then another. In moments a half dozen residents, garbed in long flannel nightgowns and baggy pajamas, are in the hallway.

"Well, isn't this just what we wanted? A pajama party in the hospice unit." Stilwell mutters a string of obscenities. "Let's get out of here, Jesse."

They quickly move toward the exit, as the old woman calls after them. "Roger, don't leave me."

∾∾

Josh has now come fully awake, as the realization of what a middle-of-the-night scream, if in fact he really heard a scream, could mean. The men may be in the building. He considers seeing if Evangelina's okay. He presses an ear to the door but hears nothing. He raises his hand to knock, then pulls it back. It's better to check this out first.

The hallway is empty in both directions from where he stands beside the sofa. He can't be sure, but he believes the scream came from the rear of the building. He stays close to one wall, as he slides his way down to the junction, where light streams in from an intersecting hallway. Just before he reaches the corner, he hears a shuffle, like soft shoes sliding across the floor. He freezes in place. Moments pass, he hears nothing more.

Taking a deep breath, Josh pokes his head around the corner into the other hallway and looks into the face of another man, just inches away. He jumps back with an audible gasp before realizing that the face belongs to another resident, who had also jumped back.

"Holy God, you scared me," barks the old man, as if Josh had intentionally tired to startle him.

Josh steps into the other hallway. "Sorry about that. I thought I heard a scream."

"That was just Maggie. Thinks she saw Roger again."

Josh gives a drowsy nod and returns to his couch, where he sits and reflects on the dream, reliving the details. It was so real. He thinks about the many times he'd seen his father give lectures before large audiences. How proud he had been of his father. And it seemed like his father was proud of him too, back before the injury to his leg, before the disappointing SAT scores. Back before his father had all but abandoned him.

He wants to knock on the door, awaken Evangelina. Tell her everything. Everything about his father that he has not told her. He wants her to know and doesn't understand why he hasn't told her yet. On the other side of the door she sleeps, just a few feet away. He will wake her. He doesn't care how it makes him look. She will understand. He stands at the door, breathing hard, hand poised to knock. But he doesn't. He returns to the couch, where he lies awake for a long time, not wanting to fall back to sleep, lest the dream continue.

◈

He is awakened by the walker of one of the residents, as it squeaks past him. Somehow Josh had fallen back into a deep sleep. This time without dreams. An elderly woman he doesn't know is heading down for breakfast. She slowly shuffles past him as if he isn't there. Either she doesn't see him or she doesn't know how to greet a strange man sleeping on a couch in the hallway.

Josh rises from the couch, runs his fingers through his hair, in lieu of a comb, and knocks on the door. No answer. Evangelina could be in the shower. Or she has already gone down for breakfast. He grasps the knob and considers entering, but decides against it. They are no longer just roommates, after all.

He saunters down towards the breakfast area. He would have liked to have washed his face and brushed his teeth before breakfast, but he'll tend to that later. He is somewhat surprised to see the dining area full of residents, well into their meals. He has overslept.

He makes his way to his table, but quickly notices that Evangelina is not there. Only Rosey and Bud are seated at the table.

"Where is everybody?" he asks.

"I don't know," says Rosey. "I'm worried about Maggie. She's always down here early."

"And you haven't seen Evangelina?"

"No. Haven't seen her or Hollister," says Rosey. "Maybe they're looking for Maggie."

Josh looks around the room, then nods at his breakfast companions. "Maggie was out in the halls in the middle of the night."

"You saw her?"

"No, but someone else did. Apparently she was looking for Roger and Gwen."

Rosey shakes her head, her lips pursed with sadness. "That poor woman. Josh, would you mind checking her room?"

"Sure. I need to find Evangelina, too."

When Josh comes to Maggie's room, he sees the door is partially open. He knocks gently and calls out her name. No answer. He then pushes the door open and enters. She's not in the room. He checks the bathroom. No sign of her. For a moment he stands in the middle of her small room, scratches his head and ponders what to do.

He notices a large photo album, lying open across Maggie's unmade bed. He pages through the album. A faded picture of a young mother holding a baby. Could this be Maggie and Roger? Next a picture of a backyard family barbeque. The slender mom is clearly Maggie. She wears shorts and a tank top and is laughing, while a small boy clings to her leg. A carefree summer scene. Josh thumbs ahead through the album. A wedding picture of a good looking couple. Must be Roger and Gwen. A few pages further the couple again, now probably in their forties, standing in front of an office building, wearing tee shirts with the letters UN written in bold print on them. Another photo shows them next to a Jeep in a desert with a group of children. Looks like the Middle East.

As he thumbs through the pages, a news clipping falls to the floor. Josh picks it up and sees another photo of Roger and Gwen wearing their UN shirts. The headline of the article, dated November, 2006, reads "UN Staffers Killed in Iraq." Josh quickly scans through the text and stops at these words: "Two United Nations staffers from the United States, Roger and Gwen Stillings, both 45, were killed Wednesday when their SUV detonated an improvised explosive device outside the city of Basra."

Josh lets out a great sigh and feels tears welling up. He carefully places the clipping back in the album, which he then closes and places back on the bed. He quickly heads down the hall to find Maggie.

Josh stops at the door to his room and knocks. No answer. He carefully opens the door to find the bed made and Evangelina gone. Maybe she is looking for Maggie. He closes the door and heads toward the rear of the building. His heart almost stops when he finds the service entrance door open and the dead bolt mechanism lying broken on the floor.

Now the pieces come together. Maggie did indeed see a man in the middle of the night, who she thought was Roger. But it was Ferguson. He shakes uncontrollably now, gooseflesh rising on his arms. But what happened next? Did Ferguson take Maggie? Oh God, did he take Evangelina? No, that doesn't fit. Her bed was made, and in any case Ferguson would have had to walk right past his bed in the hallway. But one thing is clear: Copper Point is no longer a safe place for them. The killers know they are here. They will be back. Soon. His instinct is to flee. Get Evangelina, then make a run for it.

But where is Maggie? And why didn't the killers stay to finish their work last night? He remembers the scream.

Must have been Maggie's scream. And the other residents in the hallway. Maybe they scared the killers away. But where is Maggie?

Josh steps into the loading dock area, carefully scanning all directions for anything suspicious. He stops in his tracks when he sees that the back gate has been rolled open, the heavy chain lying on the ground. He quickly retreats to the service entrance door and stands there for a few moments trying to decide what to do. The men could be, in fact they likely are, watching from somewhere nearby. But Maggie is almost certainly out there. His knees feel weak and on the verge of buckling. His mouth is dry and it feels like his windpipe is closing off. His whole body trembles with panic. He knows that he must fight these things off. If Maggie's out there, she will be easy prey for the coyotes that Hollister told him about. Not to mention the coyotes of the human variety.

Josh steps toward the gate, but stops just short of the opening. He cannot make himself go on. Convenient rationalizations surface. He will go find Evangelina and Hollister first, and they will join in the search. More importantly, he must warn Evangelina about the break-in and the danger they are now in. No, now is not the time to search for Maggie, especially alone. After all, he's not completely sure she's even out there. With this decided, Josh turns and purposefully heads back into the building to find Evangelina. But even with his rationalizations he cannot completely ignore the familiar cloak of shame that covers him.

❧❧

At the door to their room, he knocks again. No answer.

He enters the room. Atop the neatly made bed, Evangelina's nightgown is neatly folded atop the pillow. There is no trace of her.

At first he misses it, but then he spots the note, lying in the middle of the bed, almost invisible against the white chenille bedspread. Sensing something ominous, he sits down on the bed and reads the note.

Dear Josh,

I should have told you in person, but you would have tried to stop me or tried to go with me, and I'm not sure I could have resisted. I have gone home to Uncle Reynaldo's. I asked Hollister to drive me this morning, and he agreed. I have to be with Serena. That's my place right now. That's always been my place.

Please do not try to follow me. This is your chance to get free of this mess. It's me they are after. They still do not know where my uncle lives, and anyway he can protect our family, I believe.

I am so sorry I got you involved and endangered your life. You are a very kind man, a good man.

Josh, we must be realistic. You and I are from two different worlds. Parallel universes, you might say. We could never make it, you and I. My world and your world are just too different.

I wish you the very best of good fortune. I hope you learn to find faith in your life. I think there might be some hope for me to do just that, thanks to Esther. Please look after her while you are still there. I hate to leave her, but Serena comes first.

It has been a blessing for me to know you Josh. Again, please do not try to follow me.

Good Bye.
Evangelina.

The note falls from Josh's trembling hands. She must have walked out right past him while he slept. Why hadn't he awakened? Maybe he could have stopped her. Maybe he could have gone with her. No. He knows that would not have worked. So this is how it ends. He swallows hard and fights back tears.

◈

"I think it's okay to sit up now," Hollister says to Evangelina. "We've gone a good five miles and there's no sign of them."

Evangelina, who has been crouched into almost a fetal position on the floor of the passenger seat, stretches and slides up into the seat, looking back to be sure they are not being followed.

"Thank you, Hollister, for taking me," she says. "And thanks for not telling Rosey where you were headed. I couldn't risk anything preventing me from getting home."

"No problem. I do think you should have told Josh, though."

"I feel bad about that too. But I couldn't. He was dead-set against my leaving, and he would have tried to persuade me to stay and I might have given in. Or he would have wanted to go with me."

"I've got room in the back seat. Could've swung that."

"I know. But this is best. The least I could do for him is to let him get free from the killers. Once we are separated, they'll lose interest in him."

"You sure about that?"

She shakes her head slowly. "I'm not sure about anything." She looks back over her shoulder again. Still no one following them.

"Well, there's one thing I'm sure about," says Hollister, "and maybe you don't realize it."

"What?"

"Josh is really crazy about you." He says this matter of factly, but gives her a quick serious look.

"What do you mean?" She feels her face flushing.

"It's obvious, girl. Plus, he told me. Guess there's no harm in betraying that confidence now. I think he's in love with you."

"That's ridiculous. We've only known each other a few days. Yeah, we shared some pretty intense times together. But I think you're reading it all wrong to say he's ..." She can't say the word. Love. She's shaking inexplicably. This is silly, she thinks. *Get a grip on yourself, girl.*

"I'm just sayin.' And I don't think I'm wrong about this. I think he's a pretty great guy, frankly."

"You think I don't know that?" she says, rather defensively. She's turned to look directly at the huge man, hunched into the driver's seat of the little Escort.

"I'm sure you must know that. But if you don't have the same kind of feelings for him, that he—"

"I'm not saying I don't have feelings for him, I'm just saying ..." She trails off. She turns and looks out the window. The familiar scenery of northern New Mexico, the rough sun-baked hills sloping up to majestic mesa tops, slashed with narrow canyons and peppered with piñon pines. People spend thousands for a Georgia O'Keeffe representation of this, but for Evangelina it is the familiar scenery of every day. The familiar scenery of her home. She turns back to Hollister. "The problem for us is that we're too different. Think about it, Hollister. Josh is an eastern guy, grew up in Connecticut, went to Yale. He knows cities. He's a physicist, used to living an elite life. Associating with the smartest people in the world. See that countryside out there?" She waves her hand toward the panorama before them. "That's me. That's my country. Tradition. My Hispanic roots. I can't see that the two mix very well."

"Hmm," says Hollister. That's all he says for a few moments, mulling this over. "So that's what you see, huh?" He shoots her a quick but penetrating glance. "Well, what I see is a great guy and a cool lady who seem to like each other. Maybe a lot. All that other stuff you mentioned? It matters, yes it does." He gives her a broad smile. "It's just that in the final analysis, it doesn't matter very much." He turns his eyes back to the road.

Evangelina's mouth falls open, but she doesn't say anything. She crosses her arms, then turns abruptly back toward the window and watches the piñons fly by.

Chapter Ten

Monday, October 17

His first instinct is to follow Evangelina, explain things. Pacing the small room, he quickly realizes how silly this idea is. She's already told him what she wants from him. *Do not try to follow me.* Then she had written *Good Bye.* So final. But of course, he couldn't follow her anyway. No car. And he doesn't even know where she's gone. Somewhere near Rinconada, that's all he knows. He needs to talk to someone. He has no real friend to call. No confidant that he can lean on. He wanders out into the hallway, but has no destination in mind.

"Waverly." Bud's voice comes from behind him. He turns to see Bud standing in his open doorway down the hall. "Waverly," he calls again. "Where are you going in such a hurry?" With a wave of his hand, he invites Josh to join him.

Josh stays in the doorway to Bud's room, where the air is a bit fresher, while Bud ambles slowly through the smoky haze toward the only chair. He wears a faded blue sweatshirt that appears several sizes too large, with a large tear under one arm, and baggy gray sweat pants. And of course the USMC cap. Some TV show, a game show it sounds like, is blaring behind Bud. The picture is fuzzy.

"So, did you find Maggie?"

Josh keeps his answer short. "Not yet."

"So what's up with you? Frankly, you look like something the dog puked up," Bud growls.

"Well, it's been kind of a tough morning so far, sir. Didn't sleep too good either."

"Those men still after you and your woman friend?" He pops a cigarette from his pack of Camels, extends the pack toward Josh, then pulls it back. "That's right, you don't smoke."

"I think they are. But I guess I'm thinking about Evangelina a lot right now."

"Come on over and pull up a seat," Bud says, gesturing toward the edge of the bed. He finds the remote and kills the TV. "Are you two married?"

"No. We just met a few days ago. But …" He pauses.

"But what? Spit it out."

"Well, we've become rather close." Josh pauses again. "At least I'm feeling close. I mean …" He's sort of stammering now and he realizes it. He stops and takes a deep breath and starts again. "She left this morning to go back to her family. She left me a note that basically said good bye. I'm worried about her. Out there where those dangerous men might find her."

"Yeah, the dangerous men. But that's not what you're worried about right now. You're about as transparent as a pane of glass. You're worried that you've lost her." Bud's eyes, magnified through the thick gasses, are like searchlights, exposing him. He wants to turn away, but doesn't.

"Yes, that's true."

"So I have a question for you, young man. You up for a question?"

Josh nods.

"Have you ever taken a risk in your whole life?"

"Of course." Josh bristles a little at the implications of this question.

"I mean a real risk, where if you fail, you might get your butt kicked real hard, where if you don't make it, you could lose everything? Ever taken a risk like that?"

Josh says nothing. His mind is racing, but he cannot think of a time when he took such a risk. The thought of his aborted search for Maggie pops into his mind, but he quickly pushes it away.

"I didn't think so. You know what? I look at you, and here's what I see. Now, I'm not sayin' this to hurt you, hell, son, you're already hurting. I'm sayin' this because you need to hear the truth, and anything less won't do you a nickel's worth of any good. When I look at you, I see a guy who's always been in control. Always needed to have answers for everything. Nothing messy. Everything all neat and tidy. No loose ends. And so—"

Josh interrupts. "That's not quite fair to say—"

"Hear me out, son, or just walk out of here and stew in your juices. If you want to learn something, just shut up and listen."

Josh is quiet.

"So in order to stay in control, you've always been a guy who avoids risks. Why? Simple, because if you take a risk, you just might lose, and your control goes right out the window."

Josh opens his mouth to speak, but says nothing.

"I'm not done yet, almost, but not quite. So, you avoid risks. And you know what happens when you avoid risks?" The old man pauses for Josh to answer.

Josh has some ideas but just shrugs his shoulders.

"Well two things happen when you avoid risks. First is, you wind up living a narrow life, a small life, a safe life. You simply can't ever expect to win much unless you're willing to risk much. I'm guessing you're in that boat."

Josh starts to respond, but Bud isn't finished. "And the second thing that happens is that you wind up with regrets. Got any regrets, son?" Bud now pauses and raises one bushy eyebrow as if waiting for Josh's answer.

Josh clears his throat. "Of course I do. Everybody has regrets."

"That's right, son. Everybody has regrets. That's why I know what I'm talking about." Bud turns his gaze to the pictures above his desk. "That's my son, David."

Josh sees the graduation picture. Probably high school, perhaps college. "He was a good looking young man," Josh says, relieved to feel the heat turned away from him for a moment, although he suspects this is just a temporary respite.

"Yes, he was. I haven't seen him in years, and it's my own fault."

"I'm sure, sir, that you—"

"Just shut up for a minute. It was my fault. I was this tough guy, this macho idiot who was all caught up in his identity as a Marine. Don't get me wrong, I love the Marines. It was my whole life. But that's the trouble. It was my whole life. I let Carol raise David. Hell, I was just back from Korea, I was all screwed up. I didn't know what to do with a kid. I was out drinking with my buddies, swaggering and being the conquering hero and all that crap. Carol, she was taking David to the dentist and the Little League games and going to the parent-teacher conferences. And when I did interact with David, I was like some merciless drill sergeant. I was tough on him. Really tough."

Josh wonders if his own father ever had any regrets about the way he treated him.

After blowing his nose into a used napkin that was wadded up on his desk, Bud takes another drag on his Camel and continues. "I had chances to change my ways. Over time I figured out how I'd made a mess of things. But somehow, I just couldn't change. I wanted to, but I couldn't. I wanted to start being a real dad to David, but when I got around him, this drill-sergeant side of me would just come out. And you know why?"

Josh shakes his head.

"It's because I was afraid. That's right, GI Joe here was afraid. Afraid to tell my son that ..." Now Bud chokes up for a second and Josh thinks he might be about to cry. But he doesn't. "Afraid to tell him that I loved him. I was afraid that he would reject me, I guess. I was afraid to take the risk."

"I'm sorry."

"So now all I have are regrets."

"Couldn't you call him now?"

"Hell, I've tried that, but it's too late. He won't even talk to me."

Again Josh says, "I'm sorry."

"So, damn ... I didn't mean to get off into that. What I was tryin' to tell you is that you have two choices. You can live a life that is safe and risk-free. And I guarantee that you'll wind up with regrets. Or you can take a risk now and then, stick your neck out, fly by the seat of your pants, shoot your mouth off, and you know what?"

"What?"

"Well, you may get your head chopped off." Bud laughs at this, which starts a cigarette-induced coughing fit for a few moments. Then he continues, "Yeah, you may get your head chopped off, but you will live a life that is free, a life that is true."

"Sounds like good advice, Bud, but how does that apply to my situation?"

"Good Lord, Waverly, you went to college and all that, and you have to ask a stupid question like that?"

Josh begins to respond, but Bud keeps right on going. "Here's how it applies. Yesterday you tell me you don't believe in God. Why? You say some pseudo-scientific babble about needing evidence, blah, blah, blah. When in truth, you've been afraid to explore this God thing because there's a risk. Not a risk that you might discover that God doesn't exist, but a risk that you might find out that he does. And that could be kind of scary for a control freak like you."

Josh feels himself shaking with nerves and he hopes Bud doesn't see it. "Now, Bud, I seriously don't think—"

"And one more thing."

Josh sighs with resignation. "What?"

"You don't sit here whimpering to some old man about, Oh geez, my girlfriend left me and now I'm so sad. That's how you will wind up with regrets, one hundred percent guaranteed."

"What should I do?"

"See, this is what I mean. For crying out loud, don't ask me what to do. Get up off your skinny butt and do something! Make a mistake. Do something stupid. But take a risk. Or decide you're willing to live with regrets for the rest of your life. Have I made myself clear?"

Josh cannot answer. He nods his head at the old man with fire in his eyes.

∽

As they get closer to Rinconada, Evangelina's excitement builds. She's now on the edge of her seat, craning her neck for familiar sights. It's like she's been gone for ten years. "Where's home for you, Hollister?"

"Originally Illinois. Until my mother died when I was in high school."

"Oh I'm sorry. Where is your father?"

"Good question. Haven't ever seen him. He split when I was three. Never came back."

"So what happened when your mother died?"

"I went to live with an aunt in Milwaukee for awhile. Then I found out my grandmother, that's Rosey, had been putting away money for years to pay my tuition to Creighton. Well, most of my tuition anyway. Fortunately I was able to get a partial scholarship for basketball that covered the rest."

"Why Creighton?"

"She had a brother who went there. Sentimental reasons I guess. So I headed off to Omaha for four years."

"Is Rosey from there?"

"Oh no. She's from Albuquerque. So on breaks I'd head down to New Mexico to see her. What I didn't realize at the time was that she was living near the poverty level. She had a so-so apartment in Albuquerque, but then she lost that. Couldn't pay the rent. Just living on a little Social Security. Can you imagine that?"

"What?"

"Here's my grandma starving and yet she refused to touch my tuition money, which she could've done. I would've insisted on it if I'd known." Hollister looks at Evangelina with sorrowful eyes that are now misty. "I hate it when I think of her suffering."

"She seems like a wonderful woman."

"She sure is. Best in the world …" His voice trails off, then he clears his throat.

"So home for you has been a lot of places."

"Yeah. That's okay though. I guess I'm not too hung up on places. For me, home ought to be where the love is." Hollister has clearly given this some thought. "And right now that's close to Rosey." They are quiet for a few moments, then he asks, "How long have you been in Rinconada?"

"Almost all my life. It's the only home I've ever known."

"Wow. You must know everyone in town."

"Just about." She's leaning forward, hands on the dashboard now, to get a better look as they approach the village. It's like she's seeing it all through fresh eyes.

She points off to the left. "See that creek? My dad used to take me swimming over there when I was a little girl. The water's only ankle deep, but I always loved that." She's almost giddy with excitement now, no doubt because soon she will be seeing Serena.

Rinconada is not laid out on a rectangular grid like most pre-planned cities elsewhere. As the main road enters the village it turns to gravel. From this road other streets, dirt and gravel, radiate out almost randomly, one leading down into a shaded gully, another disappearing into a grove of cottonwoods. With a population of three hundred, there's not a lot to see here, but for Evangelina every turn holds a precious memory. And seldom does she get the chance to show off her hometown to a friend.

They enter the small plaza, a square central park area filled with towering cottonwoods and several rustic benches on which several elderly men have already gathered to watch the day unfold. The only large building around the plaza is the church, a large adobe structure where Evangelina worshiped every Sunday until five years ago. Across from the church is the small market, La Tienda, where most everyone shops, visits with neighbors and plugs into the local gossip, ably led by Mrs. Maestas.

Another low-slung adobe occupies another corner of the plaza. "That's the weaver's place," she points out to Hollister. "If you'd ever like to get Rosey a nice present, that's your place. They've been making rugs there for hundreds of years. Oh, and there's La Comida, best food in town."

"It would be hard to beat your cooking, Evangelina."

"Oh, theirs is better, but it's not even close to how my mama can cook. Maybe you can stay for lunch."

Hollister says, "I must say, Evangelina, I'm quite envious of you. You must have a ton of friends around here."

Evangelina turns quiet for a moment. She glances back at the church and La Tienda. In fact, she doesn't.

Evangelina directs Hollister through a maze of narrow roads, winding between lush trees and tall fences, called coyote fences, formed from vertical rows of aspen limbs.

"Here we are," beams Evangelina.

The road has ended in a broad field, at the rear of which sits a rambling but modest adobe house. Out front sits a large long-haul truck. "Whose semi?" asks Hollister.

"Uncle Rey's. It's a Peterbilt 386. He just got it last year. Isn't it a beauty? Finally traded the old 352 in. I told him to get a red one. Isn't it slick?"

"So where'd you learn about big rigs?" Hollister chuckles.

"Been ridin' in them since I was a little girl. They've been an important part of my life."

The car is barely stopped before Evangelina is bounding out. "Come on in," she beckons, almost jumping for joy. "Come on in and meet my family."

≈≈

He has no reason to stay. No reason to linger around this depressing place any longer. He'll call Hal. Have him pick him up. Get back to his routine. Back to things he understands. Back to his detector calibrations, where the only drama is an occasional pesky bug in some computer program. Back to where life is more predictable, more manageable. Yes, he'll call Hal now.

But he knows he won't. Not yet anyway. He knows, down deep, that Maggie is out there, somewhere, and that if he doesn't do something, she'll die.

Slowly but deliberately he steps outside the service entrance and moves toward the open gate.

He stands quiet for several minutes at the opening of the gate, carefully studying the desert wilderness beyond. All he can see is a forest of head-high chamisa in all directions, a stunning mustard yellow in the bright morning sun. Beyond the chamisa the rugged mountain range stands in silhouette against a deep blue cloudless sky. All is quiet. No sign of Maggie. He stares at the ground wondering if he might be able to detect her footprints, but the hardpack gravel reveals nothing.

Suddenly there's a motion off to the left. Something shifting beyond a chamisa. He hears a soft whispering sound. He lunges back behind the gate and waits. Now it's quiet again. He peeks out around the edge of the gate. A huge tumbleweed lies before him, rocking gently as the wind subsides. Then a soft gust stirs the tumbleweed again, and with a whishing sound it bounds off to the right.

Josh steps out beyond the wall and looks in both directions. A dirt access road heads to the right and disappears around the edge of the building. All the rest is wilderness. If Maggie walked out here, she couldn't have gone far, but which way would she have gone? Most likely she followed the access road, but in that case she'll be easy to find. If she headed straight off into the desert, she might never be found. Except by the coyotes, which may have already found her.

Josh takes a few tentative steps out into desert. He realizes that the sea of chamisa is thick and just tall enough that he could easily become lost, even just a few feet away from the gate. He turns to check the building, to be sure he hasn't lost sight of it yet.

"Maggie," he calls out, not using his loudest voice, aware that he's risking being heard by the killers, if they are nearby. But there's no time to lose. No answer. And there's no sign of her anywhere. *This was a bad idea.*

Another motion nearby paralyzes Josh, but again it's a tumbleweed rustling against a chamisa, where it has become lodged. He takes a few more steps. Nothing. He should go back. Geez, he isn't even sure she's not still somewhere in the building. The question of where Maggie might be vies for his attention along with the question of where the coyote pack might be. What's he doing out here?

Then he sees it. Her walker, lying on its side just a few feet ahead. But no Maggie. *She must be nearby.* He picks up the pace. Then he sees her. Motionless, lying in a curled up position beneath a chamisa. *Is she alive?*

Thank God, he almost says aloud, then plunges ahead toward her. A sudden chill knifes through him, and he stops so abruptly that he almost falls forward. He gasps, but it feels like the air has been sucked out of him. Frozen, he looks down toward Maggie's still body. No more than twelve inches from her head, on a flat rock that catches the warmth of the sun, a huge rattlesnake is coiled. Very slowly Josh backs away to a safe distance, not that he really knows what a safe distance from a rattler actually is.

This is the first rattlesnake Josh has ever seen, except for one in a zoo when he was a small child, and that experience gave him nightmares for a week. The snake is a dull gray, with diamond-shaped scales that look like battle armor. Some of the scales are brown, others a dirty white. Its head, the size of a fist, has a classic viper shape and the small beady eyes are open. A primitive reaction of terror wrenches his stomach.

But he cannot turn away from this, as much as every cell in his body is telling him to. The snake has not moved.

It appears to be sunning itself. But if Maggie stirs, he knows the snake could be aroused and strike her. He is faced with a dilemma, and he may not have much time to figure out what to do. His mind races through his meager knowledge of rattlesnakes. Mostly he has questions. Is the snake asleep? Does it know he's here? Can it see him, does it sense the heat from his body, does it feel the vibrations from his footsteps? What would MacGyver do? He wishes he knew more. Would it be possible for him to pick up Maggie and carry her away without disturbing the snake? Not likely. What would happen if he intentionally startled the snake by throwing a rock at it or one of those huge tumbleweeds? Perhaps it would retreat to safety, and he could retrieve Maggie. But this risks awakening Maggie and having the snake strike her. These options do battle in his panicked mind, and no one of them appears attractive. He remains frozen in place.

Then Maggie moves. She rolls onto her other side, extending her arm over her head, as Josh watches in horror. Her hand comes to rest just inches from the snake. Moments that seem like hours pass. The snake does not move, nor does Maggie.

Josh feels paralyzed. He cannot seem to catch his breath, like the wind's been knocked out of him. His racing mind, chaotically lunging through all his options, keeps making its way to the obvious. There is nothing he can do. The only rational course of action is to retreat, get some help, find someone who knows how to deal with snakes. He's beginning to have some enthusiasm for this plan. After all, Maggie and the snake apparently have been here for awhile. She's probably safe for awhile longer. Relief begins to flow through him, now that he has a plan, especially one that involves moving away from the rattler.

He begins to back away, but stops. Something else is flowing through him also. Something that is not relief. Something unfamiliar that feels wild and angry, something that is not rational or safe. Something that is overwhelming.

He can wait no longer. Josh takes a deep breath, then steps softly toward Maggie, careful that his shadow does not cross the snake, just in case it might be sensitive to such things. Slowly, keeping his eyes on the snake, he leans in toward her body. Gently he slips his hands beneath her. So far she has not moved again. His face is now no more than two feet from the rattler. Now he has her cradled in his arms, but as he rises Maggie awakens.

"Roger!" she blurts out, and with that the rattlesnake stirs. Instantly it reconfigures its body for a strike, as Josh leaps backward with Maggie. The snake strikes, lunging forward with lightening speed, but it falls just short of Josh. It recoils to strike again, but now Josh is safely away. He stands breathless for several moments as the angry rattler now slithers away into the chamisa, its rattle still producing the unmistakable ugly sound of imminent death.

"Maggie, are you okay?" Josh is still shaking.

"You're not Roger," she pronounces. But then she smiles. "But I saw him last night. I really did. He was here. He came to see me. I have to find him."

"First, Maggie, we're going inside and make sure you're okay." Maggie looks up at Josh with hollow eyes. He looks into her aged face and sees the young mother with her son in the backyard at a summertime barbeque. He holds her close to him as they make their way back into Copper Point.

As he strides back toward the building, there is a new energy in his step. Maybe he can't elude a couple of killers forever, but he did just outsmart a stupid snake. He imagines that Bud sees him now. He imagines that Evangelina sees him now. He imagines that his father sees him now. But then he sags under the realization that he is very much alone.

❧

"Are you still here?" It's Olive, the receptionist, just settling in behind the desk. The abrasive little bureaucrat who tried to toss them out into the street. She's got the tired Monday-morning look of someone not quite ready for the work week to begin.

Josh has gotten Maggie back to her room and into bed. She seemed fine and very talkative. But she looked exhausted, and once she was tucked in fell asleep in the midst of a sentence. He's come out to the lobby to call Lauren, unable to go back into the room – thick with the memory of Evangelina -- right now.

Am I still here? That's actually a good question, thinks Josh. "Yes." That's about all the conversation Josh can muster right now. "Look, we need to call—"

"Where's your girlfriend?"

"She had to leave. We need to call Lauren—"

"Are you guys married?"

What? The Enforcer has now become Chatty Kathy. Okay, so I'm in a nasty mood. Is it any wonder? He stops to face her. "No," he snaps, turning to go down the hallway again. He'll go back to the room. He'll call the clinic from there.

"Why did you come here the other day?"

Josh has had just about enough of Olive. He strides back to the counter, leans on his forearms and looks down at her. He starts to speak, but before he can get a word out she says, "Gee, I'm kinda sorry how I treated you guys on Saturday. I'm new here and I'm still learning how things operate. I felt bad about it all weekend."

Josh, after the morning he's gone through, was about ready to give her a piece of his mind, but now he's at a loss for words. Olive looks like she's in her late twenties. Her pale narrow face, curious and anxious, peers up at him through pink-rimmed cat eye glasses, straight out of the seventies. And her stringy brown hair is in need of one of those conditioners you see in TV commercials. She wears a simple drab blouse that could have come from Goodwill, or should soon be going there. "It's okay," he says, crumbling. "No problem. It takes a while to get the hang of a new job."

Behind him a loud crash at the door causes Josh to jump and turn. It's Lauren, kicking the push bar of the sticky glass door open ahead of her. She's carrying her medical bag in one hand and a spray of flowers in the other. She groans, "Cheesh, they really need to fix that door."

"I could say something to Mrs. Harshburn," offers a suddenly helpful Olive.

"Don't bother. It's probably been that way for years. So how's our girl today?"

"Uh, I haven't been down to see her yet. She was doing well last night. And you need to look in on another person, Maggie Stillings, who's just down the hall."

"Yeah, I've seen Maggie before. Wanders off from time to time. Why don't you take me down to see them now?" Lauren is wearing the same outdoorsy outfit she had on yesterday.

"Who's sick?" asks the curious Olive.

"Esther fell yesterday. Lauren's looking after her."

"Oh my God," gasps Olive, putting a hand over her mouth. "Is she going to be okay?"

"We'll see." says Lauren, "She's a strong old girl."

Josh leads the way down to Esther's room.

"Come in," beams Esther's cheery voice, almost song-like, when they knock.

"Well, you're looking chipper today," says Lauren, placing the flowers on the small table next to Esther's bed.

"Oh, they're so pretty! Move them over to the desk where I can see them. What are they?"

"Not sure," laughs Lauren. "Something I picked up in Santa Fe on my way in this morning. How are you feeling today?"

"Oh, I'm feeling great. Ready to get out of this bed, I can tell you that."

"Well, as soon as I check your hip we'll see about that."

"Where's Evangelina?" Esther asks, looking at Josh. Lauren looks at him too.

"She went home this morning."

"Great," says Lauren. "She needed to see that little girl of hers."

"Yes," agrees Josh, although he's certain his lack of enthusiasm shows.

"So why don't you step outside for a minute, Josh, while I check Esther's bones. We may have her in that triathlon this afternoon yet."

When Josh comes back in, Esther is beaming. "She says I can be up walking this afternoon."

"Yes," chimes in Lauren, "but I want you using that walker for awhile. You gotta promise."

Esther nods submissively.

"I'll check on you tomorrow," says a smiling Lauren, heading for the door. "I'll go see Maggie now," she whispers to Josh in a soft voice intended not to alarm Esther.

"I'll walk you over," says Josh, not wanting to be alone with Esther right now.

"Josh," says Esther, "why don't you stay behind for a minute?"

"Sure." He sighs.

"You don't have to stand. Pull up that chair, so you can be close."

Josh sits next to Esther. She looks so frail and tiny in the bed. Her porcelain skin makes her look like a doll propped up against the pillow. "I'm glad you're feeling better." He doesn't know what else to say.

She nods, then says, "So Evangelina went home this morning. You didn't seem real happy about that."

"Oh, it's fine. She had to go home sometime. She's got a little girl to take care of. I was just worried about the men who are after her."

"Yes, that scares me too. I hope she's safe. How did she go? It's not like we have a bus stopping out front every fifteen minutes." She smiles.

"Hollister has a car. He took her."

"Good. He's a sensible man. He'll watch out for her." She pauses, then asks, "So why didn't you go too?"

"She didn't ask me." He can't meet her eyes while he's saying this. "Said she didn't want to put me in any more danger."

"So what are you going to do?"

"Guess I'll go home. I was thinking about calling a friend of mine to come pick me up."

"Get back to your physics, huh?"

"Yeah. It is Monday, after all, and I do have a job."

"So, Josh, I'm wondering …" She looks hard at his face like she's searching for a clue.

"What?"

"What are you looking for?"

"What do you mean?"

"I mean, you don't seem very happy."

"I'll be okay. I just had a bad dream last night, that's all—"

"About those men? I'd probably be having nightmares about them."

"Yeah, I hear you. But it wasn't about that."

"Oh?" She's waiting for more information.

"I dreamed about my father," he finally says, not really wanting to talk about this now.

"Hmm. And it was a bad dream?"

"Yes."

"Maybe church yesterday caused it, you think? That story was about a father and a son."

Josh hadn't thought about that. Maybe so. It was about an inheritance, after all. "I guess I really don't want to talk about it."

"That's okay. You don't have to. But if something's bothering you, it's not going to do you much good just holding it in. And surely you aren't afraid to talk to a sick old lady in a bed out in the middle of nowhere." She looks at him with raised eyebrows. "But maybe I'm wrong."

"This is just stuff that happened a long time ago."

She smiles. "Last night sounds pretty recent to me."

Josh sags into his chair. "Okay, so here's the dream." He shakes his head slowly, wondering how he's allowed himself to get into this. "My dad was a famous physicist. I think I mentioned that before."

"Parallel universes, I seem to recall."

"That's right." Josh recounts the dream to Esther, whose eyes never leave him while he talks.

When he is finished, Esther says, "Lordy, Josh, I can see why that would be upsetting. Did your father really die like that?"

"Pretty much. Except I wasn't there. He had an aneurism. He died four days later."

"What do you think the thing about the physics committee giving the seminar means?"

"I'm pretty sure it has to do with his will." Josh takes a deep breath. "I haven't really ever talked to anyone about this before. You see, when my father died, he left everything he had to the American Institute of Physics."

"Why did he do that?" There's a note of indignation in her voice.

"I guess he was disappointed in me." He gulps. "Ashamed, maybe."

"You must have felt awful."

"Yeah. It was kind of a shock. Not that I cared about the money. I really didn't. It's just that ..." His voice trails off, and he's silent for awhile before continuing. "... I didn't turn out to be the kind of son he was hoping for." Her questioning face prompts him to continue. "Since I was little he was grooming me to be a great physicist. I just didn't have it in me, I guess."

"So you feel like you let him down."

Josh nods.

"I haven't heard you say anything about your mother."

Josh looks away. For a moment he studies the chest of drawers on the far wall. The delicate carving. The frilly runner across the top. The jewelry boxes. So out of place here. He looks back at Esther. He thinks about Bud's lecture about regrets. What kind of regrets, he wonders, does Esther have? "My mother." He pauses again. "My mother and I weren't close. My father was the dominant parent. He called all the shots. What I remember of my mother is that she was always in the background. She was quiet. It was like I never really got to know her. Then when I was seven, she left my father."

"Did you see her after that?"

"My parents had joint custody for awhile, until I was fourteen. Then I went to live with my father."

"Didn't your mother put up a fight?" Esther seems to find this hard to believe.

"Not that I know of, but of course I only heard my father's version of things. He hardly ever talked about her, but when he did he would remind me that my mom had left us, and he said she was an unfit mother. I grew up believing this. I did learn that she remarried and moved to California … didn't even come to my father's funeral. Hey, I don't want to make this into some tragic story. Lots of folks have it a lot worse than me."

"Yes, that's true. But I suspect that fact isn't helping much to make your pain go away."

"I mean like …" his eyes scan the room.

"You mean like me?"

"Yes, in fact. You have so little."

"Well, maybe it looks like I don't have much. In fact, I don't have a lot. But the truth is, I have enough. More than enough." She smiles, then says, "Have you tried to contact your mother?"

"No. But I've thought that, I don't know, maybe I should. But what if she doesn't want to see me?"

"She's your mother, Josh." A gentle smile says without words, "Call her."

Josh says nothing.

"So what I'm hearing is that dad wanted you to grow up to be a little Einstein, but you didn't. And so now you're carrying around a lot of guilt about that." She looks at him with inquiring eyes. Eyes that he cannot look away from. They're like a laser that's locked onto its target. Yet they are inviting. Affirming. Forgiving. "In fact, I'd guess that this has burdened your whole life, has sort of formed the whole way you look at yourself—"

"I wouldn't say that," he quickly protests, then sighs. "I guess that's probably true."

"So tell me, Josh. What do you believe?" This is asked without judgment.

He's not sure how to answer this question, maybe not even sure what she means. He ponders it for awhile, then says, "You mean about life?" The recent conversation with Evangelina is still fresh in his mind.

She nods.

"Well, I'm not sure. I guess I think … well, I'm not sure … I don't think about those kinds of things much."

"Hmm. If I might say so, I'm seeing a man who has let the past control his life. Yet he's not thinking about the important things that might guide his future. Seems like you've got it all backwards, Josh. The past is over, all you've got is the future. I worry that I'm looking at a man, a really good man, who has a lot of knowledge about facts and data. Yet he doesn't really believe anything."

Josh swallows hard, feels like there's a billiard ball caught in his throat. He looks away toward the small window and the broken venetian blinds and the white frilly curtains that frame them. Is there a mistiness forming in his eyes? Lord, he doesn't want Esther to see this. But then he looks back at her. Her kind eyes caress him with compassion, understanding, love. And it all lets loose. Tears come flowing. And a sob. He stands abruptly and turns away so that she cannot see him. He paces the room, wiping away the flow from his face with the back of his hand. After a few moments, he turns back to Esther. "I'm so sorry. I don't know what caused that."

"Come sit back down, son."

Josh sits back down next to Esther. She takes his hand in hers. "Josh. That's a wonderful name. You know why your parents named you that?"

"Not really. They never said." He's still wiping the last of the tears. "But I assumed I was named after Joshua Singleton, the famous theoretical physicist. But I'm not sure."

"Let me tell you about another Joshua. And I think this one actually describes you."

Josh nods.

"This Joshua lived a long time ago. He was the successor to the greatest leader the Hebrew people had ever known. That was Moses, who led the people out from slavery, taught them the laws that the Lord had given him. He spent forty years leading his people to a new home land. The Promised Land. Do you know that story, Josh?"

He nods. Of course he's heard of Moses, but knows little about what Esther is saying to him or where she's headed with this.

"So Moses led his people for forty years. But he never did make it to the Promised Land himself. Died before they got there. And so it was left up to Joshua to lead the people onward into a new life. Don't you wonder how he did it? I mean he didn't have the experience, didn't have the reputation that Moses had. Don't you wonder how he could carry on after the great Moses died? How he could accomplish something the greatest leader of all time could not?"

"So how did he do it?"

"I'm sure it wasn't easy for him. But here's how he did it. Hand me that book over there." She's pointing to the worn bible on her desk.

Josh hands it to her. Esther thumbs through the book, apparently knowing exactly what she's looking for. "Ah, here it is," she says, then hands the book to Josh. "Here, read this. Out loud."

Josh sees that the book is opened to the Book of Joshua, chapter one. He begins to read, "After the death of Moses ..." He reads for awhile, then Esther stops him. "Read that last part again," she says.

Josh reads aloud what the Lord said to Joshua, "I hereby command you: Be strong and courageous; do not be frightened or dismayed, for the Lord your God is with you wherever you go."

"That's it. That's the key, I believe. You see, it doesn't say that Joshua was the greatest leader of all. It doesn't say that he had the most skill, the greatest education, was smarter than Moses or anything else. It just says that the Lord told him that he would be with him wherever he went. And I suspect the key to Joshua's success was that he believed it."

Josh opens his mouth but remains silent.

"So I'm thinking this Joshua sitting next to me is a little like that original Joshua. He doesn't measure up to his predecessor, or at least he doesn't think he does. Yet he is the one who will accomplish what that predecessor never could. Not because he had become the little Einstein, not because he had become mister big shot at the university, not because he could give the great lecture on parallel universes. No, he would be called to do something different, and he will do it because he knows that the Lord is with him. Knows that he can be strong and courageous."

Josh nods his head, not sure how to process all this.

Esther holds his hand protectively, like she's holding a kitten, in both of hers, as she continues. "That's who I believe you are, Josh. Be strong and courageous." There's a serenity in her face now, a calmness that Josh feels like a soothing balm. "Be strong and courageous in your work. Be strong and courageous with all the threats you face, even those evil men. And, Josh, be strong and courageous with Evangelina. I truly believe the Lord has great things planned for you." She smiles and there's a glow about her that causes Josh's mouth to fall open again.

◈

Stilwell's phone rings. Seldom has the Contact called him so often. Must be panicking.

"Have you made the hits?"

"Not yet, But I'm—"

"It's got to be done now." There is an urgency in the Contact's voice. Stilwell can imagine the beads of sweat running down the Contact's forehead, the knots of fear welling up inside the gut. He loves it. It will not hurt the Contact to have a little taste of what this business is really all about.

"Oh?" He sounds relaxed and carefree, his best Stilwell Ferguson voice.

"Don't worry about clean. You've got to finish it off now, anyway you can. And then disappear."

Stilwell ponders this. Hmm. Not clean. Disappear. Why, yes, he can certainly handle this. He likes these new guidelines. He remains silent.

The Contact continues. "You'll need the kid." The Contact gives Stilwell the details of the plan then hangs up.

Jesse is stretched out on the hood of the car, catching a few early morning rays. He jumps as Stilwell kicks him. "Time to go back to work, my friend. Time to take care of business."

❧❧

Evangelina pushes the front door open and announces at the top of her voice, "Hey, everybody, I'm home!"

Grace Gomez appears from the kitchen. "Evangelina!" She wipes her hands on her apron, as she runs toward her daughter for a hug. Then she holds her daughter's shoulders at arm's length in both hands to get a better look. "It is so good to see you." Her curious eyes move beyond Evangelina to the towering Hollister behind her.

"Mama, this is Hollister, who drove me down."

"Welcome, Hollister," she says, but there's still curiosity in her face as she looks around. "Where's Serena?"

Evangelina is dumbfounded. "What do you mean, 'where's Serena?'"

Grace now looks serious. "She's with you, right? Della picked her up an hour ago to take her to you."

Evangelina is not comprehending this. "What do you mean?"

"She talked with you, right? You said to bring Serena to be with you." A look of deep concern is spreading over Grace's face. "She said—"

"Wait a second," interrupts Evangelina. "Della says she talked with me? You let her take Serena?" A wave of terror threatens her balance. Hollister puts a steadying hand on her shoulder as she begins to wobble.

"You didn't talk with Della?" Grace's voice is shaky.

"No." She gasps for air, suddenly feeling light headed. "Where did they go?"

"She said they were going to see you, that it wasn't far away. That's all I know. Oh, God, Vangie, I'm sorry ..."

Evangelina is putting two and two together. She paces quickly in small circles, head down, her fingers to her temples. *Fight off the panic.* She turns to Hollister. "We've got to get back up there, now."

Hollister nods. "You got it girl."

"Reynaldo and Esteban are down on the plaza. Shall I get them?" Grace is starting to cry.

"Yes. Have you still got Della's cell phone?"

"No. She took it with her, said she needed to be in touch with you. Oh God, Vangie—"

Evangelina looks at Hollister, but he shakes his head helplessly. "My phone's back at the home."

"Mama, run to La Tienda . . . Call the police right now." Her words come in breathless bursts. "And the FBI.

Tell them to come to the Copper Point home in Santuario. I think Serena is in danger. Go now. Run." She spins and grabs Hollister's arm, already heading toward the door. "Let's go."

Chapter Eleven

Stilwell pulls up to the general store in Santuario, the same building they had chased the couple into just two days before. Standing in front of the store, next to the Coke machine, just as the Contact promised, is the girl.

"What are we doing here?" Jesse asks.

"We're picking up our trump card."

"That kid?"

"Yep."

"What good can she do us?" Jesse has a stupid look on his face.

"You'll see."

Stilwell steps from the car and approaches the girl. "Good morning, Serena." His voice is cheerful and happy. "We met a couple days ago at your house. Remember?"

The girl looks scared, clinging to the Coke machine as if it were some kind of surrogate parent. She nods cautiously. "Are you taking me to Mommy?"

"Yes, she's very close to here. I'm going to take you over there right now. Why don't we get into the car?"

"Why didn't Della take me?"

Della, hmm. Could that be the Contact's name? Useful information for another time, perhaps. "She had to hurry back. That's why she asked me to take you. Ready to go?"

Serena looks left then right, as if considering her options. "I'm scared." She starts to cry.

"We're going to your mama right now. Then everything will be better. Why don't we get into the car?"

"Okay," she says in a meek voice and moves toward the car.

He closes the door gently once Serena has climbed into the back. Let her sit by herself for now. No need to panic her before it's time. This is a first, thinks Stilwell. He's never had to take out a kid before, but if this is what it takes to finish out this project, then this is the way it will have to go. *Don't get soft,* Stilwell rebukes himself.

Still, once this project is complete, it will be a good time to head for Montevideo for awhile.

৵৩৵

Something has cut into him, but is it a wound or has it been surgery? Has he been offered a challenge or an opportunity? Josh's mind turns these questions over and over, as he stands quietly in the hallway, leaning against the wall and staring unfocused into the middle distance. These are analytical questions. But he has no answers. Or maybe he has received answers that elude words, that evade being nicely packaged into some tidy rational analysis which he has always demanded.

What kind of place is this? One thing for sure. In all his life he's never encountered people like Hollister, Bud and Esther. People who could penetrate through all his facades, crack open all his defenses, shatter all his arguments of self-justification. People who seemed to genuinely care about him. He scans the long hallway before him. The stained, worn carpet. The stark concrete walls, the garish light from the poorly maintained fluorescent fixtures. But it is down these shabby hallways that he has encountered something like ... what? Could it be that it seems like home?

What does he do now? He runs his hand through his hair, takes a deep breath, then heads back to the room to call Hal.

"Gullickson," a bored monotone voice says.

Hal's voice jolts Josh back into a reality that seems a hundred years away. A place that is familiar yet now strangely alien. He almost hangs up. But doesn't. "Hal? It's Josh."

Hal seems to come to life. "Hey Bro, where are you? Sleeping off a binge?"

"No, nothing like that—"

Hal cuts in, talking fast. "Hey everybody's wondering why you didn't make it into work this morning. And the division leader himself was down looking for you. Talking to everyone about your great seminar last week. Don't get the bossman all juiced up like that every day. "

Josh doubts that any of this is true, but it doesn't matter. "Hal, can you come pick me up?"

"Sure, but where's your wheels? Or did you lose them in a poker game?"

Josh ignores the question. "Look, I'm in Santuario. You know where that is?"

Silence for a moment. "Santuario? Isn't that a ghost town?"

"Not quite. I'm at the Copper Point Senior Living Center. It's easy to find—"

"Hold on, stud. You're saying you're at an old folk's home in a ghost town and you don't have your car? Just a second, let me check the caller ID. I thought this was Josh Waverly I was talking to. Must be some other Josh … what have you gotten yourself into?"

"A bit of a problem, yes. But I'm ready to come home. One more thing. When you come, can you pull up in the back? We'll have to be careful getting me into the car unseen. And, Hal, if you see a gray sedan in the area, just keep going. Under no conditions talk with the men in that car—"

"You're creeping me out now, Bro. What's going on?"

"I'll tell you everything when I see you."

"I'll be there. Is it okay if I get up there after lunch?"

"That's fine. I'm not going anywhere." He looks down at Evangelina's nightgown on the pillow and has to choke back a sob. "I'll be watching for you."

"Q. E. D., Bro, just don't go practicing your moves on any of those old cougars, got it?"

Hal's attempts at mirth stir no response from Josh. He returns the receiver to its cradle and sits on the bed, his hand resting on the nightgown. "Evangelina," he says out loud, as his fingers gently trace across the soft cotton.

He closes his eyes and tries to picture her face, recall her scent, the taste of her lips. In his mind, he tries to hear her voice, replay snippets of conversations, relive the moments of these past few days that made him feel so alive. And he wonders if he'll ever see her again.

Then he looks up and there she is, standing in the doorway. He leaps to his feet. "Evangelina," he gasps.

She runs to him and throws her arms around him. Immediately she's sobbing.

"Evangelina, what is it?" He holds her at arm's length and looks into her face. It's filled with what can only be described as sheer terror.

"I think they've got Serena," she blurts out. Josh's mouth falls open, as she continues. "I'm sure they're headed here."

Just then, Olive appears in the doorway. She's smiling. "I have some good news. Your little girl is here to see you."

"Where is she?" Evangelina is bolting for the door.

"Out in the lobby—"

Evangelina's already halfway down the hall before she can finish her sentence.

"… with a nice man."

Stilwell stands by the reception desk with Serena. He wears grey wool slacks and the black Ferragamo loafers. A navy Versace blazer with gold buttons hangs open over a white dress shirt. He had checked his appearance in the gas station john before picking up the girl. Even though he's been stuck in this God-forsaken dump of a town for too long, he looks good. Cool and relaxed. He always tries to look good when closing out a project. A matter of professional pride.

He has one hand firmly on the girl's shoulder, the other hand lightly cradling the Glock 22 in his jacket pocket. The sleek polycarbonate feel of the barrel against his palm is soothing. The 15-round magazine is full, and Stilwell has considered that he may need all fifteen rounds to shoot his way out of this situation. That doesn't even count the fifteen rounds that Smith has. Plenty of firepower.

Jesse Smith waits just outside the glass doors, ready to move when the moment arrives. Everything is working perfectly. The ditzy receptionist fell for it and without asking questions went in search of the couple. And the place is deserted for the most part. No sign of the brassy old dame or the black version of the Incredible Hulk he ran into the other day. But he's ready for them if they do appear. Just one feeble old man hanging out around the fireplace. Looks senile. If the receptionist does indeed fetch the couple -- and the little girl as bait should be irresistible -- then the operation should go swiftly. Stilwell, always feeling pumped and at the top of his game at such moments, whistles a cheerful tune as he waits.

Moments later Evangelina Gomez appears in the opening to the hallway. She stops abruptly when she sees him, but then she looks at the kid and keeps coming. "Serena, oh my God, Serena," she gasps.

"Mommy," Serena cries and tries to run to her mother, but Stilwell's strong hand on her shoulder holds her back.

Now it's time for Jesse to make his move. He quickly shoulders the glass doors open and before Evangelina evens notices his presence, he has his hands on her, while Stilwell tightens his grip on the child. Jesse is strong and brutal, and he clasps her so hard that she cannot move her arms. She begins to scream, but a rough hand quickly clamps down over her mouth.

Stilwell calmly turns toward Evangelina. "So, Miss Gomez, it's nice to see you again. You know that was a pretty rude way you treated me the other day back in that parking lot." He smiles. "I must say that I was offended by your behavior. And now that we're together again, I hope I'll be able to hear your apology."

Evangelina twists under the vice-like clutch of Smith. She grunts into the hand clamped over her mouth, her eyes blazing with hatred and fear.

"But of course," says Stilwell, "I didn't expect you to say anything. You're just a very impolite young lady, one who needs to be taught a lesson. And my friend Jesse here and I, we're gonna teach you a lesson. Oh are we ever." He laughs. "You and Mr. Waverly. I do hope he's on his way. He won't want to miss this. And Serena. You need to know, Miss Gomez, that your bad behavior is going to cost your daughter. Yep, it's a crying shame, but she's going to get hurt real bad in all this. Just thought you'd want to know that."

Evangelina twists again, thrashing helplessly against the strong arms of Jesse, who growls a deep gurgly laugh. Serena has started to cry.

"Well, here you are," Stilwell says happily as Waverly appears at the opening to the hallway. His eyes are wide and his mouth is agape, and there is a look of terror washed across his face. He stops abruptly in his tracks, then quickly retreats back into the hallway.

Stilwell lets out a big laugh. "So, Miss Gomez, it looks like your boyfriend is a cringing wimp, after all. He's probably back there calling his mommy. No big surprise, I'd say."

☙ ❧

The man's breath is like a sewer. His jaw, like gritty sandpaper, scrapes rough against the side of her face. His low chuckle is like the hungry growl of a predator. His filthy body is arched obscenely against her back, his arm constricting her waist so hard that her ribs ache and she cannot breathe. But Evangelina is only dimly aware of these things as she watches Stilwell Ferguson holding tight to the hand of her crying daughter. "Oh God," she cries out in her heart, "Please help Serena. Please help, please help." Over and over again she silently wails this prayer, while her body writhes and thrashes ineffectively in her captor's grip.

Somehow Esther's words pour into her mind. *Evangelina, you are good news.* But she rejects the words, as she senses impending horror, horror for her innocent daughter brought on somehow by her failed life. *Evangelina, you are good news.*

When Josh had appeared at the opening to the hallway, this only added to her terror, bringing in a instant another cascade of contradictory thoughts flashing chaotically through her panicked brain. His face was ashen. Then he ducked back into the hallway. Was he running away? *Josh help us*, she wants to cry. But another part of her realizes that he should not subject himself to this horror. *Run, Josh, this is not your fight.* This is not his responsibility. Yet, *Josh, help us* are the words trying to escape her mouth.

≈≈≈

Josh stands in the hallway, just feet away from the opening into the lobby, where the killers hold Evangelina and her daughter. His back is pressed against the wall and he is beginning to hyperventilate. His head spins and he thinks he might faint. He glances at the opening where almost certain death awaits. He had seen them for only a moment, but he had seen enough. They are not here to talk.

He considers his options. He can confront them, but what good would it do? His eyes scan the hallway for some kind of weapon. He spots a fire extinguisher mounted on the wall, but that would be almost useless. They are almost certainly armed, and he would just be one more casualty. No, his best bet is to go back to their room, call the police. Hadn't he been the one who wanted to do this from the beginning? He had been right, after all. After calling the police, he would make sure the residents stay away from the lobby, where they could be harmed. This would be the smart thing to do, an almost heroic thing to do. But he recognizes these ideas for what they are, the justifications produced by fear. What he really wants to do is race out the back door and keep running, run until he drops, far from here, far from this mess he never volunteered to be a part of. These people are strangers, after all. Evangelina's already made that much clear. God, he's been such a fool. He let his emotions rule his better judgment, and now look where he is.

He glances toward the entrance to the lobby again. He can even hear Ferguson's laughter from here. Gasping hard, he turns toward the rear of the building and begins to run. Bursting into the room, he lunges toward the phone. But then he sees her nightgown. Soft. Fragrant. Like her.

≈≈

"I love you, Serena. Don't be afraid." This is what Evangelina longs to say to her child, to cry it out loud, but she is prevented from speaking by the man's coarse hand clamped over her face. She thinks these words, over and over, praying that somehow Serena might hear her, might know of her mother's love, even if it has led her to this awful place. Her writhing is in vain, her struggle against this gross assailant is in vain. But she does not surrender, she does not let up in her desperate attempt to break free.

"Do you want me to go get him?" the man asks Ferguson, after Josh has disappeared back into the hallway.

"Not yet, Jesse. Take her out, then go fetch lover boy."

"Oh yeah," cackles the man with obvious joy. "So lady, excuse me while I break your little neck. Gonna break it like a chicken's." He makes a low 'cluck, cluck" sound as he laughs. She feels his gut, pressed against her back, shake with laughter. Then his right arm comes up and across her face, drowning her in his foul body odor, and blocking out her sight as he prepares to end her life.

But in the instant before her sight is extinguished, she is certain that she has seen Josh reappear in the opening to the hall.

At Ferguson's command, the man drops his arm. "Let's keep her around for a few more minutes," Ferguson says, "now that the conquering hero has returned." Then he laughs. "Ah, Mr. Waverly, you almost missed all the fun. Now we have the whole family together. Isn't that wonderful. Kinda makes me warm all over."

Josh stands quiet in the opening to the hallway, says nothing. He averts Ferguson's eyes and looks straight at Evangelina, just for a fraction of a second. It's a look that's hard to read. But it speaks to her of solidarity, of determination, of loyalty. Even in her desperate state she is lifted by his eyes.

"Now Mr. Waverly, here's what we're going to do. I need you to just walk slowly over here near me. We need to talk. If you're a good boy, nobody's going to get hurt. We just need a little information from you."

Josh doesn't move.

"I think you'd better come right now, Mr. Waverly. You're trying my patience, and if I lose my patience I just tend to lash out and hurt somebody. It would probably be this pretty little girl. And it would be all your fault."

Evangelina watches Josh step slowly toward Ferguson, limping. Evangelina sees Ferguson's hand slip deeper into his pocket. Then suddenly, Josh tucks his head down and charges Ferguson. His speed is amazing. Ferguson pulls out a large handgun, pointing it directly at Josh. As Ferguson steps backward, Josh suddenly sweeps low, pulling Serena from Ferguson's grasp.

The gun fires, and Josh is bolted backward, wounded, but his motion is stalled only for a moment. With Serena in tow he lunges toward the man who holds Evangelina. The man is now fishing for his weapon, which gives Evangelina the opportunity to plant a quick elbow into his gut. As the man grunts, Josh rips Evangelina away from him. His momentum carries Evangelina and Serena back into the corner of the lobby, behind the L-shaped receptionist's desk. It is the only place they can go, but there is no way out. Evangelina feels Josh pushing them both to the floor and covering them with his body.

"Don't let her see," he shouts to Evangelina. "Don't let her see." He is on top of them now, his back pressing them down, as he has turned to face the men. Evangelina clutches Serena beneath her. A warm taste is in her mouth now.

It is his blood.

❧❧

Stilwell and Jesse draw their guns and turn to finish them off. Behind the counter there is no escape. Like sitting ducks. *This will be fun.*

But out of the corner of his eye, Stilwell sees something that Jesse misses. The old man, who had been hanging out in the corner of the lobby, is now approaching Jesse.

"Behind you, Jesse," barks Stilwell, and Jesse spins.

The old man is coming at him carrying a poker from the fireplace set, almost stumbling. He wears a USMC cap, which prompts a derisive comment from Jesse. "Semper Fi, you pathetic old fart," he laughs, as he fires point blank into the man's chest.

Stilwell watches in amazement as the old man, gravely wounded, continues toward Jesse. Smith prepares to fire again, but not before the old man has buried the poker deep into Jesse's midsection. A loud grunt is expelled by Jesse, as he fires wildly toward the ceiling. The old man and Jesse fall together motionless onto the carpet, their blood pooling onto the floor.

Stilwell feels no remorse at Jesse's death, feels no fear. Smith was an idiot. Being taken down by an old geezer, probably wearing Depends, is somehow a poetic ending for the stupid Jesse Smith. Acknowledging aloud, with genuine awe, the bold charge of the old man, Stilwell laughs. "Semper Fi, indeed."

He turns back toward the three still huddled on the floor behind the counter. This is a moment to savor. The Glock feels comfortable in his hand, an old friend. Perhaps his only true friend. Waverly is covering the girl and the kid with his body. He is on his back facing Stilwell. There's something about the look in his eyes. What is it? Not quite the level of fear he was hoping for. He wonders for a moment if he could kill all three of them with one shot. Just an academic question, he muses. In actuality, he does not want this to go too quickly. It would be like rushing through a gourmet dinner. He needs to see more fear in Waverly's eyes than he sees. There'll be time for that.

In his peripheral vision, Stilwell picks up a motion. He spins toward the hallway to see a large dark figure coming at him. Fast. Quickly and with an assassin's precision he fires repeatedly into the big man's chest. But the man keeps coming, barely slowed by the deadly barrage of gunfire, his momentum carrying him into Stilwell, sending them both to the floor, the gun skittering across the carpet just out of Stilwell's reach. The huge body of the black man, now motionless, has him pinned.

Josh watches in horror as first Bud and then Hollister are gunned down. But instead of being paralyzed by this bloody violence, he is oddly mobilized. Their courage infuses him with determination. He is about to die, but it will be a death of dignity, it will be a courageous death.

When the gun slides from Stilwell's hand, as Hollister's body falls across him, Josh sees an opportunity and seizes it. He shifts away from Evangelina and Serena. "Run," he orders. "Run." Evangelina looks into his eyes. It is a look of awe. "Now. Don't stop."

She grabs her daughter's hand and jumps onto the receptionist's desk like a springbok. In a flash she hops off the other side, shoulders open the door and disappears, Serena easily keeping pace with her speedy mother.

Josh feels a surge of pure relief as he sees them flee. Whatever awaits him now, however this turns out, he has accomplished something truly important. Hollister and Bud have not died in vain. He will not die in vain. This may be his end, but now he sees clearly that he will no longer live as a coward. He may only have moments left, but they will be moments not cringing in fear. He rises to his feet, then looks at his shirt. Soaked with blood. He feels faint. He is going to pass out.

Stilwell Ferguson finally pushes the large mass of the black man's body away from him. On his hands and knees, he lunges for the Glock. He glances back at Waverly, motionless and bleeding on the floor behind him. The girl and the kid are gone. Then he notices the gathering crowd. Ten, maybe a dozen residents, many leaning on walkers, are glaring at him. "Go," screams one old woman. "Get out of here."

If there's one thing about Stilwell Ferguson, he's a shrewd realist. He knows when to press on, and he knows when to call it a day. Montevideo beckons. A fleeting image of the sun-soaked beach in front of the Hotel Corazon tantalizes him.

In a quick move, he grabs his gun and stands. Poised and even enjoying this moment of being center stage, he gracefully bows to the assembled gawkers. Then he runs out the door.

Immediately there is a problem. The Maxima is parked in by a large red semi. He shoots a quick look back at the building. The cops no doubt will be arriving soon. Time to get out.

A man is climbing down from the high cab of the truck, his back to Stilwell. Well isn't this working out nicely, he muses. The Glock, warm from use and comfortable in his hand, is pointed at the man's back.

જ⁹ે

Josh's head is still spinning. He rises on one arm, still woozy, to see Ferguson bolting out the door. It takes everything he's got to get to his feet, and then he needs to lean against the reception desk for balance. He cannot let himself pass out again. He looks around the lobby in horror. Bud, Hollister and the other killer lie motionless. He scans the room and sees Olive, amidst the gathered crowd. "Olive," he shouts, "Call 911 right now. And Lauren."

Olive, like a deer caught in the headlights, is frozen in place, but Josh's sharp command somehow activates her, and she heads for the phone.

Josh fights back sobs, as he steps around the still bodies of Bud and Hollister, but he must trust them to Olive. Ferguson is out there with Evangelina and Serena. He takes a deep breath and charges for the door. He cannot allow a gunshot to the chest or a bum leg slow him down now.

On the other side of the glass doors he sees Ferguson just ahead. He is aiming his gun at a man climbing down from a truck. With all the strength he can summon, Josh lunges toward Ferguson, airborne, arms outstretched, reaching for a leg. Just as the gun goes off.

Then all is black.

༄

Stilwell has gone down hard. Something from behind tripped him. But he comes up to his knees quickly, ready to shoot his way out of this dump. His field of vision is dominated by the bright red of the huge cab, but then his eyes focus closer. He sees the hard brown face of a man looking down at him. Then closer still the twin barrels of a shotgun, just inches from his face.

Chapter Twelve

The Denny's on St. Michael's fits right in with the strip malls, car dealerships and gas stations along this busy boulevard in the new section south of the Santa Fe plaza. It's bustling and loud. A steady din of clinking glasses and coffee cups, the white-noise blend of a dozen conversations, and the periodic ka-ching of the nearby cash register create a noisy ambiance that Eric Sandoval loves. And it's the perfect atmosphere to conduct business, certainly better than that depressing little rented space over on Cerrillos. People coming and going, waitresses bearing platters of burgers and carafes of coffee, and the general fast-paced flow of life assure anonymity.

They've all gone through their first cup of coffee, and Eric has just ordered a prime rib sandwich, which is a special today. Loaded with fat and cholesterol, it will likely cancel out the effects of a week's worth of the statins he takes faithfully and the two mile walk he took this morning. Agent Carol Shepherd gets a small dinner salad, asking the waiter to hold the croutons, which creates a brief pang of guilt in Eric.

The past few hours have been intense and productive. They arrived at the scene after the state police had hauled Ferguson away and the ambulances had removed the carnage. But they had been able to interview the ditzy receptionist, who, though borderline hysterical even an hour after the incident, filled them in on what had happened. They had interviewed a friend of Waverly's, who arrived after the incident and had little useful information to add other than providing a little background information on Waverly. And, later in the afternoon, they had arrested and interrogated Della Wright.

Across from them in the small booth sits Evangelina Gomez. She's ordered nothing, said she isn't hungry. She looks exhausted. They got the core pieces of information from her up at Santuario, but she had been too traumatized for much of a discussion. Now, four hours later, they are hoping for a more relaxed conversation.

The preliminary chit chat is over. In fact there's been very little preliminary chit chat at all. Eric leans forward and says, "Miss Gomez, thanks for coming over this afternoon. I know you're busy and need to get back, but we just wanted to follow up with you a bit. We covered most of the bases with you up in Santuario. But that was a crazy time. I don't know how you went through all that. You're a very brave woman."

"I don't feel very brave." She looks down at the water glass the waitress has left in front of her and encircles it with both hands, like she is cradling a wounded bird. "In fact, I don't know what to feel right now at all." She swallows hard and looks like she may be about to cry.

"Your daughter is safe," says Carol Shepherd in a soothing voice. "That's the main thing right now. How is she doing?"

"She's doing okay. She's with my parents while I'm here. She's an amazing girl."

"Look, Miss Gomez, I know there has been such tragedy." He sighs. "Mr. Ewing, Mr. Williams, and Mr. Waverly." He pauses and shakes his head slowly, as if absorbing the impact of bad news. "What they did was truly heroic. They saved you and your daughter. And they brought down a crime ring that has hurt a lot of people."

Evangelina shakes her head, clearly unable to talk about them right now. She has pasted on a brave look, even though her eyes are filled with tears. She asks, "What happened to Della?"

"Della Wright was arrested just a couple of hours ago. She spilled the beans on the whole operation. She was the main contact for one big industrial muckity muck who was paying a lot of money to secure proprietary information from the Lab's industrial partnerships. And I'm pleased to say he is being taken into custody as we speak."

"Why would she do such a thing?"

"Who knows? She's an odd one. When we interrogated her, she was in complete denial that she'd done anything wrong, even after what she did to your daughter. She's had at least two employees killed, as best we can tell, and, of course …" His voice trails off. "… Now there are more." He's silent for a moment and takes a sip of coffee. "It's hard to figure. She's full of anger about what she perceives as the old boys network at the Lab. Seems to think she was somehow evening things out. Actually sees herself as the real victim. The psych folks are going to have a field day with her."

"So who were those men and why were they after me?" Her voice is steady but lifeless. Still in shock, no doubt.

"Ferguson and Smith. A couple of bad hombres. They'd killed those two other Lab employees, under Della's Wright's instructions I might add, this guy Wessel, who we found last week, and we're sure they murdered a man named Tucker a few years ago, also from your department. We think they went after you because Wessel had set you up to deflect attention from himself. Apparently he thought a Lab audit was closing in on him, so he planted some incriminating evidence on you and fingered you to Ferguson."

"And about Ferguson," interjects Carol Shepherd, reaching over and placing a reassuring hand on Evangelina's arm. "You won't have to be worrying about him anymore. We've got enough to put him away for the rest of his life."

The waitress brings the food, which causes a silence at the table. After she refills the coffee cups and leaves, Evangelina asks, "Do you have any more questions of me?" Her voice shakes as she asks this.

"Not right now, Miss Gomez. In fact, we're sorry we've had to take your time. We know you were an innocent bystander in all this. So you're free to go, unless you have anything you want to ask us."

Evangelina is quiet for a moment, then says, "No, nothing." She rises from the booth to leave. "Thank you," she adds.

Sandoval and Shepherd watch Evangelina hurry out the door. "Darndest thing I've ever seen, if you ask me," mutters Sandoval as he considers his sandwich.

"Yeah," says Shepherd. "A bunch of amateurs taking down a gang of murderous criminals. Folks like that just might put you and me out of business."

"Ain't that the truth," says Eric, shaking his head before he takes a big bite. "Still, I feel bad for that Gomez girl. What she's had to go through. And her little girl, too."

❧

Evangelina is grateful the meeting is over. She needs to get back to St. Vincent's and she needs to see Serena.

She hurries to the Tundra that Lauren has loaned her, but something causes her to pause. It is the image of Josh's face, as he looked at her in that moment before he lunged at Ferguson, before he took that bullet for her. What was it in his face at that moment? Loyalty and determination, for sure. But there was more. There was a look of courage that she has rarely seen, a courage that had not replaced fear, but instead had prevailed in spite of fear. It was the look of sacrifice. The look on Josh's face and the action it foretold cannot be forgotten. It was a look that demands a response.

She stands motionless, her fingers resting on the door handle. Then she looks back toward the coffee shop, bites her lip and leans her head against the side of the car, struggling with the next step she is contemplating. She looks around at the parking lot, the traffic out on St. Michael's, the hospital across the street, with the high Sangre de Cristo Mountains towering behind it. It's as if a new clarity has been given to her. She walks, almost runs, back into the coffee shop, where agents Sandoval and Shepherd still sit at the booth.

"Mr. Sandoval?" Sandoval and Shepherd look up, apparently surprised to see her.

"Yes, Miss Gomez? You think of something else?"

"As a matter of fact …" She pauses, then says, "Maybe this isn't a good time."

"Why don't you sit down, Miss Gomez, and we can talk."

"No, I've really got to be going. I mean, I have to be at …" She pauses again. Then she slides back into the booth. "I need to tell you about me."

Sandoval nods, as he finishes chewing a French fry. "What do you want to tell us?"

"Everything." Evangelina takes a deep breath, feels a resolve she has never felt before. A certainty. "I'm in this country illegally." This is how she begins. For the next half hour she tells them her whole story, as they give her their full attention.

Finally she is quiet. She trembles, feeling alternating waves of relief and dread sweep across her. *Oh God, maybe this was a huge mistake.* She studies Sandoval's face, searching for a clue. It is a kind face, a wise face. This is probably why she has picked him, picked now, to make her confession. But Sandoval shows little emotion, nothing she can read.

"That's it?" asks Sandoval. He doesn't sound especially excited about her story.

"Yes." She can barely breathe.

"So why are you telling us? We don't handle immigration issues. That would be Homeland Security."

"I have to tell somebody. I'm tired of holding it all in. I refuse to live my life with secrets any longer." She sees Josh's face in those fateful moments when he confronted Ferguson, as her words gush out, and she realizes that what she is doing is for Serena as much as for herself. It doesn't matter what Sandoval says or what he does now. She has done the right thing.

"Well, I'm no expert on these kinds of situations, Miss Gomez. As you know, the politics is changing daily."

Evangelina is quiet for a moment, then says, "What do you think will happen?"

Sandoval looks over at Agent Shepherd, who says nothing but nods supportively. He looks back at Evangelina, scratches his chin, then says, "So, here's my take. You've got some things in your favor. You were brought into the country by someone else, so you didn't commit a crime. And you helped bring down some serious criminals. And you turned yourself in." He pauses, then adds, "But you got those phony papers for your job at the Lab. I'm thinking that may be a felony. So I'm guessing, and I hate to say this, but this will likely mean deportation for you, you know. And just where they would send you, since no one knows where you came from, well that's anybody's guess."

Evangelina is suddenly concerned that she might be arrested on the spot, and for a moment considers bolting for the door. She even slides her feet toward the aisle, readying herself for an escape if needed. But now there's a softness in Sandoval's eyes, and she decides that she has no choice but to trust him. "I know that. I'm willing to take my chances. As long as Serena and I can stay together, it doesn't matter. I need to set an example for her."

Eric Sandoval is quiet for a few moments, apparently thinking this through. He runs a hand through his thinning grey hair and takes another sip of coffee. "Evangelina Gomez, you are quite a woman, I must say." He pauses and looks over at Agent Shepherd again, who is smiling. "Tell you what. Let me chew on this for awhile. I know a few people over at DHS. Okay?"

Evangelina nods.

"I can't promise you anything, you must understand. You'll probably be deported. And you'll undoubtedly have to testify against that outfit that got you the phony ID."

"I understand." She wants to thank him, but he hasn't really done anything for her. But she knows that's not true. What he has done is patiently listen, while she has cast a lifetime of burdens from her shoulders.

❧❧

A chill. Shaking uncontrollably with a chill. It's so cold. Bright garish lights. White figures move around like silent phantoms. Like ghosts. Words are said, but they sound slurred, make no sense.

Time passes. He is now able to mouth some words, "I'm so cold." He feels himself shiver, his teeth chattering.

A woman in white, leaning near him, speaks. "I'm putting another blanket on you right now. You're just coming out of general anesthesia. That chill will go away pretty soon."

"Where am I?"

"You're in St. Vincent's Hospital in Santa Fe. You've just come through surgery."

"Surgery?"

"You had a pretty nasty gunshot wound, Josh. In case you don't remember."

The woman's features, at first blurry, begin to sharpen. It's Lauren. "Did you operate on me?"

"No. Doctor Romero took care of that. I assisted. It was the least I could do after hauling you down here."

"The others. What about the others?" Josh wants to rise from the bed, but he is unable to move. His body feels like it's pinned under a ton of concrete. "Is Evangelina okay?"

"Well, why don't you ask her?" She slides over a bit, and suddenly he sees Evangelina's face, filled with tears.

"Thank God, you're going to be okay," she gasps.

He can't speak. Just seeing her face is all he can handle for now.

❧

He would seem to be out of options. That's what they probably think, the two laughing cops in the front seat. His hands are cuffed behind his back, the heavy steel rings, with unbreakable locks, biting into his wrists. He slumps motionless in the narrow seat behind the thick glass that separates him from them. A small opening covered with a dense metal grating allows them to speak to him. It's like a cage, a small foretaste of the prison life that awaits him.

But Stilwell Ferguson is not out of options. He has not gotten to this point in life without learning a few tricks. Tricks that will be implemented. Soon.

He's not sure where these two state troopers are taking him, but it will likely be a local jail, where he'll await transfer to a larger and more secure facility. He knows that it will be necessary to act soon. The longer he waits before making his move, the more difficult it will be. One thing for sure. He won't go to prison again.

He thinks through his strategy. Fortunately his ankles are not cuffed, but that will likely change as soon as he is prepared for transfer. That would make his escape much harder. Another reason to act soon. The first thing to do is break free of the cuffs. And there's only one way he knows to do this. It's a technique he learned long ago back in Chicago. Not a Houdini trick. You can't pull those off with modern police cuffs. And he won't be able to pick the locks, not from the back of the car, and especially with his hands behind his back. But there is a way.

He runs the fingers of his right hand over the large carpal trapezium bone of his left hand, the protruding bone just below the thumb, the bone that prevents the cuff from sliding off. Though his face shows no expression, he smiles inwardly as he prepares for the action. It must be swift and powerful. The pain will be overpowering, so he must make it brief. He may pass out, but he will survive. And most importantly, his hands will be free. Free to take advantage of the first opportunity he gets, most likely as soon as he is removed from the back seat.

He expects to be free in the next hour. His present passivity should lull the two cops into just enough complacency. The trendy blazer and the Ferragamos will likely project the image of a gentleman criminal, more of the white collar type of crook. Not the kind of lethal danger he really is.

After his escape, his plans are clear. He is now free from the Contact, free from Jesse. He is completely on his own again, just the way he prefers. He has connections that will make his escape to Montevideo quick and sure. That's where he will go.

But he has unfinished business here, a score to settle. This is no longer a professional action. That part is over. This will be an action of fury and revenge, fast and bloody. And it will provide many moments of pleasant reflection, when he is languishing on the warm South American beaches this winter.

But first things first. The thumb of his right hand finds the base of the carpal trapezium, caresses it gently for a moment, then presses violently inward with crushing force.

❧

Over the next several hours, Josh mostly sleeps, working his way back from the general anesthesia. A few times he awakes for brief moments, groggy and incoherent, then drifts back into sleep. He'd been in ICU for several hours, until he had stabilized enough for the surgery. But now he's been in a regular room since coming out of recovery.

Evangelina paces the small room. Every few moments she stops at the bedside to check on him. Each time she studies him intently. He lies unconscious, his mouth slightly open, breathing gently. A transparent nasal oxygen mask connected by soft plastic tubes is held in place by a thin cord draped around his ears. When his slight movements cause the mask to fall away from his nostrils, Evangelina readjusts it.

His sandy hair is tousled. His faded hospital gown is open at the neck, and she gently touches the light hair of his chest, just above the edge of the heavy bandages that cover the surgical area.

Next to Josh's bed is a pole holding several bags for his IV and a rack with beeping monitors and electronic devices. The bed is surrounded by a plastic curtain hung from a metal ceiling rail. Another bed is unoccupied on the other side of the curtain. A small TV hangs from the wall and stares down toward Josh like a surveillance camera.

The walls are a drab blue, but the late afternoon Santa Fe sun casts long golden streaks into the room, offsetting the sterile glare of the room's fluorescent lights, and Evangelina is grateful for this light, which helps cheer up the room, as well as her spirits. She's alternating between the hospital room and the waiting room around the corner, where Serena waits with Esteban, Grace and Uncle Rey.

In the room with Evangelina are Lauren, who has been a big help, and a friend of Josh's named Hal. Lauren has been busy checking the IV and the electronic devices, consulting with the nurses and reassuring Evangelina. She's here both as a professional and a friend. Hal sits in the corner, busily turning pages through a stack of magazines he has brought in from the waiting room.

Josh stirs.

"I think he's coming around," Lauren says, and Evangelina and Hal quickly gather at his bedside.

"Well, stud, it's about time you woke up." Hal, with his thick glasses and sweaty forehead, is leaning close in to Josh. Josh looks confused, scans the room to see who else is there.

Lauren gently tugs at Hal's sleeve. "Why don't you and I get a cup of coffee and let these two talk?"

Hal, clueless, nods with a big grin and follows Lauren to the door.

Evangelina silently forms the words "Thank you" to Lauren as they leave.

"How are you feeling?" Her voice is soft.

"I feel okay. I had surgery?"

"Yes. The gunshot ..." She shudders, takes a deep breath then continues. "The gunshot just barely missed your heart and lungs. But it required surgery. You lost quite a lot of blood." She pauses again, swallows hard. "But you're going to be okay. I'm so glad you're awake."

"And are you okay? Is your daughter okay?"

"Yes. Yes. We're okay. Josh, you saved our lives. And you saved Uncle Rey's life. I don't know what to say. You were amazing."

"And Hollister? And Bud?"

Evangelina looks down, shaking her head slowly. She doesn't want to talk about this now. "Bud is dead … and Hollister …" She's not sure she can get the words out. As long as she doesn't have to say the words, somehow the realities of the past twenty-four hours can be kept at a safe distance, in a manageable place where she can cope with the present. She bites her lip, and her chest heaves as she suppresses a sob.

Before she has to say more, Josh has drifted back into sleep. She holds his hand for a long time.

It's another hour before Josh stirs again. This time he awakens with a convulsive shake, like he's had a nightmare. His eyes have a panicked look as they scan the room.

"I'm right here, Josh."

His breaths are gasps for a few moments, then he quiets down and says, "The last thing I remember …" He is silent for a moment. "The last thing I remember is I was lunging through the air. My feet were off the ground."

"That's when you stopped Ferguson. Kept him from shooting Uncle Rey." She keeps her hands on his arm, reassuring.

"I feel like my feet are still off the ground."

"That's okay. You'll feel like your feet are back on the ground soon enough."

"I'm not sure."

"Not sure of what?"

"When I was in the air. It must have been just a second. But for that second I felt something. I felt out of control. I felt like I was going on pure instinct. And it was a good instinct. There was a knowledge that maybe I was going to die. But it was okay, because in that moment I felt free. I'm sure this doesn't make any sense at all." He's rapidly blurting out his words, and Evangelina is nodding as he talks. "So what I'm not sure of is, I'm not sure I want my feet to ever be back on the ground again."

Evangelina smiles and brushes his hair with her hand. She's not sure her feet are on the ground either.

♂♀

Eric Sandoval made it back to Albuquerque early enough on Monday night to watch *Dancing with the Stars* with Sally. She had a meatloaf ready for him, and they enjoyed it in front of the TV. Now, during the last commercial break of the show, Eric mutes the TV and turns to his wife. "I must say, I'm really glad to see you tonight. How about you and I do our own little dance after the show?"

She glows. "Eric dear, you are one romantic—" The telephone rings. Without missing a beat, she adds, "If that's work, I think I'm going to strangle somebody."

"Well, you can put those lovely arms around my neck any time you want," he teases, while reaching for the phone.

It's Erica Wang. Eric lets out a sigh, while averting the glare of his wife. "Geez, Erica, don't you ever sleep?"

Sally groans in the background, then loud enough that the Special Agent in Charge can probably hear her, she says,

"Tell her that just because she's your boss, doesn't mean she has a leash on you twenty-four-seven."

If Erica's heard the background words, she ignores them and says, unfazed, "So we have a little problem."

Eric nods at his wife and blows her a kiss. "What's up, chief?"

"Your buddy Ferguson has escaped."

"What? What happened?"

"State cops were taking him down to the Española jail—"

"What? That's just a podunk jail, isn't it?"

"Guess they wanted to secure him better before transporting him into Santa Fe, but yeah, good question. But that doesn't really matter. They had him cuffed behind the back in a cruiser. Somehow he got free from the cuffs. When they stopped, Ferguson jumped them. Element of surprise situation, I guess. They're still interrogating the officers about it. Anyway, he's on the loose."

Eric stands and paces, upset. "Were the cops hurt?"

"They're okay, just banged up a bit. He hit them hard and ran. Just disappeared down the street."

"How long ago?"

"Report says three twenty, so about five hours ago."

"Broad daylight. And he's on foot? Surely he couldn't have gotten very far away."

"They've been looking, but so far no luck."

"Any idea where he may be headed?"

"Could be anywhere. From what we've learned about him so far, our friend Ferguson has quite a resume. He's well connected. Mob ties back in Chicago at one time. He's probably already on a plane out of the country."

"Are the police sending anyone over to the hospital?"

"They're convinced that's the last place he'll go, especially now that his network's been busted. But they've got a cop in the lobby tonight, and one outside the room, just in case anybody suspicious wanders in."

"That doesn't sound like enough security." Eric pictures a hundred movie scenes where the killer makes it in past the sleepy cop outside the door. "I don't feel good about this."

"I don't either, but we don't tell state police what to do." Erica Wang says no more, apparently waiting for Eric to suggest the next move.

"Okay," he sighs, "I'll call Carol. We'll go up and take a look around."

He replaces the receiver and turns toward his wife, bracing himself for her words. But all she says is, "Poor Eric, you are such a good man."

❧❧

Evangelina stays with Josh until nine, but he doesn't wake up again. Lauren and Hal left a couple of hours ago. She'll come back to see him tomorrow, but she's already kept her daughter waiting long enough. As she leaves the room, she is startled by a man standing quietly next to the door.

"Oh my Lord," she gasps, "I didn't see you." It's a policeman.

"I'm sorry to frighten you, ma'am. Officer Jerry Wade, State Police. I'm gonna be outside the room tonight—"

"Is something wrong?" She's still shaking.

"Just a routine precaution in a case like this. Nothing to worry about. Have a good evening."

She finds her family in the waiting room, the only people still there at this hour. Serena is watching a cartoon on the TV, something she never gets to do at home. When she sees her mother, she jumps up and runs to her. "Mommy," she yelps with joy. The events of the day do not seem to have fazed her, but Evangelina worries that the full impact of her experience may still lie ahead. She's also concerned that the full impact of this awful day has yet to be felt by herself.

But as they make their way out to the Tundra, Evangelina is aware of a gratitude that overwhelms her exhaustion. Josh is alive. She's back with Serena and her family. And she's aware of a new lightness, following her confession to Agent Sandoval this afternoon.

Her thoughts are interrupted by a shadow darting behind the cars in the next row. She stops and looks hard in that direction, her heart suddenly in her throat. But there is nothing. Her mother gently tugs on her sleeve. "You okay, dear?"

Evangelina sighs. "Yes, I'm fine, Mama. Just jumpy, that's all. Let's go home."

Suddenly, a man appears from behind a car, approaching her, quickly. Evangelina gasps, then pushes her family towards the Tundra.

"Don't be afraid, Miss Gomez, it's Agent Sandoval."

"Gee, you really scared me." She then sees Agent Shepherd appear next to him.

"I'm sorry. But I need to speak with you. Can I have a moment?"

Evangelina hands the car keys to her mother. "Can you wait for me in the car?" She suspects he wants to talk to her about her confession this afternoon, which she hasn't informed her family about yet.

"I'm sorry to bother you tonight, especially after this day, Miss Gomez. But I'm afraid I've got some unsettling news."

"What?"

"Stilwell Ferguson has escaped, and we—"

"Oh, God." Evangelina extends a hand to steady herself against a car. "So that's why there's a policeman outside the hospital room."

"They didn't tell you?"

"The officer said it was just a routine precaution."

"Probably not wanting to unduly alarm you. In fact, there's no indication he's around here. We're pretty certain he's headed out of the country. But I wanted you to know. Just keep your eyes open. Where are you staying?"

"We're at the Super 8 down the street for a couple nights, until Josh is better."

"I'll make sure the police are watching that place too, but I'm sure they've already got that covered. Like I said, I don't think there's anything to worry about, but we're just trying to be careful." He hands her a card. "Look, if you need anything at all, please call me."

Evangelina nods as she backs toward the Tundra. *Nothing to worry about, huh? So, why then are two FBI agents out here in this parking lot in the middle of the night?*

⋞⋟

State Trooper Jerry Wade still sits by the door to Josh's room, absorbed in a Kindle, when Evangelina arrives the next morning. "Everything okay?" she asks, apprehensive.

"It's been quiet, Miss Gomez, just the way we like it."

Inside the room she finds that the nurse has Josh up and out of bed, sitting in the chair in the corner. "Am I glad to see you up and about!" she beams.

"I'm still pretty wobbly. Couldn't have made it into this chair without the nurse."

"No problem. The marathon isn't scheduled until later this afternoon. You'll be ready by then." She shoots him a cute smile, then pulls a chair over from the corner so she can sit next to him.

"Don't get me laughing," he says, "that's when it hurts."

Evangelina lays a hand on his wrist, just above the IV needle, and strokes him gently. "I'll try not to laugh, but seeing you better sure gives me a lot to smile about."

Later in the morning, Josh is able to take a short walk, with a nurse guiding him on one side, while Evangelina pushes the IV pole on the other side. They go only a few feet beyond the door before they return.

In the afternoon, Evangelina is allowed to take him out by herself, to walk him all the way to the end of the hall.

Josh wears a faded cotton robe over his hospital gown and throw-away cotton slippers. He ambles slowly down the hall, but his strength is returning quickly and everyone is pleased.

"I think I'm ready," he says to her.

"Let's check with the nurse. We'll probably need a wheelchair."

A few minutes later, Evangelina wheels Josh into the elevator and takes them down to the second floor, to ICU.

"Only family members are allowed," says a protective nurse at the reception desk in ICU. "Anyway, I can only allow one visitor at a time and there's already someone back there—"

"They're family," shouts a voice from a room across from the desk. "And we need them both now."

"Well, I guess you can go back for just a minute."

Evangelina wheels Josh into the small room, where Rosey stands beside Hollister. He lies still in the bed, several tubes running into his mouth. The steady 'whish, whish' sound of the ventilator vies with a dozen other electronic sounds of the large array of sensors and displays around the bed. A small bench has been pushed up to the end of the bed to accommodate the feet of Hollister's six-nine frame.

Evangelina gives Rosey a hug, but says nothing.

"It doesn't look good," says Rosey, barely holding it together. "I've been praying real hard. I don't know what I'll do if he's taken away from me." There are sagging dark shadows under her eyes.

"Oh, Rosey," Evangelina says, "has he been conscious at all?"

"No. They've got him in an induced coma right now, while the ventilator is in. They say his chances are better this way. He's had several transfusions, but they're not sure he can make it through today." Rosey's voice trembles as she says these words.

Josh wheels himself up closer and gently touches one of Hollister's large feet. "Hollister, it's Josh. I don't know if you can hear me, but I want you to know I'm rooting for you." He pauses, then adds while choking back a sob, "And I want you to know that I think you're just about the best person I've ever known."

Rosey places a hand on Josh's shoulder. "Thank you, Josh. I'm so grateful you're doing better. I've been praying for you, too."

Josh looks up at Rosey with watery eyes, but says nothing.

Evangelina says, "Rosey, I'll be praying for Hollister too." Then she falls apart. "I'm so sorry he had to get caught up in this. This is all my—"

"It's nothing of the sort," Rosey interrupts. "Don't you be talking that way. You never made Hollister do anything. What he did, he did on his own. He's a good and brave man, that's all."

Evangelina is quiet for a minute, then nods and whispers, "Good and brave. He is that."

She pushes the wheelchair back toward the elevator, but as they pass a small chapel outside the ICU, Josh says, "Can we go in there for a minute?"

The chapel is a small room, paneled in light wood, with two rows of pews, softly illuminated by the light coming in through stained glass windows and an electric candle atop a small altar.

Josh slides forward in his wheel chair, as if he wants to kneel, but he's unable to get out of the chair.

"I don't think you should get out of the chair, Josh."

He nods, then slides back into the chair and bows his head. Evangelina says nothing, but keeps her hand resting gently on his shoulder.

❧

Eric Sandoval sits with Carol Shepherd at the Denny's across from St. Michael's Hospital, in the same booth where they met with Evangelina Gomez, sipping his second cup of coffee and finishing off a Grand Slam, today's special of eggs, sausage and pancakes.

"So, maybe Ferguson has split the scene. What do you think, Carol?"

"Probably, but he could be lying low until the police protection is withdrawn."

"Which is today. He doesn't show for twenty-four hours and the cops conclude he's gone for good. Not sure I like that thinking."

"Yeah, but what else are they going to do? Just how long are they supposed to be spending taxpayers' money on a threat that probably doesn't exist?"

Eric shrugs, not wanting to get into a discussion about taxpayers' money. "So what are we going to do?"

"I don't see much that we can do here." She laughs, then says, "And anyway, if you eat too many more of these meals, I don't want to be the one who has to tell Sally about your coronary."

Eric feels a shiver of guilt about the Grand Slam, but doesn't show it. "Maybe you're right, about not being able to do any more here, but I'm thinking we may want to hang around for another day, just in case." His cell rings. It's Erica Wang.

"I think we've got ourselves a lead on Ferguson," she says.

"I'm all ears."

"A plane ticket was purchased for a Continental flight leaving tonight from Albuquerque, connecting in Houston, and then onto Rio de Janeiro."

"Surely Ferguson wouldn't use a credit card with his name on—"

"He didn't. It was a Visa card, in the name of Louis Wessel. Needless to say, we'll have a nice little greeting party there for him."

"Hmm." Eric ponders what to make of this.

"So you and Shepherd can get your tails back down here. The taxpayers aren't paying for you to shop for jewelry on the Santa Fe plaza."

Eric starts to respond to this second comment about the taxpayers' money, but Wang has hung up.

"So we're going home?" asks Shepherd.

Eric says nothing. He takes another sip of coffee and looks out at the traffic on St. Michael's Boulevard.

✑✑

The trip to see Hollister has taken a lot out of Josh, and once they are back in the room Evangelina helps him back into the bed.

"Evangelina."

"Yes?"

"I want you to know that I don't want to lose you again."

"I'm right here, silly."

"I mean ..." He pauses. "Remember what I said about my feet being off the ground, being out of control?"

"Yes."

"I am out of control. Out of control in love with you."

"Oh, Josh ..." She looks embarrassed.

"Cheesh, I shouldn't have said that. I'm sorry."

"You don't need to be sorry." She busies herself with pulling the blanket up around Josh's shoulders.

"I mean, this is so premature, I know. But I remember Bud telling me to not let any opportunities slip away. I've seen things slip away, and I don't want that to happen again."

"What opportunities are you talking about?"

"I mean about us. Look, I know this is fast, good grief, I'm about the last guy in the world anyone would ever accuse of going too fast. But, Evangelina, what you said about us being in parallel universes. I'm not sure that has to keep us—"

Evangelina interrupts. "Josh, I need to tell you something. I didn't want to tell you until you were feeling better. But, I told the FBI about my being an illegal—"

"That's okay, Evangelina. I'm proud of you for telling them. That doesn't change anything about how I—"

"But it means they'll probably deport me."

"I don't care. I'll go with you. Evangelina, I know I'm moving way too fast, but I need to know if someday you might learn to love me too."

"Oh, Josh," she gushes, laughing and blushing. "I think that's impossible—"

"I see," he says quickly. "Oh gee, now I feel a little embarrassed."

"Josh, will you listen to me, you silly man?"

He is quiet.

"I don't think it's possible that I might learn to love you." Her fingertips trail gently across his shoulder. She plants a soft kiss on his forehead. "Because, dear Josh, I already do."

❧

The dream begins as it always has. The sensation of being trapped in darkness. Suffocating. Then the screams, becoming louder and louder. But this time something different happens. A shaft of light appears in the darkness, and a hand reaches out toward her. It's Josh's hand, a hand of rescue. She stirs awake, not in panic, as in the past, but with a sense of safety. It takes a moment to realize where she is. She has fallen asleep in Josh's room, in the straight-back chair near the door. How long has she been out? Suddenly she realizes that the shaft of light is real, it slices across the dark room as the door opens. Startled,

Evangelina bolts upright, presses her back against the wall, holds her breath.

The nurse enters the room pushing a small wheeled cart. Evangelina exhales, and laughs. "You scared me," she says.

"Oh, I'm sorry, I was just trying to be quiet. We don't want to awaken folks. I just need to make a few tests, and I'll be out of here in a moment."

Evangelina settles back into the chair, with a sigh of relief, as the nurse tends to the sleeping Josh. She checks her watch. Eleven thirty. Her parents and Serena are back at the Super 8. She told them not to stay up late for her tonight, that she would be staying in the room for awhile with Josh.

She thinks about Bud, Hollister and Josh, and their courage in saving her. Never has she seen such a thing. Never has anyone done anything like this for her. And she relives, almost word for word, her conversation with Josh this afternoon. A warmth fills her, as she considers this man, lying just across the room from her. She sees him now in shadows, as the nurse gathers her data. What does the future hold for them? There are so many questions, so many barriers. But right now, none of these seem insurmountable. Maybe it's the late hour and her sleepy stupor, but for the first time in a long time none of the barriers in her life seem insurmountable at all.

She apparently has fallen back to sleep when she senses the door opening again. Again the shaft of light spreading across the floor. Must be the nurse again. She begins to nod off again, then realizes that this is different. Immediately a jolt of terror surges through her body as she realizes that it is not the nurse.

It is a man. It is Stilwell Ferguson.

She's frozen in her chair, not breathing, and apparently in the dark he has not seen her. Ferguson slowly makes his way toward the bed, and in disbelief, unable to breathe, Evangelina watches as the light from the hallway flashes off a long silvery blade, now raised above the bed.

Something happens inside her. A sudden change. A transformation. She is no longer afraid, but instead is now mobilized, focused. There is a sense of mission energizing every sinew, pumping adrenaline through her body, enhancing the flow of blood in her veins. Stilwell Ferguson represents death to her, the incarnation of everything evil. He cannot be allowed to harm her Josh again.

She scans the dark room for a weapon, a stick, a bar, a broom, anything she can use for her attack. There is nothing. Silently she rises to her feet. There is not a second to lose. With the stealth and quickness of a puma, she springs toward Ferguson. He begins to turn, but cannot make the rotation before Evangelina has leapt upon his back.

She holds on like she's riding a bucking bronco as he twists violently, thrashing, trying to throw her off. She does not know if he still holds the knife. Hopefully he has dropped it in the attack. She lets out a piercing scream, screeching into Ferguson's ear. "You will not hurt him! You will not hurt him! You will not hurt him!"

Josh has come awake and apparently is trying to sit up, but Evangelina has to focus on Ferguson. She has no plan beyond the immediate desperation to keep him away from Josh. Over and over she screams, a wild, primitive scream, a scream that releases the rage, the fear, and everything that has built up inside her in twenty-five years of life. Her hands are around his neck, squeezing with strength that surpasses what a small woman should be able to produce, her fingernails digging in like tiger claws. It is super-human strength that fights for Josh, for Serena, for Hollister, for Bud, for everyone who has ever suffered.

But Ferguson is too strong. He spins his way to the door, toward the light of the hallway, Evangelina still clinging to his back. He twists and thrashes until she has lost her grip on him. She is flung violently against one of the walls in the deserted hallway. Her body smashes hard against the wall, and it hurts. But, fighting through the pain, she quickly makes it back to her knees and is ready to stand, when she see it. Ferguson still has the knife. And now he holds it high, as he moves in on her.

"You poor fool. Prepare for your bloody death. And then, as you lie dying, think about me plunging this knife into your boyfriend, because that's just what I'm going to do. And, by the way, maybe after that I'll be stopping by the Super 8 down the street. There isn't anyone there you'd like me to pay a visit to, is there?" Ferguson lets out a laugh that seems to be one of pure pleasure.

"Oh, God, please help me," she pleads silently. On her knees she knows there is no way she can elude the deadly plunge of the knife. She screams again, but no help appears. *Where are the nurses?*

He's above her now, has her pinned against the wall with a strong foot, ready to plunge the knife home. "I'm going to be relishing this for a long time," he says in a steady, almost objective way.

It is then that Evangelina notices Ferguson's left hand, heavily bandaged. Writhing, she is able to free one arm, and get just enough of an angle to give the injured hand a hard thump. Ferguson recoils in obvious pain, and this might give Evangelina just the moment she needs to break free.

But Ferguson is too fast, and her escape is cut off by a leg that blocks her path. With a kick, Ferguson knocks her back to the floor, then quickly a foot pins her. He kneels down low and close to her, raising the knife for the kill, as Evangelina cries out, "Dios mio! Dios mio!"

She closes her eyes to accept the blade, just as a peel of thunder echoes in the hallway. The blade does not come.

Trembling, she opens her eyes to see his murderous face just inches from hers. She sees his eyes filled with hatred and the coldness of evil. But then Ferguson twists slightly, and the knife falls away harmlessly. Stilwell Ferguson tumbles toward the floor, then lies motionless, a pool of blood forming rapidly around his head. His eyes are open, looking cold and dead, not much different from how they looked when he was alive. Behind him, Agent Carol Shepherd crouches at the end of the hall in a shooting stance, her revolver still poised in firing position.

In moments Shepherd and Eric Sandoval, as well as several nurses, who have raced down the hall, are beside Evangelina.

They lift her to her feet, then hold her for several moments as she shudders, before taking her into the bedside, where Josh is still trying to lift himself from the bed. "It's over, Josh," she sobs. "Dear God, it's finally over."

❧

"How come you always figure stuff like that out?" They're back at Denny's, after getting Josh and Evangelina calmed down and turning the routine cleanup details over to the local cops.

"Well, Carol, you don't get to be an old guy like me unless you've figured out a few things." Eric Sandoval is sipping a decaf, having refused to look at the dessert menu, still smarting from Carol's coronary remarks this afternoon.

"I mean, that plane ticket to Rio. How come you didn't fall for that? How did you know it was a ruse?"

"I didn't know it was a ruse. But I figured a guy like Ferguson is too smart to make mistakes that others would easily catch. I could've been wrong about that, but it looks like this time I wasn't."

"I've still got a few things to learn, it looks like."

"Well, I must say, Carol, the way you took Ferguson down tonight was impressive. Not sure I could've pulled that off. You saved Miss Gomez's life, that's for sure."

Carol smiles. "So this time," she says, "can we really go home?"

Sandoval lays a twenty on top of the check and says, "I think that's a great idea."

Chapter Thirteen

Two months later

Josh doesn't know his way around Santa Fe very well, especially the side streets in the oldest parts of town. The roads are narrow and winding, many of them unpaved, and are lined with adobe compounds and coyote fences that give the old neighborhoods an aura of mystery. Night has fallen and a light dusting of snow has made everything white, and it would be difficult to even stay on the road if it weren't for the festive little lanterns, the farolitos, lit for the Christmas season and lining the edges of the streets. The small Prius is perfect for navigating these meandering lanes.

Evangelina fumbles with a city map, illuminated by the dim light in the visor, while Josh steers through the narrow streets. "I think we're getting close," she says. "Have we passed Delgado Street yet?"

"We just passed it."

"Okay, so turn right at the next intersection."

A few minutes later they pull into a narrow dirt driveway and park behind an old white Escort. "Yes, this is it," smiles Evangelina, relieved.

A red gravel path leads to a weathered wood door in a rough adobe wall. An opening in the door is filled with an irregular vertical array of small aspen branches. An old metal lantern illuminates the entrance. All part of the legendary Santa Fe charm.

Before they can knock, the door opens. Hollister grins and invites them in. "So you found it. Way to go. I know it isn't easy."

They follow Hollister, who moves smoothly and without a trace of any lingering effects from his wounds, through a small patio, past a gurgling fountain, to another door and into a small living room. The ceilings are high and lined with rough-hewn vigas, the floors are a coarse Mexican tile. A kiva fireplace in the corner is ablaze, providing welcomed heat on this chilly night. The room is sparsely furnished. They take their seat on a large worn sofa facing the fireplace. "Welcome to our home," Hollister says.

"This place is beautiful," says Evangelina.

"Well, I am just renting, but yeah, it's pretty nice digs."

"And it's also beautiful," adds Josh, "to see you up and about. You are amazing, Hollister."

"Guess it takes more than three bullets to bring down a big dude like me."

Just then Rosey comes in from the kitchen, carrying a platter of cheese quesadillas, cut up into bite sized strips. "Hey you guys, I hope you enjoy this," she laughs.

"Remember, I'm still learning how to cook this New Mexican food, I'm not a pro like you, Evangelina."

Evangelina helps Rosey with the platter, then gives her a hug. "Gee, it's good to see you, Rosey. You look great."

"Well, I feel great, too. It's awfully kind of this grandson of mine to take me in."

"Hey, you took me in when I needed a place, grandma," says Hollister. "And besides, I for one love your cooking." They all laugh.

Evangelina says, "Hollister, congratulations on your new job. It sounds really great."

"Yeah, it's funny how things work out. All the publicity after that day at Copper Point. Got a call out of the blue from *The New Mexican*, said they were looking for a communications guy to be sort of an official greeter for the city, write articles for people moving into town, attend public ceremonies and all that. They said a hero like me, can you imagine them thinking that, and with my background, would be perfect. It's sort of a dream job, if you ask me."

Dinner is an enchilada casserole. They sit around a small pine table that Evangelina says reminds her of the table in her father's house. As Josh reaches for seconds, he asks Hollister and Rosey, "So have you seen Esther recently?"

Hollister says, "We've seen her once since we moved. She's doing well. No more falls. She's amazing, if you ask me."

"Yes she is. We drove up to Santuario last weekend. First time we'd been back since Bud's funeral." Josh pauses and for a moment there is a pall over the conversation. No additional words are said about Bud, because no words need to be said. Josh sighs then continues, "It is amazing how she's pulled that place back together." Josh shakes his head, then adds, "I wish there was something we could do to help, maybe shed some light on the conditions up there."

"As a matter of fact, I'm working on that now. In my new job I've got some connections, some people who might be able to turn this whole thing around. It may take awhile, but it's time to get those folks some help. Meanwhile, Esther's there and that gives me hope."

"I miss her church services," says Evangelina, "even though I only ever went to one."

"Me too," says Rosey. "She's just what that place needs right now, after what happened."

"Speaking of church," Josh says. "Got a question to ask you, Hollister."

"Well, glad to hear you want to talk about church, mister science whiz. What's your question?"

Josh looks at Evangelina, who nods with an impish smile, then back at Hollister. "Well, we've got some pretty big news."

"Uh oh," laughs Hollister with fake wariness.

"We're getting married next month."

"Holy moly!" Hollister jumps up and almost hits his head on the hammered metal chandelier. "Married! Married? That's awesome. So you really did go for it, after all, Josh!"

"Yes, I did," Josh says, feeling a warm glow. "Next month at a church here in Santa Fe. In fact, Esther helped set that up. Convinced the priest to take a chance on a lapsed Catholic and a struggling sort like me. We're going through the premarital counseling now."

"So this calls for a toast!" Hollister hoists his glass of sangria with such enthusiasm that some of it sloshes on the table, but no one cares. "Here's to Josh and Evangelina, a beautiful couple. May they know God's richest blessings."

"Thank you." Josh feels a lump in his throat and he thinks he might cry. Evangelina has slipped her hand into his.

"And you said you had a question for me? You're not challenging me to a game of HORSE, are you?" Hollister leans forward and says this in mock seriousness, with his best James Earl Jones voice.

"No, that game of HORSE will come later. Tonight I'm asking you to be my best man."

Tears well up in Hollister's eyes, and soon they are in everyone else's eyes as well.

◆◆◆

St. Luke's Episcopal Church faces East Palace Avenue, just two blocks off the famous plaza. Strollers by the thousands pass the church headed for the next art gallery down the block or seeking some nearby secluded adobe-walled courtyard, which hides a legendary New Mexican restaurant. The church, however, looks nothing like the famous examples of pueblo architecture that surround it in this historic city. With its grey stone façade and square-cornered bell tower, it could easily be part of the scenery in an English village.

It's a crisp January morning, but there is ample bright sunshine and only a few remnants of last week's snowfall. A beautiful day for a wedding.

Josh is there early, waiting in the sacristy with the groom's party. Hollister is almost as nervous as Josh, and a joking banter among the men, aimed at keeping Josh's nerves under control, only gives evidence to how anxious they all are. Josh cannot help but chuckle as he surveys the three members of his groom's party, who on the surface seem to have absolutely nothing in common.

"So, bro, the big day is here. I still can't believe you pulled this off. After everything I taught you, you had to go out and pull off the greatest stunt of all. Taking a bullet in the chest for your honey. Now that's a move! I tell you, babes -- even ones like that fox you landed -- can't resist a move like that. Gotta say, I'm pretty proud of my protégé today."

"Thanks, Hal. Guess I'll take that as a compliment. And I gotta say, all you guys look great." They are all wearing black tuxes, the three of them. Hollister, standing at six-nine, with Reynaldo barely reaching up to Hollister's chest. And Hal, with his bright reflective forehead in contrast to Hollister's dreadlocks. If Bud were here, leaning on his walker and puffing on a Camel, this would be a perfect group.

They're waiting for Father Wellman to come in and give them final instructions about the service and announce, as Hollister had called it, the 'two minute warning.' Josh senses this day as a defining moment in his life, and there have been several such moments -- spectacular, transforming moments -- in the past few months, moments that have reshaped and redirected a life that had seemed monotonous and stale, that had seemed devoid of hope.

Father Wellman and Josh have become quite close these past two months, as Josh and Evangelina met with him almost weekly to discuss their marriage. Their discussions covered everything, even the difficult topics that could blindside them in the future. Like, how would Josh be as a father to Serena? What special needs might Serena have following the incident at Copper Point, and what demands might this place on their marriage? How will the different cultural backgrounds of Josh and Evangelina manifest themselves in their life together? How will Josh's issues with his father affect his role as a husband? And, perhaps most urgently, what will they do if Evangelina is deported?

All these issues were treated with love and humor, and both Josh and Evangelina came to feel quite comfortable discussing these topics with Father Wellman. While they hadn't come up with concrete answers to some of the questions, they had come to realize that the key to their healthy marriage would be honest and open communications.

Father Wellman had also stressed the importance of religious faith in their lives. Evangelina had easily accepted this as a foundation for the marriage, and in fact they both agreed that they would continue attending St. Luke's after the wedding. Evangelina had told Josh that she felt it was like home being there.

For Josh's part, his conversations about faith with Father Wellman covered the waterfront. They discussed the conflict between science and religion, and Josh was coming around to accepting that there is no conflict. They discussed the meanings of faith and hope, as opposed to scientific knowledge. Father Wellman, it turned out, was deeply knowledgeable in all these things, and over and over he could skillfully challenge Josh's knee-jerk objections. Six months earlier these conversations would have fallen on deaf ears for Josh. But after his times with Esther and Bud -- he believed he could recall every word of their important conversations -- he was now open to what Father Wellman had to say.

All of these things had begun to change the way Josh looked at the world, looked at himself. But none of these things was sufficient alone to change what he believed. What changed him, what made him open to seeing things in a new way, was Evangelina. It was her love, her kindness, her authenticity, her beauty that had clubbed him over the head. And over the heart.

And so, just three weeks prior to his wedding day, in this same church, with Evangelina and Father Wellman, Josh was baptized. He was baptized, not because he had finally done some analysis that convinced him about God's existence. In face he still had many questions, many concerns about this new topic of faith. He was baptized not because of a new certainty, but because of a new direction he saw his life was taking, a new direction based on love. And even though this physicist did not have all the details worked out, he was ready for this new direction.

Another turning point had occurred in the past three weeks. For all the same reasons that led to Josh's baptism, he called his mother. It hadn't been hard to find her number, with the help of the internet. But when he picked up the handset to make the call, there was a moment of uncertainty when it was not clear that he could follow through. As he sat, almost paralyzed, with the receiver in his hand, Evangelina had said to him, "Oh, so are your feet now back on the ground?" She then gave him a big smile and a gentle kiss. Immediately he dialed the number.

A woman answered, and it was an initially unfamiliar voice, a detached voice that was probably prepared to deal with another telephone solicitation. But within moments, something unexpected occurred. A longing in Josh was exposed. Apparently long hidden and suppressed, but residing just beneath the surface, there was an immediate longing to know all about this woman. To see her. To touch her. Josh's hands trembled as he heard for the first time in many years, the sound of his mother's voice.

His mother's response was that this must be a crank call, and she seemed prepared to hang up. But Josh quickly convinced her it was real, and her shock was obvious to him. There were moments of awkward silence during their conversation, and there were moments when one or both of them was crying. But, in the end, it was a life-changing experience. His mother and her new husband arrived in Santa Fe two days ago, in advance of the wedding. They had spent a quiet evening with Evangelina and him, and there much was said, though much of it was nonverbal. They all learned that the love that exists between a mother and her child can never be extinguished.

The next night his mother and her husband attended the rehearsal dinner, and now they are seated out in the sanctuary, waiting for the service to begin. When the priest asks, "Who presents this woman and this man to be married to each other?" his mother will join her voice with those of Esteban and Grace in saying, "I do."

Josh has not seen Evangelina this morning, but he knows he is minutes away from seeing her come down the aisle. He cannot wait to see her face, and he imagines that moment like a freezing man waiting for the sunrise.

"Are you ready?" Hollister has put his arm around Josh's shoulder as he whispers in that deep voice.

Josh smiles up at him. "Yes, Hollister, I am ready."

Then Father Wellman comes in and says, "Gentlemen, it's time. Let's join hands and say a prayer."

৵৵৵

The nave of St. Luke's is stunning, with a high arched ceiling supported by intricately carved beams, tall stained glass windows on all sides of the sanctuary and a high altar, backed by a beautifully carved reredos. But Josh sees none of this today. His eyes are glued to the rear of the church, where Evangelina will appear shortly.

The prelude music has ended, and the processional has begun. Serena, the flower girl, makes her way alone up the center aisle, casting rose petals around her. She draws oohs and ahs from everyone and threatens to steal the whole show. Then Evangelina's attendants begin their procession forward. First comes Rosey, with an amazing smile on her face. Then Evangelina's maid of honor, Lauren, who looks beautiful in a light green dress. Josh notes that this is first time he's seen her without hiking boots.

Then the music rises and everyone stands as Evangelina begins her way up the aisle.

Josh's knees almost buckle at her beauty, and Hollister even reaches out a supportive hand, just in case. Her flowing white gown is magnificent, but it is her face, radiant and glowing, and her smile as her eyes meet his, that almost knocks him over.

≈

Evangelina's heart leaps with joy, as she makes her way up the aisle. She feels herself washed by the loving faces on all sides. In the center, ahead, awaits Josh.

The faces that greet her on this short walk are like the story of her life. Faces that are familiar, each telling a story, each revealing a part of who Evangelina is, each revealing hope for who she will be.

But there is one face that doesn't fit. One face she didn't expect to see here. A face she doesn't want to see here. She almost stumbles, almost comes to a complete stop. But then she looks back at Josh. His eyes, bathing her, are like a lighthouse lamp leading her home. She locks her eyes on him and continues.

Together they stand before Father Wellman as the liturgy begins. Before he speaks to the congregation, he whispers to Josh and Evangelina, "You two look awesome today," and this helps neutralize the butterflies that Josh is experiencing and suspects that his Evangelina is too. Then he welcomes the congregation, announces the purpose of the occasion, and offers a prayer. Then everyone sits for the readings. At the conclusion of the readings, it is time for the sermon. Father Wellman steps forward and says to the congregation, "Please join me in welcoming our guest preacher this morning."

Esther makes her way to a low lectern in front of the congregation. There is no way she could make it up to the high pulpit. She moves slowly and deliberately, leaning on a metal cane that she's been using since the fall. Josh wonders if she's ever spoken before a large church congregation before. But if she's nervous, she certainly doesn't show it. She has no notes.

"I wonder if somebody could read that Gospel passage again." A deacon, a middle-aged woman vested in white, stands and opens the Gospel book to read again, "Jesus said, 'I have said these things to you so that my joy may be in you, and that your joy may be complete. This is my commandment, that you love one another as I have loved you.'" She sets the book down and returns to her seat.

"Thank you, dear. That was beautiful." She smiles at the deacon, who smiles back.

"So, did you all hear that? Did you all hear those radical words? Josh and Evangelina, did you hear those words that will be the foundation of your marriage? I heard them. And what I heard were two important things. And yes, they are two pretty radical things. They stand against much of what our modern culture would have us believe. I believe you both already understand these two things. The first is about what God wants *for* you, and the second is about what God wants *from* you.

"What God wants for you is joy. Oh, yes, joy! No, this is not the finger-pointing, gotcha, dour-and-grim grumpy old God that some folks would have you believe. But this is a God who wants to have joy in us and wants our joy to be complete. Do you get this?" Esther walks slowly over to where Josh and Evangelina sit and leans over toward them. "Josh and Evangelina, what God wants for you is for your joy to be complete!" Evangelina is gripping Josh's hand tight, and at these words from Esther, she squeezes even harder.

Esther continues. "Too many times we don't understand this about God. That he wants us to have joy. So we go through life burdened down by guilt and shame, by worries and regrets, by low self-esteem. We let fear control our lives, when what God wants for us is joy!" Her voice rises on this last sentence. "So, what God is asking of you this afternoon, Josh and Evangelina, is that this marriage means you are going to live your lives, from this moment on, guided not by fear but by love.

"Now it won't always be easy. I'm not sayin' that you're just gonna sit back and let God do all the work. Nosiree! That's how our culture sometimes treats marriage, like it's an entity that has a life of its own, something that the man and woman just sort of stand back and watch. 'If it works out ...' We hear couples say that all the time, as if the success of the marriage is something that is beyond their control.

"But a marriage requires maintenance and nurture and constant loving care. You wouldn't buy a new car – and, by the way, this marriage is a Rolls Royce and not a '68 Corvair -- and never maintain it. Like that new car, your marriage needs care. It needs maintenance and polishing. What it takes is love. Not just romantic love when the moon is high and the lights are low, and Luther Vandross crooning on the stereo." Esther actually dances around a bit as she almost sings this last rhyming line, and everyone chuckles. "Oh yeah, it takes that kind of love, too. Remember, Jesus wants complete joy for you. But he wants more *from* you.

"That's right, more from you will be required if this marriage is going to be a Rolls Royce and not a '68 Corvair. It will require sacrificial love. What Jesus says next is a commandment not a suggestion. He doesn't say, hey, why don't you give this a try? It's a commandment. He says, 'love one another as I have loved you.'

"And just how has he loved us? Well, he gave everything for us. He died for us. Scripture says that 'while we were yet sinners, Christ died for us.' That is, even though we had turned our backs on him, he went ahead and gave his life for us anyway.

"Now, there are some folks here who know a lot about sacrificial love." Esther looks over at Rosey. "There are folks here who would do anything for their families. That's sacrificial love." Rosey's eyes are misting up. Next she looks right at Lauren, and this makes her squirm. "And there are folks here who will come and help those in need, even when it's not a great career move or even though that person is never gonna make a lot of money out of it. That's sacrificial love. And there are those here who would do anything in this world to protect their little daughter." At this, Evangelina, already misty eyed, looks over at Serena, seating in the second row with Esteban and Grace.

"And there are folks here who would even step in front of a murderer's gun, who would risk their own lives, to save another person." She looks over at Hollister, who smiles at her then modestly looks down. Then she looks at Josh, as he swallows hard and licks his lips as if his mouth has suddenly dried out.

"Yes, those folks are here. And, my oh my, wouldn't our friend Bud Ewing, that brave Marine, who died a hero on a beach head of red carpet in an old folks home, wouldn't it be great to see him here today? I can tell you though, I suspect he's got a big smile on his face right now.

"So, Josh and Evangelina, what does that mean for your marriage? It means you are to give to one another, exceeding what is fair, exceeding what is deserved. Give and give and give. Forgive and forgive and forgive. Love and love and love.

"Now there's one last thing I gotta say, and then I'll shut up and go sit down. Josh here is a very good scientist, a physicist. Awhile back, he told me about parallel universes, a new-fangled idea that maybe there are more universes out there than just this one we know about. He said how it was unlikely these universes would ever be able to communicate with each other, that they'd just go on existing without ever knowing anything that was going on at all in the other universes.

"Well, that sounds kinda sad to me, if it's true. But then I already know a little something about parallel universes, and most likely you do too. I live in a parallel universe, a little old folks home out in the boondocks that almost no one knows anything about. You see, while life goes on around here, while folks are shopping at the mall, mowing their back yards, or meeting for margaritas over at the local restaurant, the folks up at our little home wait alone. Wait for someone to come and see them, wait for someone to love them. That little old folk's home where I live is a parallel universe. But it doesn't have to stay that way. Once in awhile, people like Josh and Evangelina, people like Lauren and Hollister, come by bringing joy and love and hope with them. And the separation of these two universes just goes poof.

"Josh and Evangelina, as you begin your lives together, you must know that you may experience what seems like parallel universes from time to time. Separations that come from your different backgrounds and cultures, from your histories. But you will not let these things separate you. It won't be easy every day, but I can assure you that it will be wonderful. Because God wants and is prepared to play an active role in your lives together – because his will for you is joy and love beyond your wildest dreams."

There is total quiet in the church as Esther makes her way back to her seat.

A few minutes later Josh and Evangelina stand before Father Wellman and say their vows, Josh first taking Evangelina's right hand in his and repeating after the priest, "In the Name of God, I, Josh, take you, Evangelina, to be my wife, to have and to hold from this day forward, for better or worse, for richer or poorer, in sickness and in health, to love and to cherish, until we are parted by death. This is my solemn vow."

When Evangelina's vows are said, Father Wellman pronounces them husband and wife, concluding with this admonition to the world from the Church: "Those whom God has joined together let no one put asunder."

These final words jar one of the guests. In the midst of so much celebration, one person sits near the back of the church with a troubled look. Eric Sandoval doesn't know when he is going to tell her. Not certain about how he will tell her. But he must tell her soon. Indeed he is here to put this marriage asunder.

Chapter Fourteen

A million centuries ago, a star a million times more massive than our sun shuddered violently under the collapse in its own gravitational field, on its way to becoming a black hole. Its dying gasp was the emission of an intense burst of gamma rays, lasting only a few minutes. Yet, this brief burst contained more energy than our sun has emitted in all the ages since it was formed five thousand million years ago.

The germanium detector that Josh had calibrated now orbits the earth aboard the Advent satellite, poised and pointed toward the distant corners of the universe, waiting to detect and analyze such intense bursts of radiation.

Josh peers intently into the large monitor before him. Small blips are scattered across the screen, signatures of the gamma ray burst, which arrived at Advent just last week. His group has been studying the data for days, and the excitement is high among everyone on the international team of which Josh is a part. In the past he has only calibrated the detectors, then turned them over to others who would use them in experiments like this one. Now he is a principal investigator on such as experiment.

With one click on his mouse, Josh brings up a different software program, which contains a new mathematical model of intense gamma ray bursts, in yet another attempt to fit the data to an improved physics theory of black hole production. He is able to adjust parameters in the software package from his workstation, and he will tweak the output until the mathematically-generated curves match the blips on his screen. From those optimized parameters, Josh will be able to deduce such amazing things as the size of the star that collapsed a hundred million years ago and whose light is just now reaching earth, the energy of the gamma rays in the burst, and perhaps, if the data are good enough, some insight into the dynamics of how a black hole comes into being.

He now pushes his office chair back from the monitor, after he's been going at it for hours, and emits a deep sigh. He glances over at the clock to the left of a rack of electronics. How the afternoon has gotten away from him. His brain has been completely engaged in mathematical and physics details all day, minutia so specialized that it's easy to lose sight of the staggering reality that he is among a handful of people privileged to use such data to peer into the most mysterious and elusive reaches of the universe.

He stares up at the ceiling for a moment, toward the humming fluorescent lights. But he's not looking at them. His mind is reeling with other things. As compelling as the gamma ray measurements are, they cannot compete with the images of a child's face or the twinkle in a lover's eye.

When he steps outside the Institute, he does a quick three sixty to evaluate his new surroundings. Faculty and students scurry across the huge plaza, around which sit several ultra-modern glass buildings. In the midst of Science City, the Institute of Astronomy is a core part of the famous National Autonomous University of Mexico. He's been here three months, thanks to Hal's help in quickly landing a cushy sabbatical assignment, and he still can't believe it. It is not lost on him that inside the institute he spends his day studying the mysteries of the universe, yet right out here in the swarm of this great city he is in a part of the universe every bit as mysterious as the one he is paid to study.

The subway station is just on the other side of the plaza, and from there it's a fifteen minute ride, more or less beneath the Paseo de la Reforma, the grand boulevard that crosses the central section of Mexico City. He loves this part of the day. The people watching at rush hour in this city of eighteen million is an education in itself. But what he loves most is that he is almost home.

He emerges from the subway station onto the Paseo de la Reforma, and as always it almost takes his breath away. The shiny skyscrapers towering above the tree-lined boulevard, the imposing statues of famous people he does not yet know about, and the endless traffic that makes driving to work a poor alternative to riding the subway. But two blocks off the Paseo, past a Starbucks and a small trendy restaurant, he turns into a narrow quiet street and there, a hundred yards down, is his apartment.

On the second floor, the apartment is no larger than his old one in New Mexico. It is starkly furnished. Josh gave his telescope to Hal before leaving the old apartment. And giving away the home theatre system had been quite an experience. With the help of Lauren, they carried it up to Copper Point in the back of her Tundra. They also purchased a hundred movie DVDs to go along with the theatre system. Picking them out had taken a whole afternoon. At first there was apprehension, as they set up the big 52-inch screen in the lobby at Copper Point. Mrs. Harshburn initially objected, but with Esther's smooth influence and probably because she was still somewhat intimidated by Josh, the system was accepted.

Soon they had the couches arranged around the TV, and it wasn't long before *Mr. Smith Goes to Washington* was on the big screen, with Maggie and others nearly swooning over Jimmy Stewart.

The telescope and home theatre system had not prevented the old apartment from feeling empty and cold. But the new apartment is anything but cold. It always gives him a jolt of joy and warmth to open the door and find Evangelina and Serena there.

It is true that the first month here had been trying for them. After Mr. Sandoval told Evangelina that she would soon be deported, at their wedding reception no less, their lives had changed fast. Sandoval had made the case for leniency for Evangelina and her family to Homeland Security, and she had several things going in her favor. She had turned herself in, she was a hero of sorts after helping to defeat Della's sinister operation, and she had been brought into the country as a small child. He was able to secure the dropping of criminal charges for using false identification, in exchange for her testimony against the outfit that was selling the phony papers. And no charges would be brought against Esteban, Grace or Reynaldo. But she would be deported. DHS had somehow negotiated with Mexico to accept her, even though no one knew her country of origin. She had one month to leave the country on her own or face forcible deportation.

For awhile their lives were a swirl of panic and fear. Then Josh landed the one-year appointment in Mexico City, thanks to Hal's help pushing the paperwork through with the Institute of Astronomy.

When they had first come to Mexico City, the burning issue was whether Evangelina might apply for a green card in a year, when they might be able to return home. While it remains uncertain whether this might be possible, that's no longer a burning issue for them and they have come to a place of peace about whatever may lie ahead. The burning issues now are enrolling Serena for kindergarten in the Fall at the excellent American School, just a short distance from their apartment. And Evangelina's preparing to enroll for Fall classes at the university to continue her major in history. Thanks to the flexibility in Josh's schedule and the fact that he can work at home some days, he will be able care for Serena while she is in school.

The apartment is small, but it has two bedrooms and Serena has her own room. She has taken to the move so well, bouncing with the excitement and sense of adventure of living in this new place. All three of them have been caught up in the new adventures. As much as this little apartment has become their home, it's the city itself that has enthralled them. On Saturdays they wander for hours through the many museums nearby, especially the Museum of Anthropology, where Evangelina lingers amidst the historical exhibits, and the Museum of Modern Art, where Josh is learning more about painting. In fact his evening class in oil painting will begin in a few weeks.

But tonight they will be at home, Skyping first with Esteban and Grace, then with Josh's mother. Josh got them both set up with internet connections and new laptops just before they left. Now the video visits are a much anticipated part of their weekly schedules.

All these things are highpoints in their busy weeks, but they all are but little sparkles on the great sea of romance and love that Evangelina finds herself sailing on. And now her husband has just come home. Yes, it is home, her real home. The place where, just as Hollister said, love resides.

Josh stands on the small terrace of the apartment, looking down at the street below.

A peace that he has never known fills him. He is Joshua, leading his people into a new homeland, accomplishing something his famous forebears could not. His father talked about the parallel universes, but Josh has visited them. And now he is learning about something even more amazing and mysterious than parallel universes. Every day he sees it, and recognizes it for what it is, in the small electronic blips coming in from the far reaches of the universe. He sees it, and recognizes it for what it is, in the laughing bouncy energy of his daughter who spontaneously called him daddy last week. And he sees it every minute of his life, and recognizes it for what it is, in the pervasive love of his wife.

She joins him now on the terrace. Night is falling on their avenue. A few couples stroll toward the boulevard. Two children laugh as they wobble on small bikes along the sidewalk. A dog across the street stretches lazily and looks at them, then goes back to sleep. Her fingers move lightly along his arm, and her head rests against his shoulder. Someday there may be a another promised land to which he will go, to which he will take his family. But he cannot imagine how it could be any better than this.

Acknowledgements

I am grateful to my wife Mary and to our children Erica, Karl and Lucas, all who provided encouragement, ideas and editorial guidance throughout this project. Thank you to my sister Patty, a critical editor, who provided much input into improving the story and fixing many mistakes in earlier versions. Thanks to Laurie Scheer, UW Madison, for critical review of parts of the manuscript and suggestions about the title. Finally, I offer my appreciation to the great institution of Los Alamos National Laboratory, where I was privileged to work, and where so many gifted scientists serve today for the betterment of our country.

About the Author

Jim Trainor is both a physicist and ordained priest. He holds a doctorate in physics from the University of California and has served in some of the world's premier scientific laboratories. He is also an ordained Episcopal priest, serving as senior pastor to congregations in New Mexico, Texas, and Wisconsin. He and his wife Mary have three grown children and live in central Wisconsin.

Jim's website is rjtrainor.com.

Jim's blog is r-j-trainor.blogspot.com

Also by Jim Trainor

We have big questions about the meaning of life.

ISBN 978-1456354084